# *Skin Deep*

Catherine Barry



POCKET BOOKS

LONDON • SYDNEY • NEW YORK • TORONTO

First published in Great Britain by
Pocket Books, 2004
An imprint of Simon & Schuster UK Ltd

Simon & Schuster UK is a Viacom company



1 3 5 7 9 10 8 6 4 2

Simon & Schuster UK Ltd
Africa House
64-78 Kingsway
London WC2B 6AH

Simon & Schuster Australia
Sydney

www.simonsays.co.uk

A CIP catalogue record for this book is available from the British Library

ISBN 0 7434 9221 8

EAN 9780743492218



Typeset by Palimpsest Book Production Limited, Polmont, Stirlingshire
Printed and bound in Great Britain by Cox & Wyman Ltd,
Reading, Berkshire

*For Frances*

My gratitude, love and thanks to the following:

My family.

Pat Sullivan, Rose Shiel, Suzanne Erskine.

Des, Carole, Alex, Eileen, Liz, Bernadette
and all connected to D.U.A.G.

My buddies in the Bill and Bob Club.

Peter and Sheila Sheridan.

Rose Doyle.

Cathy Kelly, Martina Devlin, Marisa Mackle,
Martina Reilly, Annie Sparrow, Colette Caddle, and
Catherine Dunne.

The Darley Anderson Agency.

Suzanne Baboneau, Jane Ellis, Jane Pizzey
and Ian Chapman of Simon & Schuster (UK).

Treasa Coady and staff of TownHouse Publishing (Dublin).

Clare Ledingham, my amazing editor.

Greg Dark.

My children Caitriona and Davitt.

If you want to become whole, let yourself be partial.
If you want to become straight, let yourself become crooked.
If you want to become full, let yourself be empty.
If you want to be reborn, let yourself die.
If you want to be given everything . . .
Give everything up.

Tao Te Ching

# Chapter 1

From a very early age I refused to use my Christian name. My mother had seen it only right and fitting to christen me with a name that was truly cruel. I dealt with it as best I could. I simply insisted my name was Finn. Everybody called me Finn, and if they didn't, they soon learned to.

I chose the name Finn because some of the kids had nicknamed me that. It sounded cool and I didn't know of any other Finns and that was the final deciding factor. It was different, and I wanted to be different. I was Finn O'Farrell as far as everybody was concerned. I had kept my secret well hidden. In fact, I had almost forgotten my real name, until the day I did the interview for the Credit Union and my cover was blown for good. I wanted this permanent position. I wanted it real bad.

The last job interview I had done was a complete waste of time. It was for a sales position in the basement of a second-hand bookstore in a tenement building on Marlborough Street. The pay was pathetic and the place smelt of mouse droppings and mouldy sawdust. The manager had chirpily tried to rope me in with the amazing perk of having 33 per cent off all books. Great, I had thought. Now, let me get this straight. You pay me a hundred pounds a week and I buy all your crappy books with 33 per cent off, which will probably leave me with about thirty pounds after tax? Yes. He had nodded excitedly. No extra points for figuring out what I told him to do with his 'amazing perk'.

I didn't hold out much hope for the Credit Union job either. For one, I gave a really poor performance from the minute I parked my butt in the seat opposite my future manager, Mark Adams.

'So. You live locally, I see?' He raised an eyebrow at me as he perused my two-page curriculum vitae.

Actually it was really only one page. I had double-spaced everything to make it look more impressive. No matter how hard I tried I just couldn't disguise the employment-history section: it boasted a solitary three-week period of employment at McDonald's in Grafton Street. I had been fired rather abruptly when a customer complained they had choked on a foreign object discreetly embedded in their Big Mac.

It turned out to be a false nail, which I had been trying to glue on my forefinger between flipping 100 per cent pure Irish Beef burgers and wrenching the lever of the milkshake machine clean off its writhing, shuddering body. There was more writhing and shuddering as I refused to leave. I gave in resentfully when a security guard, who looked distinctly like the guy out of the movie *The Green Mile*, offered to escort me out of the premises.

'Yes. Actually your Credit Union is only about a fifteen-minute walk from my flat.' I beamed.

'Well, that certainly helps. We like to employ local people, if at all possible.' Mark Adams smiled.

I smiled back, hoping he wouldn't notice I wasn't a local.

*So far so good.*

He peered again at the CV and took in a deep breath. 'So, Finn?' He looked at me.

'Yes. That's my name,' I replied.

'Yes. That's what it says here,' he confirmed, looking from me to the CV.

'Well, actually Finn isn't my real name,' I blurted suddenly. What if he asked for my birth cert and found out I was lying?

'Oh?' He looked puzzled.

'It's a little difficult to explain,' I started. 'You see, my real name is Fainche.' I cringed. [Fawncha.]

'Oh?' He nodded nonchalantly.

'Yes, it's a bit of a mouthful. That's why my friends call me Finn. Have done ever since I was little.' I tried to wriggle out of the inevitable.

'Fainche, eh? A most unusual name,' he commented.

A fucking infliction, I thought.

'Irish, eh?' he enquired.

'Yes, it is,' I squirmed.

'Mmm.' He rubbed his chin. 'What does it mean? Does it have an English translation?'

'Yes, it does.' Now I wished I'd never mentioned it.

'And what is it?' He waited.

Long pause.

*'Fanny.'*

I mean there's just no way of saying it nicely. It's like curse words – they sound so aggressive and loud. Mark Adams recoiled, and I could see the struggle between his mouth and his brain as he tried to remain serious and dignified. 'Excuse me?' He coughed.

'It means Fanny!' It came out crass and uncouth again.

I felt certain the job opportunity was ruined now so it didn't matter what else I said. I blathered on, trying to explain why my mother had lost her marbles and given me a name that also pertained to a vagina.

'You see, it originated from the name of two saintly Irish virgins, one the sister of St Enda of Aran, and patroness of Rossory, on Lough Erne, whose feast was kept on the first of January. I've no idea why my mother chose it because I wasn't born on the first of January or anything. In fact I was born in April. But my brothers – I have two by the way – were born in January so I suppose she might have had them in mind when she did it. Anyway, the other patroness of Cluain-caoi, in the neighbourhood of Cashel, was venerated on the twenty-first of the same month. What that has to do with anything is about as obvious to me as the visions of Our Lady crying blood in Mount Mellary. That's the gist of it anyway,' I finished.

Then, without warning, I let out a robust, unplanned burp. The kind that has a little one tapering off at the end of it, like the little spaceship following the Mammy and Daddy spaceship round the bend in the film *Close Encounters of the Third Kind*. My hand flew to my mouth. *For fuck sake, Finn . . .*

'Excuse me. I'm very sorry.' It always happened when I was nervous, but why now, in the middle of a very important interview? I was so embarrassed and annoyed with my body.

A kind of bewilderment settled in Mark Adams's eyes. I was certain he was reaching under the table for the panic button when he stunned me into silence with his next question. 'Can you do that at will?' He leaned over the desk earnestly.

'I beg your pardon?' I asked.

'Can you do that, you know, when you want to, or does it happen by accident?'

'Which? The burping or the inability to stop talking?'
'The . . .' He gestured to his throat.

'Oh, that. I can do it at will but I don't usually. That one was involuntary. My brothers taught me how to do it properly, like from deep down inside.'

I heard my voice quiver. I was making a fool of myself. 'God, I'm sorry, going on like that. Look, thank you for your time, I'm sure you've better things to be doing.' I felt the blood rush to my face. I was ready to leave, crawl quietly into some corner and die with the humiliation.

'It's no problem. Wait till you hear the others. Dessie holds the record at the moment.' He smiled, pressed a buzzer and called someone in. I assumed I was to be accompanied to the door again, but there was no need: I would make my own way out this time.

A small blond guy stepped into the room. I could tell he wasn't naturally blond because he'd sprouted dark roots. He looked like a cross between a bale of hay and a Tesco's multi-purpose Vileda mop. He smiled, exposing the clearly marked absence of one front tooth. If it hadn't been for that he might have done well as an extra in *Rosie and Jim*.

'Dessie,' Mark Adams said, 'this is Fain – Miss Finn O'Farrell,' he corrected himself politely.

'Yo.' Dessie nodded, chewing methodically. He wore a glazed expression, like the lights were on but there was no one at home.

'I think you two will find you have a lot in common.' Mark Adams smirked.

Dessie looked me up and down. I wasn't sure where all *this* was going but I knew where *I* was going the minute it was over: straight to the pub.

'Finn, can you type?' Mark Adams winked at me.

I wondered was this all part of the interview process.

Were they pulling a fast one on me to see was I game for a laugh? Perhaps I was on *Candid Camera*? I peered round the office, looking for the hidden lens, and gave one of my best smiles just in case. 'Yes, I—'

'Can you file?' Dessie butted in.

'Yes, of course I can,' I confirmed.

'Have you handled cash before?' Mark Adams wanted to know.

'Yes.'

'Marvellous. Bloody marvellous,' he concluded.

'What's marvellous?' Dessie asked, and stared at me with those vacant eyes. I decided he was a true fart of an individual.

'Dessie, I want you to train in Finn, like yesterday. Can you put in some extra hours?' Mark Adams asked.

'Sure.' Dessie smiled at me.

I smiled back.

He stood there, chewing away.

'That's all, Dessie. You're excused.'

'Yo,' Dessie said, and left.

'Finn, you're in.' Mark Adams stood up and extended a hand.

'You're having me on,' I choked.

'Well, I've looked over your CV. You can type, you can talk, and if you don't mind the odd burp from your fellow workers then you're the one for the job.'

'Right.' I was stupefied.

'Welcome to the Credit Union.' He shook my hand vigorously, and that was how it began.

That was how I landed in Dublin, wide-eyed and destitute except for a packed lunch. I had come 'up from the country', as they say, from a small rural suburb. I was used to small-town rules and small-town ambitions. I ached to be rid of it, to taste the wildness and freedom of a city. My life had taken a turn for the best. Things were looking up. I was happy in the job, delighted to have new friends. I had parties to go to, shopping sprees to indulge in. I had choices. It was such a relief to be away from my narrow-minded family and our neighbours back home. I had money in my pocket. I had a bank account. I had museums and cinemas and theatres to visit. But, most of all, I had an abundance of freedom. I hardly knew what to do with it.

I had managed to get a small flat on the North Circular Road. I was used to lots of room back home and the flat was cramped and poky, but it was a small price to pay for the explosion of my inner world. At last, I was able to expedite without limit or constraint. As far as I was concerned, Finn O'Farrell had arrived and she was never going home, not ever.

Oh, it was all so perfect! Life was exciting, new and fresh as a daisy. It was just dandy! I was in seventh heaven! I never entertained the thought that some day it might change. No. Life was peachy. Life was a breeze. Until the day a teenage popstar by the name of Samantha King burst on to our television screens and fucked it all up.

# Chapter 2

'It's bloody mayhem out there,' I said, as Daria closed the door behind me. I considered Daria to be my best friend. She had come to work in the Credit Union shortly after me and we were soon great buddies. We had a lot in common, especially our obsession with weight. She joined me on social occasions and signed up in the same gym. We compared notes on diets and weight loss: I lagged behind her, always playing catch-up. Daria was always one step ahead, scanning magazines and books for the latest fads in the flab war.

She had incredible self-discipline, something I sorely lacked. I had had a lifetime struggle with self-restraint and no amount of will-power could stop me having my daily five bottles of Energyade. It was my favourite sweet thing, a high powered energized drink that I could not get enough of. On bad days I could drink up to four litres of it. I fooled myself into thinking I was brimming with good health as a result. I denied emphatically that I was slowly turning pale orange, as Daria was prone to tease.

At lunchtime one day we puffed furiously on a shared cigarette on the balcony out back before the doors opened for afternoon business.

'We're going to be swamped,' she moaned, leaping from one foot to the other in an effort to get warm.

'That door is not to be opened until the dot of two. Not a second earlier, do you hear? They can freeze their goolies off for all I care,' I said. 'They've been queuing for twenty minutes. Why don't they read the opening times? The notice is right in front of them. Are they blind or what? I'm not moving until Mark appears.'

Mark Adams had my vote from the day of the interview. He was a fair-minded, balanced individual, who always treated his staff with respect. I loved him because he was unorthodox and willing to try different things. The office rarely had a bad atmosphere or an unresolved conflict, but although he was game for a laugh and joined in with most activities, in business hours we were expected to work.

Inside the office, the three other male staff were gathered round the television. The boss had purchased one in an effort to calm irate and impatient members as they queued to pay off their loans. It was perched on a corner unit at an angle and Dessie was laughing while Tom and Colm were in animated discussion about the new Samantha King video that was playing.

Daria and I eavesdropped. I was doing my bit with the Christmas decorations. No one else was bothering with them so I had taken it upon myself to add a little festive spirit to our workplace. I had made and hung paper chains and bought everyone a silly little hat. They refused to wear them, except Dessie.

Now I was on a swivel chair, precariously balanced on one leg as I hung a wreath of holly and ivy.

'I'm telling you, she had a boob job done,' Colm droned on.

'She said it was a growth spurt,' Tom disagreed.

'Some growth spurt,' Dessie said. 'I've seen her earlier

videos. She hadn't a handful. Now look at her.' He pointed to the screen.

'Hey, Skin, what do you think?' Colm called to me.

Samantha King bent down dramatically, her long hair pouring forward. She circled round and back up again, just long enough to show a mightily impressive cleavage – something I secretly yearned for but knew I could never have.

'She didn't grow them. Even an industrial heavy-duty fertilizer couldn't produce those kind of results,' I said. They all laughed, but inside I was seething with jealousy. The two things I had always wanted were long hair and big boobs. Sam had both and I hated the fucking sight of her.

'Frankly, guys, I don't care how she got them. I'd still give her one without a moment's hesitation,' Dessie concurred.

'Sure you would, Dessie.' Tom winked at Colm.

Poor Dessie, the mad thing. He loved to regale us with stories about his visits to Amsterdam, Greece and Ibiza. How hard he tried to have us believe his conquests had been made into such far-flung corners of the earth, when we knew he hadn't even explored the north side of his workstation – and that if a real woman were to approach Dessie he would probably develop penile paralysis. I humoured him because I knew it was just the bragging bravado of a young fella. His boasting was harmless gibberish. Dessie didn't seem to care a jot about the others' taunts. I think he might even have enjoyed them. He always came back for more, with an even lengthier description of his latest procreation attempt. A man of the world was our twenty-year-old Dessie. I was a more mature twenty-five and felt sorry for him; I often came to his aid when his till didn't balance or he'd made some administrative cock-up. As irksome and moronic as he was, I felt motherly towards him, as if he was some wayward son who just hadn't figured out the world yet. It wasn't unusual to find me making his lunch in the kitchen or poring over his tally rolls looking for errors. I had even sewn a button back on to his jacket and shopped for a new shirt when he'd poured tea down the front of the one he was wearing.

At that moment, though, Dessie wasn't uppermost in my thoughts. Something had started me thinking. It took a while to figure it out. Then it came to me. Samantha King had been the final straw.

Daria sniggered and nudged me in the arm. I tried to say something but my mouth wouldn't work. I stood there with it gaping open.

*Ping.*

The lightbulb appeared over my head.

*Samantha King. Boob job. Boob job. Samantha King . . .*

The words rolled round in my head, getting comfortable, carving out a little niche for themselves.

*Boob job. Samantha King . . .*

They hadn't joined forces with my sense of logic yet, but they had entered the brain cells. They were a part of my psyche, and they sounded almost familiar.

*Samantha King. Boob job.*

They kept repeating themselves like a mantra. It was like I had suddenly remembered the last verse of the national anthem. Like I had reclaimed my lost self. It was like the insides of an antique clock that hadn't worked for centuries suddenly spluttering into action. Slowly the cogwheels began to move. They turned at a snail's pace, the rusty screech begging for my attention. As they picked up speed, though, the train of my thoughts chugged in a familiar rhythm; *Samantha King. Boob job. Samantha King. Boob job . . .*

The rising noise level outside broke my concentration. Members were banging on the window. We still had twenty seconds to go. I turned to Daria. I wanted to tell her there and then what had happened at lunchtime. I wanted to tell her the obsessive thoughts that had taken hold of me. I wanted to tell her how unhappy I felt about my hair, my boobs and my body. I wanted to tell her I couldn't tolerate it any more. I wanted to tell her that the answer to my problem had suddenly dawned on me.

'Daria?'

'What?' she said.

Mark Adams appeared in the office. 'Lads! It's time.' He noticed the Samantha King video and tut-tutted.

'Get that slapper off the box,' he muttered, and changed the channel. He turned to go back into his office.

'What is it? What's wrong?' Daria asked. She was already moving towards the door to open up.

'I – I—' I tried.

But she had left me suspended in mid-sentence.

'Nothing,' I whispered after her.

The lads dispersed and took up their places. Daria turned the key and was almost trampled underfoot by the angry mob. She struggled to free both doors but the members had jammed themselves in the small entrance. They hadn't even the patience to wait until she had opened the doors fully. It was Christmas time and the turn of the millennium: the busiest period we had ever experienced since the Credit Union had been invented.

I positioned myself in the far workstation, Daria sat beside me and the lads took up the remaining desks.

Business was constant and we barely exchanged conversation. The relentless queues refused to allow for an interlude. I just got on with it, mechanically greeting the members and posting their transactions. I was quiet and pensive. I guess Daria noticed. She turned to me when a break appeared in the line.

*Samantha King. Boob job. Boob job. Samantha King.*

'Finn, are you OK?' she asked.

'Huh?' I said.

'Are you OK?' she repeated. 'You seem to be in some other world today.'

'Oh, I'm just thinking, this and that and that and this and nothing much, really.' I sighed.

'Let's go for a drink after work and have a chat, eh?' she suggested.

'Better still, let's get absolutely rat-arsed,' I enthused.

'You're on,' she smiled, 'but can we please skip O'Mahoney's, just this week?'

I had been observing her all afternoon as she casually hoovered up the best part of a large box of Cadbury's Celebrations. I gained weight just watching her. I was determined to get into a size-fourteen dress for the Christmas do and I had to be exactly ten stone to achieve it. I was certain I was there. I had only had my usual crate of Energyade and a couple of chocolates from a box of Black Magic. Before I could remember eating anything else, I stopped thinking about it. 'No, we cannot. Absolutely no way,' I said emphatically.

'OK, keep your thong on, Missus,' she said, with resignation.

I let out a weary sigh.

'Where were you at lunchtime?' she asked.

'I really don't want to answer that.'

'Sure you're OK?' Daria tried.

'Yeah, I'm OK,' I lied.

*Samantha King boob job.*

She knew about Shane, my boyfriend, and how we had recently split up. I could see the question dancing in her eyes but she knew better than to ask directly. Good friends do that: they leave well enough alone to the extent of joining you in the denial. We would both sit in the bubble of illusion until I had decided for myself that it was time to face reality. Anyway, that wasn't what was bothering me – well, it wasn't all of it: it hadn't helped that *he* had dumped *me* even though I knew he was a git.

I glanced at my buddy Daria Alexandru. I envied her flawless swarthy sallow skin. Daria was a creamy coffee colour. She looked like she had an all year round tan, like the Spaniards or Italians. Her eyes were the colour of Bournville chocolate and her hair was sleek and shiny. She wore it shoulder length in delicate spirals of coiled jet-black, A striking contrast to my mousy brown imitation perm.

I got by with the help and support of Elizabeth Arden, an expensive friend, considered myself average – plain, even. I was normally pale and anaemic-looking. My skin had never glowed (except when I didn't want it to: then I resembled an oversized beef tomato). No matter how hard I tried to explain, no one believed that I had always looked like this, even as a kid. That was why I had moved in with Elizabeth Arden and refused to go anywhere without her.

As I watched Daria, her smile disappeared. I looked up to see why.

'Uh-oh,' I whispered. Mr Marcus Myers, our favourite customer, stood at the top of the queue. Periodically, he glanced anxiously at his wristwatch.

'Next, please,' Daria called.

Mr Myers wouldn't budge.

'Next, please!' Daria called again.

He stayed rooted to the spot.

'Mr Myers?' I called.

He shuffled reluctantly to Daria's desk and threw his book into her hatch.

'What can I do for you, Mr Myers?' Daria asked him.

'Can you not read English?' he barked. 'If you can't understand plain English, you shouldn't be working here.'

'I just wanted to know if you want to pay in or withdraw,' Daria replied.

Mr Myers moved forward, pressing his ear to the glass. 'What? I can't understand a frigging word you're saying,' he mumbled.

Daria ignored him and proceeded to fill out the lodgement form. Most members knew to have that done before approaching the desk. She put his book through the printer and handed it back to him via the hatch.

He examined it closely, then shut it and put it back in the hatch. 'It's wrong,' he snapped.

Daria knew it was correct, but opened it and checked just to reassure him. 'It's correct, Mr Myers,' she said, and slipped the book back into the tray. He pushed it back immediately and caught his hand in the process. 'If you let go of the book, Mr Myers, you can retrieve your hand. It can't be pushed and pulled at the same time.'

Mr Myers let go and pulled out his hand. I was raging that it hadn't been severed in the process. At least a minor laceration. It wasn't too much to ask, was it?

'I'm telling you it's wrong. It's one pound out. My balance is wrong. It reads two hundred and forty-nine pounds instead of two hundred and fifty. Are you thick or what?' he grunted.

'The balance is correct, Mr Myers,' Daria repeated. 'The pound missing from your account is an annual debit. It goes towards fees incurred for the service we provide for you. Fifty pence goes towards the Irish League of Credit Unions and fifty pence to charity. Everybody pays it. It's a standard contribution.' A black curl came undone and plonked itself in Daria's eye.

'I never consented to that!' he snarled. 'You mean to tell me that I have no choice but to give fifty pence to charity?'

'As I already explained, Mr Myers, it is a standard contribution that all members pay at the end of the year.'

I could tell she was trying to keep the disgust out of her voice. Scrooge reincarnated, I thought. How could anyone resent paying fifty pence towards a charity? Every time I passed a poor box I had to put something in it, even if it was only a couple of pence. I just couldn't help myself. I couldn't bear poverty – it was preposterous that it still existed when there was so much to go round.

'Is it not enough to have to cough up for the likes of you refugees to stay in luxury houses with all the trimmings and benefits, eh? That isn't good enough for you, sure it isn't, eh? Now you're trying to swindle me Credit Union money as well. I will not pay another farthing towards you lot!'

Daria's face froze. She removed the stray curl from her eye and stared at him.

I wasn't having Myers give my best friend a hard time. I was sick and tired of his endless fault-finding and I hated the way he seemed to enjoy berating her. I had already planned my strategy and was on high alert.

It was time to move to Defcon 1. I came over to her desk. 'Is there a problem, Mr Myers?'

He launched into another tirade of nonsense. I let him blather on for five minutes and waited for him to wear himself out. In the meantime, I bit my tongue so hard I was sure I'd have to go to the general hospital and have it stitched back together. When he had finished banging on about Daria's supposed error, I paused a moment just to make sure he was done. When I was confident his very last invective had expired, I repeated word for word what Daria had already said.

He calmed down. 'Now, that makes sense, Miss. Now that you've explained it to me good and proper I apologize for troubling you,' he said, glaring at Daria like she had half a brain. He smiled at me as if butter wouldn't melt in his mouth.

He made me sick. He had offended Daria, and knew it. Even the cold acknowledgement I returned – a lethargic nod – was difficult to summon, but I did it. Droves of people were now queuing down the steps outside as a result of this delay.

As soon as Myers had gone, Daria put up her sign to indicate her station was temporarily closed. I watched as she walked slowly towards the ladies'. She closed the door behind her and locked it.

Dessie arrived at my side, supposedly looking for more pay-in slips. 'That miserable git, he can hear a penny drop before it hits the ground. I hope he dies roaring,' he whispered, out of the side of his mouth.

'What difference would that make? He can't take it with him. You never see a security van following a hearse, do you?'

'Why doesn't she tell him to rev up and eff off? He has no right to speak to her like that. She should tell the manager.' It would never occur to Dessie to do it himself. He was a bit of a wimp, full of encouragement in the assertiveness department but unable to articulate it.

'Look, I told you before. She won't tell Mark Adams,' I told him.

'What's she afraid of? He's a fair man,' he asked.

'She wants that promotion. Are you a dope or what?' I snapped. I continued to serve the next member while Dessie continued his feigned search.

'For God's sake. He can't hold her back for reporting an abusive member! This place wouldn't survive a day without her. What would he do a thing like that for?' He shoved some Milk Tray under my nose. We now had six boxes of chocolates circulating the office.

'No, thanks. I'm afraid I'm addicted to anything there's two of. If I have one, I have to have another.' I looked longingly at the orange cream. My hand went out to take one. *Get your bloody greedy mauler out of that box!* I pulled it back. I had felt several compulsions to eat in the toilet that afternoon and had fistfuls of sweets buried in my pockets. I was storing them for later.

'I still think she should tell him. He does nothing but complain every time he comes in here and it's always Daria he has a go at.' Dessie rammed four sweets into his mouth. He was full of wisdom and good advice.

'Well, Myers seems to have it in his pea-sized brain that she's a refugee sponging off the system and poor Daria feels she can't trust anyone any more. All this badmouthing about refugees is really getting her down. People just assume she's one too. . .Hey! You're a bloody pig, do you know that?' I added self-righteously, as if I was a saint.

He was munching the chocolates, little piggy snorts emanating from his lips, his cheeks puffed out like a hungry hamster's. 'Some of us don't have to worry about our weight. I have the body of a god.' He patted his stomach lovingly.

'Which one? Buddha?' I squeezed it playfully – I could easily pinch more than an inch.

'Get off me, you mad thing!' Dessie protested.

It was then I saw Colm out of the corner of my eye. He was smiling shyly behind a paper coffee cup, his bright eyes peering over the rim like those of a bold child. He stood up and approached my desk. I pushed Dessie aside so violently he almost toppled over.

# Chapter 3

'How's it going, Skin?' he asked, in his usual jovial manner. Colm and I had always been the best of friends; he always cheered me up.

'That man is going to be the death of us,' I told him.

'Dessie or Mr Myers?' he joked.

'Hey, now, don't be rude – Myers, of course,' I said, standing up for Dessie.

'Has he been at it again?' Colm asked.

'I don't know what his problem is but he loves to get up Daria's nose,' I confirmed.

'Something will have to be done about him sooner or later.'

I admired Colm's concern. I was also admiring his bottom, which I was prone to do on the sly. 'Where were you yesterday?' I asked.

'Had to do an errand for the manager,' Colm answered, and coughed into his closed fist.

'Must have been a big long errand. You were gone all afternoon, and we were snowed under with work – we could have done with an extra pair of hands.' I raised an eyebrow.

'I'll make up for it, I promise. Here, give me that filing.' He leaned over me and I could smell his aftershave. It reminded me of sandalwood and honey mixed together.

'Were you out chasing again, Colm?' I probed. 'I hope it wasn't that one from the hairdresser's with the Marilyn Manson haircut. Or was it the tart from the chemist? You know the one who looks like a tube of Zovirax?'

'Now, Skin, I'm surprised at you bitching. Why all these questions anyway?' he asked, as if he wasn't in the least intrigued at my blatant scrutinzing of his love life.

'Just curious, I guess.' I gave a casual flip of my wrist. The kind the Queen gives when some boring gobshite is harping on about her lovely hat.

'You're very capricious,' he observed philosophically.

I reminded myself to look up 'capricious' in the dictionary. I didn't know what it meant, but I hoped it was a compliment.

'I never ask *you* that sort of thing, now, do I?' he continued.

'No, never,' I admitted, as much to myself as to him. I was annoyed at the clarity of my own reply.

'I just had to drop in some loan forms, that's all. Boring, run-of-the-mill office-job trivia,' he went on. 'If you hadn't legged it out the door so fast at lunchtime today, you would have known I was about to ask you did you want to go to Café Olé to eat . . . and smoke all my cigarettes like you usually do.'

'Aw,' I gave him a smile, 'I'm sorry, Colm, but I had an urgent appointment to keep.' I wasn't going to tell him I had been in Arnott's getting myself fitted for a bra. I could hardly go into the details of how my breasts had been foraged by a marauding elderly woman with silver hair.

'An urgent appointment eh? Sounds mysterious. Aren't you going to fill me in?' He raised himself up on the tips of his shoes and stretched nonchalantly. His shirt rose up, exposing a small area of his tight-muscled flat stomach. I tried not to stare. He finished his yawn and fixed his shirt back into his trousers. I could have sworn it was deliberate.

I would have tried to return his saucy gesture with something sultry and seductive, but I knew I would have exposed a hefty spare tyre and I didn't think it would have the right effect on him. I had to make do with a radiant smile. 'Oh, now who's being nosy, mmm? Let me see. What had I to do today at lunchtime? Oh, yes. I remember now. I just had to attend to some boring, run-of-the-mill, office-job trivia. An errand for the manager,' I smiled cheekily, 'you know, like yourself.'

Colm leaned forward, his forehead almost touching mine. 'Well, then, we should have joined forces. We could have been bored together.' He stared right into my eyes.

I was all a-dither: the sweat was pumping out of me and I was sure my arse was permanently stuck to the seat of my leather swivel chair.

'You're very naughty, Miss O'Farrell,' he added quietly.

I was afraid to breathe: I was sure I smelt of Walnut Whip and sour cream and onion Pringles.

He began to say something else but Daria had returned to her desk. We pulled away from each other as if we had just discovered that an outbreak of the bubonic plague had been lurking in the air-conditioning system and we had just exchanged the kiss of death. There was a bit of an awkward silence.

'I'll catch you later.' Colm drew himself upright, his tone all principled and proper.

'Sure,' I answered, watching him move back to his desk. Still immersed in the magic of the moment, I decided to be extra-bold. 'Colm,' I called after him. He stopped and turned round. 'How about lunch tomorrow? You free?' I stuttered.

'I don't know.' He rubbed his chin, pensive, as if the question required serious consideration. 'I'll have to see. I may have one of those urgent appointments . . .' He grinned.

The bastard, I thought.

At lunchtime that day I had walked down Henry Street, feeling as if I was about to visit the dentist and hadn't brushed my teeth since I'd been sucking rusks. I had never owned a decent bra in my life, and in order to wear that black dress at the Christmas party I needed one that would give me some extra shape and lift.

I had turned into Arnott's and made my way to the lingerie section, where a silver-haired lady arrived at my side. 'Can I help you, dear?' she asked.

'Well. Em. Actually. I need to be fitted for a bra,' I whispered.

'Very well,' she said, and marched me into a small compartment enclosed by a limp curtain rail. I fiddled with the curtain making sure one side overlapped the other. Just in case. Sometimes you could see through the gap. I didn't want anyone seeing through the gap.

The sales lady returned with a measuring-tape and a selection of bras. I stood awkwardly, waiting for her instructions.

'Now, then,' she started, 'you will have to remove your top and your bra, dear, for an accurate reading.'

I was mortified. I hated undressing before anyone, even myself. I always avoided mirrors as if they might start speaking to me in a deep, forbidding voice. 'Hey, you? You're in the wrong fairytale,' they would bellow.

I obeyed the silver-haired woman, who seemed indifferent to my embarrassment. I was used to that. Other women stripped off without the slightest hesitation, in the gym, at the pool. They didn't give a fiddler's if their backside made tidal waves, or their thighs made earthquake shudders on the tennis courts. I wanted to be like that, but I wasn't. To me, undressing was a painful ritual I had to endure. When someone was watching, I felt like a hair follicle undergoing a DNA test.

I winced now as the woman pulled, tugged, stretched and molested my flesh. She hummed and hawed, kneading her way through my armpits. She gathered the two ends of the tape and peered at the numbers through her small spectacles. 'You're a 36A, dear,' she said finally.

I felt like someone had just tapped me on the shoulder to tell me my skirt was wedged inside my knickers.

36A.

I'm a bus without the top deck.

36A.

No wonder Shane had dumped me. He couldn't be held accountable for what was, wrongly or rightly, a man's standard expectation of any woman. I looked at her in desperation, imploring her with my eyes.

'You could try a push-up bra?' the woman suggested. She handed me a pretty black-laced buttress object. I put it on. It made something of a bulge but not on my chest: several layers gathered beneath it, giving the impression that I had grown a Siamese twin. When I put my T-shirt back on I looked like a set of tyres on a go-kart track. The bra had done its best – but you can't give a potter a kiln and expect them to create a masterpiece without any clay.

'It isn't working,' I cried.

A light came on in the woman's eyes. 'Perhaps a water-bra?' she suggested.

'Excuse me?'

'The new water-bra, dear. The latest invention for women who have . . .' She trailed off, like a gossipy Les Dawson woman in a launderette.

'What the hell is a water-bra?' I asked. I was already regretting the idea. The woman fiddled with the boxes on the floor, muttering to herself. Eventually she found one and straightened up. She held it out to me and I took it. It was soft and smooth, a padded bra filled with water. Ingenious! It even felt like the real thing. I tried it on and it made a difference. But I didn't relish the thought of a mobile aquarium hanging off my chest. I imagined the bags of water swishing away: the noise alone would put anyone off, but what if they burst in the middle of a passionate embrace and my partner was drowned in the flash flood? No. That wouldn't do at all.

'How much is it?' I asked, already decided.

'One hundred and twenty pounds.'

'What?' I laughed. 'You're kidding, right?'

'No kidding,' she said, with a hint of sarcasm.

The water-bra was my last option. She had nothing else to offer except, perhaps, a prayer for a miracle. Considering God had not heeded any of my own pleas, I didn't count on Him to grant hers either.

The silver-haired woman tapped her foot impatiently.

I bought the push-up bra. At least I would know I was trying to be more feminine. On the way back to work, I mooched into a vacant telephone kiosk and stuffed a pile of sweets down my throat. Sure what difference could they make? I'd been very good all week and I was sure I had reached my target weight.

I thought of phoning Shane again – after all, we'd been together a long time. Surely something good remained between us. Maybe something could be salvaged. I needed a man, any man, especially at this time of year. But the past interrupted and reminded me of incidents with Shane I had conveniently forgotten. Like the one and only time he had brought me a box of chocolates and how thrilled I had been – until I found out he had won them in a Kriskindle exchange at work. He hadn't even bothered to wrap them. The bollox . . .

'It's the thought that counts?' he had tried.

Yeah. What kind of a thought was that, Finn? I asked myself. I dropped the telephone idea, pronto and went back to work.

Now I turned to Daria, who was looking decidedly unhappy. I watched her raise her eyes to heaven as a member approached her desk. She had barely put her bum on the seat and the 'closed' sign was still up. She ignored the person in front of her until her computer was up and running. Nobody else had Daria's guts. I admired her confidence.

'Hey, you still pissed off?' I asked.

'No, I'm fine now, I shouldn't have risen to the bait,' she said.

'Yeah. That old bastard. Look at the thanks you got for throwing his book at him.' I tried to humour her.

'I didn't throw it at him. If I'd thrown it at him, I wouldn't have missed,' she said.

Daria was a whiz at her job and practically ran the place. I had no real career interests. I didn't show a smidgeon of intuition or ambition. As long as the door closed at five and I had my pay cheque, I was happy.

I was too shy to deal with people in any real depth. I liked to be in the background, filling the water-dispenser and putting flowers on people's desks. I turned calendars, made cups of tea and brought out little snacks.

It wasn't unusual to see me with my sleeves rolled up and my hands in the kitchen sink either.

Daria had come to Ireland from London in 1991. Later she had enrolled in college and graduated in 1997. She had applied for a permanent position in the Credit Union and was accepted immediately. She took to the work like a duck to water and the staff loved her. Although she was only three years older than me, she was game for anything.

All had been going well until last year. We had all noticed a marked upward incline in blatant prejudice. It seemed to come with the Europeans who were pouring into our country. The 'Celtic Tiger' phenomenon brought opportunities, wealth, prosperity and high standards of education. For the first time Ireland's doors were opened to the world, and foreigners from its every corner flooded the capital.

Daria's sallow skin and unusual accent was a rarity in Dublin and she became a target for careless racist remarks. Working among the public had turned her into an accessible political punch-bag.

She was tiring of people's hurtful remarks. Mostly she seemed to handle it but I knew that today Mr Myers had really upset her. I decided not to mention it again: there's nothing worse than an extra bit of kindness to rekindle the flame. Anyway, I was still listening to my own tapes: I couldn't wait for the doors to close and tell her what I was thinking.

*Samantha King. Boob job. Boob job. Samantha King . . .*

By four o'clock the lads were perking up, and the silliness had begun. We welcomed the distraction – anything to get us to the end of the day.

My telephone rang. I answered it. The Vard sisters blasted in my ear. I dialled 112.

'Hello?'

'Dessie, you little bugger. What are you trying to do? Put me asleep?'

'You've an awful face on you – are you in your flowers?' He laughed.

'You've asked me that question three times this week alone. You're a big boy now and it's time you learned that women only menstruate once a month,' I replied.

'And a happy new year to you, too. Hey, what are you pair doing after?'

'Going on a colossal bender. Why?' I asked.

'Just wondering. Guess we're doing the same,' he said.

Daria's phone rang. She grabbed it. 'Hello? Hello?' she said impatiently.

'– Madame Curio's forecasting horoscopes . . .'

It was Colm this time. I could see him sniggering at the far end of the office.

'Jesus.' She rolled her eyes and slammed down the phone.

'That's it,' I said to her. 'Let's get serious.'

Daria winked, dialled a few numbers and transferred the call to 114.

Dessie picked up the phone.

'Mr Myers is on the line, said he would like a word,' she said, in officious tones. Before he could respond, she transferred the call.

'At the signal . . . it will be sixteen thirty-three and twenty seconds . . .'

'Oh, for the love of . . .' he said into the receiver.

Two minutes later, I put in the final call.

Dessie went for the bait. He picked up the phone. 'What is it now?' He groaned. 'You girls are so predictable. Let me guess – a gay-sex line? Priests Anonymous? Psychotics Live?'

'Mr Myers wants you,' I said calmly, then transferred the call.

'Does he now?' I could hear him across the office. 'What do you take me for? I'm up to my town halls here, you know, some of us have work to do. I don't care if it's Santa Claus and the arse has fallen out of his sled. I'm fucked if I'm taking any more calls. Especially if it's from that steamer Marcus Myers.'

A temporary silence followed.

'Finn? Are you still there?' Dessie held the phone under his chin while he put a member's book through the printer.

'Hello?' an angry voice boomed back at him.

'Who is this?' Dessie asked. Probably he was putting two and two together and praying to St Jude for hopeless cases that it made five.

'This is Mr Myers.'

Dessie bowed his head down and banged it on the desk.

When we had finally closed, everybody heaved a sigh of relief. Daria wanted to eat at the office and get ready there. I didn't want to hang around and wait for her so I decided to go up town and avail myself of the late-night shopping. I thought of the little black dress I had planned to wear to the Christmas office party, and while I was confident it would do the job, I wanted to look at what else was on offer.

I wandered through the brightly lit shopping mall and passed a line of Christmas trees, inhaling their deep woody scent. I would have offered to bring one back to the Credit Union and decorate it, but the boss insisted they only made a mess. I hated the artificial ones: they never stood upright and tall.

I took in the essence of Christmas, the glitter, the flashing lights, the distant carol-singing, the bustling shoppers. Everybody looked happy. Everybody had someone, or so it seemed to me. Couples kissed, families laughed, babies gurgled in their cosy prams, their little faces aglow. I reminded myself it was a time to share, and a time to show love, a time to be jolly. Bah, humbug, and jolly, my arse, I thought. I'm alone. I'm so alone in this marauding crowd.

I tried to distract myself by visiting my favourite flower shop. Poinsettias were in full bloom, their flowers spreading outwards, petals cherry red and smooth to the touch. I decided to buy one for each of my colleagues. I couldn't carry them back so I asked the assistant to deliver them to the Credit Union. They knew me well as I haunted the place on most lunch-hours. They often gave me their leftover background filling for bouquets, bits of fern or baby's breath, dyed bamboo sticks and such. I liked to fiddle with them in the flat, and could turn any piece of shrubbery into a fine display. I loved the smell of the earth, the feel of the thick peat filtering though my fingers.

Inside A Wear, a million ant-like shoppers were whipping clothing off the rails. There was a mile-long queue outside the fitting rooms. I browsed among the black dresses. They were all beautiful, but the biggest I could find was a ten. I moved on to some others that were more flamboyant and Christmassy, with flashes of red and cerise. Very Spanish. I liked them. Why go black anyway? It's so predictable and boring. I searched for a size fourteen but, again, there were only tens. There might be an epidemic of anorexia, I thought, but as I ventured further into the store and checked out sweaters and skirts, two-pieces and trousers, they all seemed designed to fit people who had either suffered a long-term illness or had lived their entire life on lettuce. It only served to make me feel worse about myself.

What was the point in shopping for anything? What did I want a dress for anyway? I had a dress already. It was perfect, yet I couldn't help myself. I had been obsessed with dresses for years, always trying them on but never venturing to buy something new. Why did I insist on putting myself through the same torture year in year out? I was always left feeling depressed. Suddenly I wanted to get out of there and away from all the lithe slim women, slipping effortlessly into their size tens.

Slowly I made my way back to the office, feeling sorry for myself. As I ambled along, I kept thinking about how awful my life was, how lonely I was, how sad, and what a pile of self-pity I was turning out to be. I needed a kick up the backside, which was exactly what God must have been thinking.

On my travels, I passed a vagrant child sitting on the pavement, a little girl of five or six. She was shabby and unkempt. Her hair was cut short and tight and hadn't seen a brush in God knew how long. She might have been mistaken for a boy, but for the dress she wore. She was singing 'Silent Night' rather badly. Every now and then she burst into a fit of coughing. I bent down and smiled at her. She did not smile back. I rummaged about in my pocket and put all my loose change into her grubby outstretched hand. Still no smile.

'Happy Christmas, little darling.' I smiled at her again.

She stopped singing and blinked at me. Then she shoved the change into a torn pocket and started up again, singing out of tune, out of breath, with a desperation that made my heart break. She sang even harder, louder, as if nothing else mattered, and indeed it didn't. Her voice was food.

Her eyes were too old for one so young, and suddenly I could see myself reflected in them all those years ago. The dress she wore was old and grubby. It was too small for her and crept up round her thighs. The tears and rips in it had been badly darned with black wool, yet she seemed unperturbed.

I remembered my own childhood and felt ashamed. Oh, how I had wanted a party dress! Just one! I knew Mam had little money, yet I also knew that she hadn't had to beg on the street for it to buy food. Did this child even have a mother? Did she dream of having a new clean dress? A big pink dress with frills and bows to show off to everyone? Or had she forgotten how to be a little girl?

*Mary has invited me to her fifth birthday party. I won't be five for another two months and I can't wait. '"Mary, Mary, quite contrary",' Mam chants, as she peels apples into a bin on the back doorstep. Mam doesn't like me to play with Mary. It upsets Dad. 'Stick with your own, Fainche,' she says to me. I try to stick with my own but the boys only want to play football or Gaelic or hurling, like me Dad. I'm not very good at any of that. Dad says I'll get the hang of it if I practise enough. I go down to the club with him and the boys but I don't fit in. Other boys are always tripping me up when Dad isn't looking and they are always slagging off my spindly legs. When I complain to Dad, he never gives out to them.*

*Sometimes I sing to myself, mostly in the bath on Saturday night. It's the only time I get to be away from the boys. They are not allowed to have a bath with me and I don't know why. I put the taps on full so Mam can't hear me. She hates singing. It annoys Dad, too, unless I sing in Irish – he doesn't mind when I do that. And my mam doesn't have to be worried about me annoying him. I hate it when he gets angry with her because of me and they have an argument. I seem to cause a lot of arguments.*

*I really want to go to Mary's birthday party. Her mam makes treats like macaroons and chocolate Rice Krispie cakes in flowery paper cups. Mam only makes fairy cakes for Dad. Sometimes she lets me lick the wooden spoon. I love the creamy mixture and run my finger along the inside of the bowl until there's nothing left.*

*There will be Taylor Keith lemonade and American cream soda in Mary's house. There might even be an ice-cream cake. My mam gives me a green pound note and tells me to buy her a present in Kiely's on the corner. There isn't much in Kiely's by way of birthday presents. Not for a green pound note. I buy a box of iced caramels and a card with a girl roller-skating on the front. I lean the card on the ice-cream freezer in the shop. I am only learning how to do joined writing and it takes me ages to do her name. I make lots of mistakes and there are fingerprint smudges on the envelope.*

*I wish I could have a birthday party, all for myself. Mam says I don't have enough friends and the trouble of it wouldn't be worthwhile. Besides, how would she handle the boys? They would be bored. I would still like to have one. If no one came, I would eat everything myself. I get hungry at the thought of it. I peel the cellophane wrapper off the box of sweets and take out three. They are wrapped in crinkly plastic paper. There are white ones and pink ones. I make a lot of noise in the empty lane as I shove two sweets into my mouth at the one time. I keep the other to hide in the criss-cross wiring in the mattress under my bed. I scrunch up the papers and stuff them through a hole in my pocket towards the back of my brown anorak. There are a lot of papers in there now.*

*I trudge through the autumn leaves feeling the beechnuts crush beneath my wellington boots. I love the sound of the leaves, the colours I kick through. Brown like the polish me Dad uses to buff his shoes. Yellow like the kitchen lino and rust, the colour of Padraig's three-wheeler bike in the shed. Sycamore leaves, big floppy ones with five fingers stretching out to grab me by the legs. My wellies are caked with mud, a pair of old trousers tucked into the top of them. I close the box of iced caramels. No one will notice that I took a few, and sure they won't notice that they should have a cellophane wrapping on them with a silver line round the side.*

*I wrap them up in a piece of old birthday paper that Mam keeps for special occasions in the bottom kitchen drawer. She has everything in there. Bits of string and ribbon, Lyons coupons, spools of old thread and lots of squares of paper to get the fire lit. The birthday paper looks creased. I smooth it out with my hands but it still looks crumpled and worn. I can't find any Sellotape. Dad says it's too expensive and sure what would we be doing with it? I mix some flour and water together in an old saucer and use my paintbrush to glue the wrapping paper round the box of iced caramels. My hands are sticky and the present looks old but I put it over the oven, which is still warm, and hope it dries out.*

*At four o'clock I arrive at Mary's door for her birthday party. Her mam answers it and puts her hands on her hips. 'Fainche!' she says, wagging her head from side to side, and then she bursts out laughing. I'm happy because I'm going to a birthday party so I don't mind her laughing this time. I let a little laugh meself. I haven't told anyone yet that I'm changing my name. I haven't told Mam, or that Mary's mother always laughs when she hears it. 'Fainche!' she says, as if hearing it for the first time. 'Fainche!' rolling her eyes to heaven and letting an unmerciful burst of laughter into my face. Sometimes the girls in school do it too, whispering behind my back as if I'm an eejit or something.*

*Mary and six other girls are in the kitchen. I can smell*

*marshmallow and melted chocolate and the fat off ham squeezing out of the sides of the sandwiches. There are plates and plates of them. My eyes can't take in all of it. Mam always says my eyes are bigger than my stomach. I think I know what she means now. Mary is wearing a pink dress. It has broderie anglaise along the bottom and a big frill on the collar. The material is all fluffy with pink bobbles, like the ones I used to pull off my old teddy bear. I would love to feel it in my hands. She has a pink satin hairband on her head. It matches her dress. She looks really pretty. Like the doll I saw in Kiely's window that Mam said was 'daylight robbery'. I'm sure she meant something else because I never saw any robbers in Kiely's.*

*The other girls all have dresses. Some are blue, some red, but they all have big frills and sparkly white knee-length stockings. Not the grey sports socks my Mam gets in Guiney's for the boys and me. 'What's good for the goose is good for the gander,' she says. I ask her what that means. She says it is a figure of speech. I ask her what a figure of speech is. She says it is an expression. I ask her what that is and she tells me that if I don't know either I don't deserve to be answered.*

*I love party dresses. Mary gets a new one on her birthday and at Christmas. I always ask her for a feel of them when I'm allowed play in her bedroom and no one else is looking. I feel a bit funny in my grey socks. They don't always stay up. Especially the left one: it keeps gathering round my ankle and I keep pulling it back up. Mam says to put elastic bands round the tops. She says that will keep them up. Mam made me a pair of shorts out of the 'good dining-room curtains'. She bought new ones in Guiney's and hacked the others up. I have a whole new wardrobe of clothes, shorts, trousers, dungarees and two new cardigans all made from the 'good curtains'. They have orange circles and chocolate-coloured triangles on them. If you look real hard, some of the clothes have a green leaf on them too. I keep them for special occasions.*

*I am wearing the shorts because they have a leaf on them. I also have my cardigan to match and a pair of brown leather sandals that pinch my toes. I am the only girl without a dress, a nice party dress.*

*After Mary has opened all her presents, her Mam invites us all to do something special. A party piece, she calls it. Some of the girls sing a song, some do an Irish dance, but I ask can I play the piano. You see, my Dad has a piano but it is very old and battered-looking. He sometimes lets me sit on his lap and bang noises out on it. We haven't got a proper piano chair. Dad uses the one from the kitchen. I love to hear the crisp sound from the creamy-coloured ivory keys and run my fingers between the black ones. The black ones make different tones, sharper and deeper than the others.*

*Now, Mary's piano is a real one. It is big and white and the top is raised and held up by a brass lever. I sit down on the beautiful French piano stool. My legs dangle over the side. I can feel the velvet tapestry beneath my bottom. The material feels like my shorts, patchy and stiff. The piano has proper foot pedals but I can't reach them. Mary's mother is laughing again. All the girls are laughing too. I let out a little laugh meself. Sure isn't it a party? You're supposed to have fun at parties.*

# Chapter 4

Daria and I had an argument in O'Mahoney's. I knew it was coming. O'Mahoney's was the local chemist where we weighed ourselves once a week. She had nosebagged her way through half of Rowntrees' yearly supply in *Guinness Book* record time. Her aim had been to talk me out of going there at all: the others had gone to the pub and she was anxious to join them. She tried to smooth me over with the promise that if I left it for another week, I would be twice as pleased with my weight loss.

'That's the most pathetic attempt at manipulation you have ever tried to pull on me.' I stared at her in disbelief.

'I was only thinking of you,' she said demurely.

'You weren't thinking of me when you were stuffing your face. You know, if you continue to eat as much as you do, I wouldn't be surprised if NASA come looking for you.'

'Huh?' she said.

'They might want to use you to fill the hole in the ozone layer,'

'I'll be too busy,' she offered.

'Too busy eating. I could almost hear your oesophagus begging for mercy. If you keep it up, it'll collapse,' I added.

'Speak for yourself. I've heard your hips arguing. "If

you let me by, I'll let you pass,"' she replied, in a squeaky voice.

'Hey, I'm not the one who washes out the coffee in sweets under running water just so I can have the chocolate,' I reminded her.

'I'm not the one who bashes my cornflakes to a pulp so I can top up and get more in the bowl,' she hit back.

That gag was below the belt. Very few people knew about the cornflakes. I glanced around to make sure nobody had overheard. 'Shut your mouth, will you, Foghorn Leghorn?' I shushed her.

'I don't want to do this,' she said.

'Just get up and be done with it,' I snapped.

'Why do I always have to go first?' she whined.

'Why do you think elephants start throwing peanuts at me when I visit the zoo?' I answered. I heard some muffled laughs from the other shoppers. Before she could answer I grabbed her by the arm and a scuffle ensued.

I managed to get one of her feet on the scales. It shot up to four stone. 'That'll do,' she roared, and pulled herself off.

A little crowd had gathered.

'No, it won't do at all. You're a bad girl and we're going to prove it.'

I grabbed her by both legs, lifted her over my shoulder and plonked her full weight on the scales. The needle hovered between ten and eleven stone. 'Shit the bed,' she muttered. She began to undress. First the coat, hat and scarf were discarded. 'Take these,' she said. The needle barely flinched. 'Shit the bed twice,' she moaned. Her uniform jacket came off next, then the blouse. I covered my eyes just in case. The crowd was cheering now. Thank God she had a T-shirt on underneath. She struggled with her high leather boots and flung them on to the heap. She toyed with her skirt belt. The needle rested just above the ten-stone mark.

'Bloody hell!' she cried.

'The leather strap in your skirt, love,' an elderly onlooker suggested. 'That thing probably weighs a few pounds,'

The rest of the audience nodded in accord.

'Hey, it isn't an asteroid belt, you know,' she said.

It only made them laugh more.

Daria perfected a balancing act, one foot on the scales, one foot held high, as in a ballerina's pirouette. She couldn't look down now.

'What does it say?' she asked.

'"Get the fuck off",' a young bloke shouted.

The crowd went hysterical.

'Quit messing around,' she begged him.

'He's not messing,' I insisted.

'Finn?' she pleaded.

'Ten stone.' I gave in resentfully, then mumbled under my breath, 'I don't know how you manage it, you greedy cow.'

Daria jumped down and took a bow.

The crowd clapped and dispersed.

'Are you finished?' The shop-owner glared at her.

'Yes, thank you.' She flashed him an overly confident smile, then tapped her foot impatiently. 'Your turn,' she glowered at me.

'Hold my Energyade.' I shoved the bottle under her arm.

I took off my coat and said a quick prayer that she wouldn't have a rummage inside it and find all the sweets I'd saved for later. The shop-owner paused. I saw the look of concern on his face. No worries, mate. I wasn't going to discard *my* clothing: I didn't want to frighten everybody away. Besides, there was no need for me to cheat. I'd been a good girl. I really had. *I had.* No biscuits. No cakes. No crisps. No sweets. No fucking anything. I was so hungry I could have eaten a nun's arse through a hedge. But it was all going to be worth it. I was going to look devastating in my little black number.

I stepped up confidently and popped my twenty-pence piece into the machine. The needle shot upwards like the space shuttle. I held my breath until I was almost blue. I couldn't wait to see that clean level stroke on ten, to feel that sense of achievement. The excitement was nearly too much for me. I waited for the scales to have a chance to assess me fairly, then opened one eye apprehensively. I was ten stone five pounds.

*What? I can't be!*

I jumped down, grabbed my bag and rummaged through my purse, searching frantically for another twenty-pence piece. I plopped myself back on and rammed in the coin. I was still ten stone five.

'It must be broken. See? You bloody broke it,' I blamed Daria.

'There's nothing wrong with it. What's the matter with you? You're the same weight you were last week,' she reasoned.

'I can't be!' I wailed. 'You don't understand! I was so good. I walked every day. I did four aerobics classes and sweated a truckload. I didn't so much as lick a fucking lollipop. I can't be the same weight!' I was on the verge of crying.

'Finn, I'm not listening to this rubbish again. So what if you're the same weight? You didn't eat half the cocoa plantation of Brazil and put on a half-stone, did you?' She pointed at her arse and wagged it back and forth.

'It's all right for you Miss Fat Girl Slim. You can lose

it in a few days. I can't,' I said, exasperated.

'Maybe if you stopped drinking this crap. I mean, how can anyone drink so much Energyade?' she asked.

'It's a health drink,' I whispered, knowing quite well I hadn't any health issues.

'Finn, this stuff is for people when they're sick and even then you're only supposed to drink a glass of it,' she preached. I knew that, but I wasn't going to get into it. 'It's disgusting, too. Have you ever looked at what's actually in this bottle? Look at the ingredients, sugar, glucose, more sugar – and, let's see. . .oh, what a surprise, more sugar . . .' Daria went on and on but I wasn't listening to her.

My head ached with disappointment. It's typical. Like when you're playing a game of Snakes and Ladders. You get to that square three paces away from 100, the finishing line, and land on that really nasty long snake, the one that slithers you all the way back to the start.

Daria must have seen the look of dejection on my face. 'I told you we should have skipped this week. It's Christmas, Finn. Look, I went a bit hard on you there. Everybody has a little extra at Christmas, right? For God's sake, hang loose!' She pulled at my arm and tried to give me a friendly hug.

'If I hang any looser I'll end up on a clothes rail in Barry White's wardrobe.' I sighed.

'Look, I went along with you. You insisted on weighing yourself. We've done that. Now I want a drink, do you understand? Everybody is celebrating, Finn,' she said, licking her lips.

'Celebrating what?' I asked, wanting to forget about everything.

'Christmas? The millennium?' She gestured with her hands.

'I don't want to hear about it,' I moaned.

The scales had reminded me yet again of the Christmas party coming up, and how awful I would look in the black dress. Also, I was still reeling from the scenario in Arnott's earlier that day. It was a double-whammy. I was overweight and flat-chested.

# Chapter 5

Later, inside the pub, five different staff gatherings were all singing their own songs. The noise was deafening. I sang along with one, then got confused and drifted into another. I was grand with the first verse of Whitney's 'I Will Always Love You', but it sounded woeful mixed with the last verse of 'Fairytale In New York'. The fat lady sang rather badly. Eventually the lads told me to put a sock in it. I lashed back another Bacardi and Coke, but paralytic bliss was still some thirty minutes away. I was broody and sullen and being a real pain in the arse.

'Cheer up, for Christ's sake.' Daria elbowed me in the ribs.

'I'm OK.' I forced a weak smile.

'You've been a real wet rag lately,' she observed.

'I know. I'm sorry. I can't help it.'

'It's not the end of the world,' she said.

'What isn't?' I asked, uninterested.

'Splitting up with a guy. There's always a positive side to it, you know.'

She had said the forbidden words. I was annoyed. 'I'm sick and tired of training men in for the next woman.'

'See? That's something positive.' She smirked.

Daria insisted on blathering about how wonderful it was to be single again. I didn't want to acknowledge that I was in pain over a moron. 'It's not just Shane. I'm upset over my weight and my boobs,' I said.

'There's nothing wrong with either,' she insisted.

'You don't understand. Something awful happened today.'

'Well, go on.'

'I went and had myself fitted for a bra.'

'And?' Daria said.

'I'm a size 36A,' I wailed into my drink. 'Can you believe it? A size 36A! The bloody shame of it! I would have been better off buying a crop top in the children's department.'

'36A? Oh, come on, Finn, that's average,' she insisted.

'Look here, you, I wasn't born yesterday.' I sniffled into a threadbare handkerchief. '36A is for the little girlies in teen-scene magazines. You know, something you might give your twelve-year-old niece,'

Daria stifled a laugh.

I glared at her. 'It isn't funny,' I protested. 'How would you feel, eh? It's no wonder Shane left me. The relationship was too time-consuming for him. Most of our sex life was spent searching for my so-called tits.'

'Oh, Finn.' Daria couldn't help herself. She burst out laughing.

'Go ahead, laugh, it's OK for you.' I snivelled.

'I'm not laughing at you.' She hugged me. 'God, Finn, can't you see that the size of your boobs really doesn't matter? Why are you homing in on yourself and blaming your bodily proportions for this break-up? It was his fault, not yours! If I were you I'd be celebrating. Think of all the lovely guys you're going to meet from now on! I mean, what have you actually lost?'

'Nothing, I guess.'

'You have to learn to take these things with a pinch

of salt. Shane did absolutely nothing for you. In fact, I think he made you feel worse. He was a complete git. And now, to add insult to injury, you're saying the break-up was because of the size of your chest! Are you serious? Listen to what you're telling yourself. It's complete insanity.'

I thought about what she was saying, but I wasn't convinced. I had too many clear memories at the fore-front of my mind to contradict her views.

I could see Shane clearly in my mind's eye. I remem-bered that awful day when he was sitting on the couch in my flat watching MTV again. Some dark skinned beauty was performing and an entourage of gorgeous men surrounded her. I instantly felt irritated. I wanted to say something but then, enter the double-whammy, Jennifer Eden: Samantha King's Rival.

Jennifer 'If I had landed Robert De Niro's part in *Flawless*, I still couldn't sing to save my life' Eden. I swore I could see Shane's eyeballs jump right out and land on her boobs. I hated Jennifer Eden with a vengeance. Here she was again, simulating masturbation rather badly, her neckless head propped on her bosom like a crudely made snowman it was so obvious her boobs were falsies. The irony was, I wanted those boobs! I wanted to distract him, make him notice me the way he noticed her. Deliberately I stood in front of the television.

'Leeds United have been relegated,' I said.

Shane didn't flinch.

'The goalie was sold for fifty pounds,' I added.

Not a twitch.

'The manager was involved in an alien abduction and swears he was sexually molested with a Phillips screw-driver by a hairy green eunuch with huge almond-shaped eyes.'

No reaction.

He looked like he was having an out of body experience himself. He had landed on another moon. If there was anything at all that interested him, other than lingerie catalogues and scantily clad teeny bopper pop divas, it was Leeds United. The fact that he hadn't heard me alerted me to the seriousness of it all. I contemplated removing all my clothes, balancing a terracotta vase on my head and sticking a feather up my arse. I knew it was useless. If he hadn't heard the Leeds United bit we were really in trouble. I was angry with the MTV beauties who kept stealing my man away.

'You know, men love big breasts and long hair,' I said to Daria now, convinced I was right.

'Not all men,' she replied.

'Oh, yes, all men,' I contradicted her.

'You've a hang-up about your boobs, Finn,' she reminded me.

'You're right. You couldn't hang wallpaper on me.'

'Oh, be logical, will you? You can't have a relationship with two lumps of flesh. There are other bits. Like the person they're attached to?' she said.

Easy for her to say: her breasts were a respectable size 34C.

'He wasn't interested in the rest of me. They're all the same. Look at them.' I jerked my head at the lads and threw back my fifth drink.

Dessie, Colm, Tom and Mark Adams were laughing their heads off.

'What, for God's sake? They're having a bit of fun,' she said.

'They're ogling. They were ogling this morning. They're ogling this evening. It must be a national pastime.'

I watched Mark Adams turn his head as a passing blonde bombshell in a backless halter-neck dress brushed against his knee. His red moustache twitched – it always looked like it needed a conditioning treatment, all wiry and stiff-looking, like intertwining rusty coils of metal.

'Didn't you notice them watching that slut Samantha King this morning? Tom nearly came over faint.' I grinned at the memory.

'They were listening to the music.' Daria shook her head from side to side.

'We'll see about that. Dessie?' I called drunkenly.

He sidled over, his chin buried in a pint glass of Carlsberg. His streaked blond hair looked ridiculous in the middle of December – even without the piece of tinsel he was now wearing round it. With his radiant complexion – due to rapid alcohol consumption – he looked like a jolly Christmas tree. The only thing missing was the extension lead, I could have brought him home to the flat and plugged him in. He would have looked nice in the porch.

'Question,' I started. 'Two women approach you. Both are selling the exact same insurance policy. One could feed an army with her breasts. The other is as flat as a breadboard. Which one would you buy the policy off?' I asked him.

'I would be sensible and buy the correct policy, no matter what the women looked like,' he said, without hesitation.

'You lying bastard,' I slurred.

Colm had moved over. 'What?' he asked.

'Sit down. I have a question for you,'

Colm draped his arm casually round my shoulders. I felt a little peculiar. I'd never fancied my chances with Colm. He was just a nice guy, a friend. Often I chose men with a physical defect – a crooked nose, a scarred face. I had even dated a guy with nine and a half fingers. I was the type to fall in love with someone who had a terminal disease or was confined to a wheelchair for life. I liked defects. Colm was a deviation: someone to romanticize and fantasize about. I felt comfortable with the knowledge that he would never make a move on me, and he always, always made me laugh. I tried not to look cross-eyed as I put the same question to Colm as I had to Dessie.

'I'd do the same as Des, of course,' he swore, without taking his eyes off me.

'You're lying, Colm, and I really thought you, of all people, would own up.' I said.

'Are you putting a question mark over my integrity?' He tried his best to look insulted by the mere suggestion.

'Heaven forbid! You know I'd never do such a thing. Still, there's more than a small question mark hanging over your acting abilities right now and I didn't put it there,' I replied, smiling.

'Look, you asked me a question and I gave an honest answer,' he insisted.

'We'll see about that,' I said confidently.

I grabbed Tom and Mark by the collar and asked them the same thing. Tom went along with his mates – he always did: as Mark Adams's right-hand man, he frequently played down his seedy side when he was in the boss's company. After three years, I felt I knew absolutely nothing about Tom O'Hare except that he was a whoring bastard who always had his hands in someone's knickers. What bothered me more was that Colm seemed to spend a lot more time than usual with him lately. I couldn't understand this: the two of them had nothing in common. Or had they?

I gave Mark Adams the Cyclops eye. As far as I was concerned, he was the only one who had any character. His future as an honest human being hung in the balance.

He paused to think about the question, wisely so, massaging his moustache as he pondered the correct response. 'OK, then. You want an honest answer?'

'Yes. An *honest* answer,' I nodded.

'I'd go for the big boobs,' he said.

The lads expelled a united horrified gasp and stared at him. I could almost hear their thoughts.

*There's a spy in the camp! Traitor! Absconder!*

'See?' I turned to Daria. 'They're not all pretentious, shallow yes-men.'

'We are, actually,' Mark said.

'What?' Dessie eyed him incredulously, as if he was playing with a short deck.

'No, we're not.' Tom perked up and then, apparently having realized he was on the wrong footing, refrained from adding more.

Colm sat quietly, nursing his pint.

'Yes, we are, lads. When a man's penis is erect, his brains are in his balls.' Mark let out a satisfied 'Aaah' as he finished off another pint, his moustache bathing in the frothy remnants.

'That's brilliant,' I said.

'It's disgusting!' Daria exclaimed.

'It's the truth,' Mark Adams reiterated.

'Who said so?' Colm asked, curious as always.

'Madame Cyn,' he answered.

'She ought to know. How many dead brain cells is she responsible for?' Daria snorted.

'At least someone knows,' I said, my tone drenched with heavy sarcasm.

'I think you're all getting sidetracked,' Colm said.

'Oh, come, now, Colm, since when did you come over all scrupulous and full of morality?' Daria quizzed him.

'Yeah, since when did you care? Don't tell me you're not the first to admire a nice pair of . . .' Tom tapered off.

'Of course I do, but I admire lots of other things too. Like the way a person smiles, the texture of their hair, how they carry themselves, their character. All those things matter, too. I would rather see a woman in a nice bathing suit than nudity for nudity's sake. Most men would, I'm sure of it,' he said.

*I knew he would mention the hair. I was willing to bet a million that he loved long hair.*

They all went quiet. Colm swirled his drink round. 'I'm not saying I'm a saint. Who doesn't ogle a beautiful woman? But I don't always judge a book by its cover,' he said, his eyes resting on me. I blushed, if that was possible: I was already puce from head to toe with the Bacardi.

'Have you ever actually read a book?' Mark asked.

We all laughed at this.

'You girls want to believe the worst about us. Which one of you hasn't succumbed to the good-looking bloke selling something? Own up, you pair,' he went on. 'And how do you know he hasn't had cosmetic surgery?' Colm asked.

I didn't.

An uncomfortable silence ensued. 'I suppose breasts have a purpose. They were created to feed our children, not purely for a man's pleasure,' Dessie pontificated with virtuous conviction. He ought to know. According to him, he had fondled more than Don Juan De Marco. The others nodded in agreement as they clung to their rickety moral scaffolding – all except Colm, who didn't seem to care about speaking his own mind in front of the boss.

I had heard enough. I went straight to the point of my earlier question. 'OK. OK. Let me get my point out once and for all. I saw all of you watching Sam King this morning. Just like regular Homer Simpsons, the lot of you. I swear I *saw* the drool rolling down your chins, and don't tell me you were studying her dance steps. You were all glued to her boobs.'

Dessie rubbed his stubbly baby fluff and Tom left for the bar. Colm went to get up, but I dragged him back down by the seat of his pants. He straightened them out. His aftershave wafted between us and I thought how unusual and distinctive it was. Not overwhelming like Dessie's Polo, which, I was certain, he drank for breakfast dinner and tea. Perhaps he hadn't realized yet that you use it on the *outside* of yourself.

'Where do you think you're going?' I slobbered.

'To the toilet.' He pinched my bottom.

I was momentarily distracted, but wasn't going to leave the conversation open-ended. 'I'm not finished with you yet,' I slurred. 'Daria, you saw them, didn't you?' I lassoed the guilt rope tightly about her pretty little neck. There was no escaping.

'Yeah, I did. You ought to be ashamed of yourselves. What worries me is that you guys think Sam King is normal, that all women should look like that. You know she's had every possible cosmetic procedure done?'

'No one knows that for sure, you're only assuming.' Tom shrugged his shoulders. It was clear it didn't matter to him one way or the other how she'd got her boobs.

'Who cares anyway? I think she's bleedin' massive,' Dessie agreed, but only because he was an eejit and wanted to keep in with the lads.

They all stared at him like he had three heads.

'From where I'm sitting it would seem that *you women*

are more obsessed with Samantha King than we are.' Colm stood up again to go to the toilet. This time I didn't make any move to keep him back.

A deafening silence followed.

By then, though, I didn't care. I didn't care if Samantha King was the work of God's hands or the surgeon's scalpel. I would have sold my soul just to look like her. Even if I couldn't have had the boobs I would have settled for the hair. That lovely long silky blonde hair. How I had yearned for that hair when I was a little girl. I could still recall vividly how Mam had flatly refused to let me grow mine past my ears. I had felt so unfeminine with that short cut she had insisted on. She had told me it was best to wear it short because of the nits. I had so desperately wanted to be a 'real' girl, but I was blocked. I was a girl who wanted plaits, ponies, buns and ringlets, anything but that scruffy mousy brown crop. Yes. My dream of long hair had been neatly folded away in a box with the fancy party dress.

*I am six years old and going to have my hair cut. Padraig and Fearghal are with me. My mam says it's quicker if we all go to the same place.*

*I don't like having to go inside Henry's barbershop. It's full of old men reading the racing pages and the castor-oil smell of greasy Brylcreem. It reminds me of my Dad's Palmolive shaving stick and brush, poking out of the white tin mug on the bathroom shelf. My Mam is talking to Henry, the owner. I don't like Henry. He always leaves me to last. I would like to go first for a change, so I can sneak across to Rosalie's.*

*Rosalie is a real hairdresser. She cuts ladies' hair. My best friend Mary had her hair done there for her communion, a lovely bun that sat stiffly on the back of her head. She had lots of brown clips holding it in place. I didn't believe she went to Rosalie's because my Mam said only 'vain' girls went there.*

*I love looking out the window of the barber's into Rosalie's parlour. There's a lovely cream net curtain in the window. It's full of pretty holes and shapes. It goes up in the middle leaving a space for a plastic bowl of yellow roses on the windowsill. My mam says it came from Spain and can't be up to any good. She says Spanish dancing is a 'decadent art'. I'm not sure what that means either but I think it might have something to do with the decades of the rosary. Maybe they don't say it at Rosalie's. They close the shop at five thirty so how can they say the rosary at six like we do? Perhaps the Spanish net curtain is the work of the devil. I shouldn't look at it so much, but I can't help myself.*

*The ladies' salon has 'Rosalie's' written across it in big brown letters. Sometimes, when we pass it on the way to the butcher's next door, I can see the mist that shoots from the hairspray bottles still floating in the air. If I sniff hard enough I can get a whiff of apple and coconut shampoo. I like to watch the ladies in a line under the hairdryers, their lips moving but no sound coming out. They sip cups of tea and read magazines.*

*They have big plastic curlers peering out from under pink hairnets with little coloured beads stuck on them. I like pink; it's my favourite colour. I wish I had a pink bow in my hair. Just once. Mam says I'm being a silly billy. I haven't enough hair to tie a bow in. Henry and she are laughing at the thought of it. Padraig and Fearghal are laughing because Mam is laughing. I don't think it's so funny. Mam is happy because Dad will be pleased. Dad is quiet when he is pleased. Mam likes it when he is quiet . . .*

# Chapter 6

On Monday I arrived into work late. There wasn't a sinner in Ireland who wasn't arriving into work late, so why break the mould? It was the day of our Christmas party. Everybody complained that we had work the next day and how awkward it would be. We'd had a choice for the party: either Monday or the following Sunday, which didn't suit either – we still had to turn in for work no matter what state we were in. We had been trying to book a venue since July, but because of the Mad Millennium, nothing was available, so we settled on the Monday night.

The working day had been quiet enough, the Christmas rush almost over. We made the best of it, as we knew in advance that the interest was set to go on the accounts the following day. It was always a curse for weeks afterwards when people who never visited the Credit Union came in for their yearly top-up. They didn't have to come in, their interest automatically went on to their books, but still they came – as if we might steal it if they didn't.

Mark Adams was in a fury, a sight for sore eyes to be sure. I had a hunch it had something to do with Mr Myers when he arrived at Dessie's side purple in the face and the veins straining to jump out of his neck. I nudged Daria, who bit her lip. We both felt guilty now. He was sure to get into trouble.

'All I know is this guy rings me up screaming down the phone that we called him and then some member of staff abused him!' he hissed into Dessie's ear, while smiling at the member at his desk.

'Mrs Moylan, how are you? Haven't seen you in ages,' Dessie smiled weakly through the hatch. He handed Mrs Moylan her book and she said goodbye. Mark Adams in a temper could make you curl up and die. He was a small wiry man, but his presence was awesome and even more so when he was angry. The only give-away was the red face and twitching moustache, a sign for us all to go and hide.

'Put your closed sign up,' he ordered.

Dessie did as he was told. 'I swear, Mark, I didn't phone him. I didn't even know he was on the phone. The internal line lit up so I answered it and you see—'

'If it wasn't the day that's in it, I would fire you on the spot,' Mark Adams spat. 'I don't care what happened out here. I've had to listen to him for over half an hour. I managed to convince him that he must have had a crossed line and been connected to some other company by mistake. That, my boy, is what's called a modern-day miracle, and if you ever do that again and you live to see the end of the day, that will also be called a modern-day miracle. Understand?'

Dessie wasn't sure if he was supposed to speak. He opened his mouth and went to say something.

'You're an awful fucking gobshite,' Mark Adams cut him down.

Dessie shut his mouth.

'It's closing time. Get out there and stand at the door and lock it each time a member leaves. Then get your arse back in here, balance up, then help the others,' he ordered.

'OK,' Dessie mumbled, and walked towards the door rattling his keys.

Poor Dessie. I felt awful guilty. I tiptoed over to his desk and stuck a Cadbury's flake in his printer.

Tom and Colm were having a good long laugh about it. I glared at them through the nine-foot-long tally toll. OK, Dessie was a bit of an arsehole, but he was young and naïve and they always made him feel left out. He just wanted to belong to the gang, but it seemed Tom and Colm were determined to keep him out of their social life. When the last member had gone, Daria and I set to work on our calculators, our nimble fingers punching away at the speed of sound. We concentrated because we knew it was worth it. It was the only time in my job that I was engrossed in my tasks. That was because I couldn't leave until the dirty deed was done. In fact, none of us could. If some idiot didn't balance we all had to stay, so it was always a tense fifteen minutes at the end of the day.

I counted my cash, cheques and coin and came up with a total. I glanced hopefully at the corresponding figure flashing on my computer. Bingo, I was balanced and to the penny! We all were, except Dessie. I noticed the two boys get up to go to the kitchen, not a helping hand forthcoming from either. I walked over to him and took his balance sheet. He was out by a sizeable figure.

'God, Dessie, how did you manage this?' I asked him. I already knew the answer. Mark Adams had scared the hell out of him and, in all likelihood, he had made a mistake then. I went through everything and paid particular attention to the last half-hour's figures. Dessie was beginning to write out a 'difference' on his balance sheet.

'You can't hand up a difference like that, not after what happened earlier. He'll skin you alive. Hold your horses, young bucko,' I said. He was a hundred and fifty pounds short. I scanned the desk and the surrounding area, and there I spotted something.

'It's OK. I have it,' I said, delighted with myself.

'Thank Christ.' Dessie heaved a sigh of relief. He ran his hand through his blond streaks, showing up the black roots.

'A hundred and fifty pounds in coins behind the bin, Dessie, you Goddamn eejit.' I kicked the bags.

Dessie bent down and gathered them up. 'Christ, I completely forgot about them. Not just a pretty face, eh?' he said.

'I have brains, you know,' I said, jotting the figures down again on a clean sheet.

'Yeah, I know,' he said, quite seriously.

'That doesn't mean you're to start getting any ideas, Dessie.' I smiled at him. I felt like the lady in the Surf washing-powder ad. It wasn't much to brag about, was it? A spotty four-eyed idiot with a crush on you? But a queue wasn't forming to take me out.

Even though I knew Shane was a dead-beat, I found myself wondering could our relationship have been worked out. Was it his fault or mine? I thought back to that last row we'd had, the one that had finally broken us up. I concluded that the Chippendales had been to blame. A bloody poster of the Chippendales had ruined our relationship, and I should have known better than to get into a row with him about it.

We had planned to go out for our first anniversary, a quiet romantic meal at a table for two in Nico's on Dame Street. I wasn't feeling in the best of form. I had a cold coming on and a bad dose of PMT. I couldn't contain my hostility. I was already angry because I had found a lingerie catalogue in Shane's pocket, which of course he denied was his. I was disgusted that he could fob it off without a hint of guilt. But I didn't want to argue with him and tried to put it to the back of my mind.

Trouble was, I was putting so many things to the back of my mind that it had become overcrowded. It was increasingly hard to ignore all the relevant grounds I had to tell him to go and get fucked. He was inconsiderate, lazy, chauvinistic, cruel, insensitive and boring – and those were his good points. I should have seen it coming. The conversation went something like this:

'What's the matter with you? You've a face on you that would turn a cowpat,' I observed. Actually, I was the real cowpat because of the PMT, but everyone knows that, no matter what's wrong, it is always, *always* the man's fault.

'There's nothing wrong with me.' He sighed.

We were standing on the North Circular Road in the middle of a torrential downpour, waiting for a bus into town. The bus shelter only barely shielded us from the east wind, which was hurling sheets of rain at us.

'There *is* something wrong with you,' I repeated.

'There's nothing wrong,' he snarled.

'You don't want to go out, do you?' I asked.

'I never said that.' He shrugged.

'It was your suggestion,' I reminded him. 'I would have been just as happy to get a takeaway and watch a movie.'

'What? Since when did you change your mind?' He stared at me.

'I didn't change my mind. I never said we had to go out,' I lied.

He grunted and dug his hands deeper in his pockets. 'Are you saying you want to go home now?' He was trying, I knew, to sound calm.

'What would you like to do?' I had confused him further. I loved doing that and seeing his temples pulsate and his throat constrict with choked-back anger. I was being a right bitch. 'I don't care what we do, just so long as you cheer up. For God's sake, your face looks like a long drop of water,' I finished.

We huddled closer, the unrelenting rain still driving in full throttle.

Shane fidgeted. I knew him too well: there was definitely something else irritating him. I followed his gaze and then I saw it. I permitted my face a cheeky, smug smile.

'What?' he barked at me.

'I know what's wrong with you.'

'Look, I told you, there's nothing wrong with me I—'

'Oh, but there is,' I broke him off. 'It's that poster of the Chippendales.'

There was a long silence.

'What poster?' He played dumb.

'That poster.' I pointed to it. 'The one with the big hunks that have oil smeared all over their muscular bodies and are wearing silly little G-strings.' I described the poster in minute detail, knowing he had seen it.

'I never even noticed it,' he lied.

'You did, so,' I pushed him.

'Well, *you* obviously saw it,' he remarked.

'I was only looking at their faces.' I had started to lie now.

'Then you must be fucking cross-eyed,' he retorted.

'I can't help it,' I stared at a particularly good-looking

Nordic blond. His chest was all puffed out, proud and confident, a Cheshire cat grin painted on his chiselled features.

'Will you please stop staring at that thing?' Shane was openly aggressive now.

It was just the reaction I wanted. In fact, any reaction was better than none at all, which was what I had acceded to over the last month. Shane had settled into as ongoing trance: nothing moved him but MTV and the smell of food. He hated the constant arguing that had become the staple diet of our union. The more he backed away, the more I nagged; the more I nagged, the more he backed away.

'What's all the fuss? I don't tell you what posters to stare at,' I defended myself.

'It's indecent. It makes me sick. All these women paying money to see some guys . . . you know . . .' He threw back his head.

'It's only a bit of fun!' I laughed. It was the kind of laugh targeted to push the 'sensitive' button. He hated being laughed at like some kind of eejit.

He wasn't amused one bit. He stepped up into his DIY moral pulpit. 'You call that fun?' He gestured to the poster, nodding like a Lamberts Theatre puppet.

'Why are you getting so upset over a bloody poster?' As if I didn't know and wasn't enjoying every single minute of it.

'You haven't taken your eyes off it since we got here!' he accused me.

'Oh, that's rubbish.' I waited for the explosion.

'Would you pay twenty pounds to go and see that show?' he asked, raising his voice a bit more.

'Why not? What's wrong with it?' I asked. 'Men have been paying thousands of pounds since the year dot to look at naked women. I don't remember you ever objecting to that.'

'It's not the same thing. I've never paid twenty pounds to go and see a stripper,' he said.

'You're right. You've never paid twenty pounds to see a stripper . . .' I agreed.

He was momentarily calmed.

'. . .more like thousands of pounds. You buy the newspapers with the page-three babes. There's the cable-link bill that gives you direct access to hard-core porn, tits and arses twenty-four seven. Oh, and the Internet. The educational discoveries of the nineties, they call it. There are more porn sites on it than anything else – and you have to include the *lingerie catalogues too*.' I gave him a sideways glance and stepped backwards.

I waited for him to placate me. I waited for him to assuage my delicate psyche. I waited for him to smooth me down with sweet nothings, to tell me he loved me, he realized how insensitive he had been, and how sorry he was. How he had been 'tricked' into looking at the lingerie catalogue like I had been tricked into staring at the Chippendales poster that I was presently denying had any effect on me. I waited and waited, and prayed that he might suddenly understand the ways of the world. Just as well I wasn't holding my breath.

He lifted the sole of his boot and looked at it. 'There's a hole in my boot. I don't believe it. They're brand new,' he complained.

I was furious. He hadn't even tried to reassure me about the catalogue. I searched for ammunition and found it to my right. A poster for a new brand of men's aftershave, depicting a young girl of perhaps thirteen or fourteen. She was completely naked, save a Crombie hat on her head.

'Tell me, darling, what comments do you have to make about this?' I nodded at it.

Shane looked wearily at it. 'What's that got to do with anything?' he asked impatiently.

'Do you not see the irony, Shane? Do you not see what's wrong with it?' I asked incredulous.

'Duh? No?'

'You don't? If I'm cross-eyed, then you must have cataracts. It's child pornography, for Christ's sake!'

'What the hell is wrong with you, huh? What do you want from me, huh? You started this stupid conversation. I mean, what do you want me to say? That I don't mind you leering at other men? I can tell you this for nothing. No girlfriend of mine is paying money to see some arse-bandit prance about a stage with his willie hanging out,' he spat.

'Shane, there's a slight difference between the Chippendales and this,' I said, pointing to the other poster.

'Like what?' he asked.

'It's a fucking girl, not a woman! She's fourteen if she's a day!' I shouted at him.

How would I know how old she is? She looks about twenty to me?' he answered.

'Oh, you should know being an expert on porn movies,' I snapped, disgusted beyond belief.

'Finn, it's no secret that young girls are often in porno movies and hey, I resent the accusation that I watch them.'

'You watched *The Art of Making Love*, didn't you?' I was quick to retort.

'That was for educational purposes, and there were no girlies in it. Remember, you watched it too.'

'Oh, for the love of – educational purposes? That's a

good one! The best yet! Well, I hate to capsize your humongous ego but *you* didn't learn much, did you?'

The eruption was inevitable. He exploded right on cue. Well, let the fucking lava flow, baby, you asked for it.

'What's that supposed to mean?' he shouted.

I wasn't intimidated. I had moved on. I was having a mini *tsunami* myself and it was too late to stop it. 'I suppose *9½ Weeks* was for educational purposes, too, huh?' I ranted.

'I thought it was about pregnancy,' he responded, knowing he was going down for a third time. His waving hand was just about visible but I wasn't about to throw him a lifebelt.

'Why did you sign up for Sky and Premier, then, huh?' I dived in.

'I only signed up for the sports channels,' he tried.

'Sports, is it?' My voice had taken on the tone of a vicious gremlin. 'You've never watched a sports programme in your entire life. You wouldn't know the difference between a goalpost and a cricket bat.' Had I been in possession of either, I would have gladly whacked him over the head.

'That's rubbish. You know I love the golf,' he said.

'Golf? Oh, please! Since when? You never played a round of golf in your life! You couldn't hit a cow's arse with a fucking banjo!' I roared.

'Pipe down. I mean it,' he threatened me. A group of green-clad Americans had arrived at the bus shelter and were huddled nearby, talking loudly.

'You're jealous, but you'll never admit it, will you?' I went on, knowing that I, too, was consumed with jealousy and that it was just too hard to hide it any more.

'Jealous? Of those morons? There's something really

wrong with you if you think that!' He chuckled.

'Well, you'd better get over it. I have tickets for the show. Daria is coming with me.' I found myself spinning a yarn.

'She would, wouldn't she? That thing's obsessed. A bucket of Mickeys couldn't satisfy her.'

I knew he was tormented by thoughts of Daria and me surrounded by half-naked, lithe, muscle-pumping toy-boys. There would be no holds barred with Daria about. I could see him imagining the scenario. Me shoving a fiver down a bloke's codpiece and Daria making *doubly sure* that it went in. He looked like he wanted to bang his head off the bus shelter.

He was choking, trying to get the next words out. 'I can't believe you! Talk about double standards. You want us men to behave like Padre Pio, while you lot go throwing your knickers at some stranger. I don't know what all the fuss is about. Look, if you must go, go. I really don't give a damn. There's something really wrong with you, though. They're all gay, for God's sake!' He hit back the way men do. His mouth was in motion before his mind had a chance to think things through.

The Americans stopped dead in their tracks and let out a collective gusty 'Oooooh!' They were earwigging and I can't say I blamed them. If nothing else, their trip to Ireland had supplied them with first-class material for a number-one best-selling novel. But I didn't care what they thought. I was hurt. I stared at Shane in disbelief, his last words resounding in my head with acute clarity. *He didn't care. He really didn't care about me at all.*

I tried to swallow the tears and defend myself. I tried to think logically. My head was doing faster laps than

Michael Schumacher. 'So what if they're all gay? Men love nothing more than to watch a pair of lesbians doing their thing! What's the bloody difference in watching some gorgeous dude strutting his stuff? I'm not going with the intention of finding the love of my life. It's all a joke. You just can't understand that, can you?' I screamed at him.

'Yeah, baby, you tell that man!' an American woman cried. Suddenly a bright flash of light exploded before my eyes. The Americans were taking photographs of us. I couldn't believe it.

Neither could Shane. He completely lost it. 'For Christ's sake! If you don't get that thing out of my face I'll rearrange your nose, do you hear me? Now, piddle off and shoot some trees!' Shane screamed.

The bus pulled in, bringing with it a tidal wave of dirty water. It splashed against Shane, giving him a free mud-wrap, compliments of Dublin Bus.

He stepped on to the bus, soggy clothes dripping, leaving a trail of water behind him. I stood on the pavement and suddenly understood what all my friends had been trying to tell me for months. I was dating a complete and utter wanker. Shane looked over his shoulder and our eyes met briefly. He made no gesture to hurry me on to the bus.

'Is this the bus for *Maldahide*?' one of the Americans shouted into the driver's face.

'Formaldehyde? No, I think that's a kind of poison,' the driver answered wearily.

'Howdya pronounce this?' The American handed him a tour brochure.

The driver read it and handed it back. 'The bus for *Malahide* is on the other side of the street,' he replied. The Americans toddled off, whispering among themselves, while I stood waiting for Shane to do the right thing by me.

'Are you getting on or wha'?' the irritated driver asked me.

'Fuck off,' I answered him.

'Suit yourself, ye toerag,' he shouted, and the doors hissed shut.

The bus pulled away, with Shane watching me through the foggy window.

I had not seen him since. He hadn't called me either. Not once. Not even to have me answer and hang up on me. That would have been enough to prove he cared something for me. I wasn't so much missing him as the familiarity of a partner. The Christmas season only exaggerated that sense of incompleteness.

All that crap they give you about family unity and brotherly love. Family unity, my arse, brotherly love, my arse. I thought about my so-called family. I hated my brothers, really hated them. It had been no fun being a girl with two brothers. Especially when they appeared to me to be the apple of my father's eye. Nothing I did seemed to interest Dad, but the boys? They stole all the attention. Dad seemed to resent my being a girl. Even my mother treated me like a boy. Maybe she had done it to please my dad. I resented her for that. I thought back. I recalled an incident that proved my theory was at least plausible. I could still hear my mam calling, 'Oh, boys, boys, where are yous?'

*I am eight. My brothers and I are playing on the sand down at the beach. I always get to be the one who's buried. All I can see is my toes. I am wriggling them to make sure they're my own because I can't feel them. They look funny sticking out of the sand. Padraig has hung seaweed on them and says it attracts the sharks from Australia. I don't mind, as long as they don't find a secret tunnel up from the sea and take a big bite out of my bum.*

*I can hear the ice-cream van at the other end of the beach. It will be another five minutes before it reaches our spot. I'm going to get a ninety-nine with raspberry ripple dribbling down the side. I'll eat it slowly until I get to the end of the cone where there's always a surprise blob of ice-cream. Then I'll bite off the end and suck it out. I'll make sure this time that Fearghal doesn't beat me to it. The last time he ran up behind me and grabbed it before I saw him coming. He had it scoffed too quickly for me to complain to Mam and Dad – sure they'd have told me to quit whingeing anyway, and if I tried another stroke like that I'd never see another ice-cream for the rest of the summer.*

*Padraig is running backwards and forwards to the sea. He has dug a trench round me. It doesn't matter how fast he runs, as soon as he pours the water into the trench it disappears. I can feel it trickling through my legs under the mound of sand. Fearghal has built a turret and planted castles all round me. They are finishing them off with shells and feathers and having a right oul World War Two battle at my expense. Fearghal always has to be a German so he always loses.*

*The ice-cream van is getting nearer. I can just about see the tips of Mam and Dad's heads over the sand dunes beyond. Mam is standing up and shaking out the grey rubber ground sheet. She is having one of those talks with Dad again. I can tell by the way she folds the sheet perfectly, packing it into the big straw basket. She is standing with her legs apart and her hands on her hips, and I know she's looking for us. The sound of the waves is fierce, but I can read her lips. I can read her fear. She has her hand over her brow now, shading the glare of the sun from her eyes. Between the loud crashing of the waves on the beach I can catch her shouts: 'Boys? Boys? Where are yous?'*

*I try to lift my hand out of the sand but it's stuck tight and I'm shouting at Fearghal to hurry up or the ice-cream man will be gone before we know it. He's too busy giving Padraig a 'Ringsend uppercut' for standing on his prize turret. It was all lopsided and crumbling anyway.*

*My mam has moved to the top of the dune. She's scanning the beach for us. Dad must be giving her a hard time again. It's always over me. I don't know what I've done this time. Mam must be blind. There's only one eejit buried in the sand and the boys are doing a war dance round me. She still can't see us and I can read her panic in the way she turns to Dad. He drops his newspaper and comes to stand beside her. I have displeased him again. I didn't answer quickly enough. Otherwise Dad wouldn't have had to get up at all. That will really annoy Mam.*

*'Patrick, where are the boys? Can you see them?' I hear her shouting to him. I have my left hand free. I wave to her and she spots us at last.*

*'We're here, Mam,' I shout, as loud as I can. 'We're here!' I say, more quietly.*

*The boys are looking at me.*

*'Since when are you a boy?' Padraig sneers.*

# Chapter 7

The Royal Hotel was anything but. It stank of disinfectant, and its staff were so inebriated we almost had to serve ourselves. Our table was at the far end of an enormous barn-type hall, along with another thirty or so. There were probably about four hundred people in all, squashed together like sardines in a can. I frequently elbowed our manager's wife in the jaw and on occasions we ate off the wrong plates or drank the wrong drinks. A white card in the centre of the table announced who we were: 'Dublin Central Credit Union'.

Mark Adams was adamant that we enjoy ourselves. To get us started he produced some party artefacts that he insisted we wore. The girls had bouncing baubles on their heads and the men sported false moustaches. We ate rubber turkey and ham with our antennae bopping and moustaches twitching.

We looked like a casting line-up auditioning for *One Flew Over the Cuckoo's Nest*. All that was missing was the medication in the little white cups. Nobody ate the Christmas pudding, so when they weren't looking I gathered up the pieces, wrapped them in a paper napkin and stuck them into my bag. I would have them later in the loo if things got really boring. The warm cherry-coloured mulled wine was going down a treat. The bowl had been emptied in minutes so Mark Adams ordered more. Red and white wine also flowed freely and the odd pint splattered the table.

Dessie amused himself solely with party-poppers and streamers, and never seemed to tire of the loud clap of the crackers, which he pulled with himself. He had gathered a small mountain of plastic ditties and marvelled that no one else seemed to think they were worthy of attention. He regaled us with the stupid jokes and laughed heartily. He had surprised us all by arriving with a fairly decent-looking girl – a little young but then, so was our Dessie. Her name was Anita, and she was a whimsical brunette with freckles galore and an overabundance of teeth. She was painfully shy and quiet but seemed totally enamoured of our Dessie, and I thought it was kind of cute. I was glad he had a girl on his arm, even if she was probably his sister.

Mark Adams's wife, Angela, looked a bit harsh, but was quite nice. She was dressed in a plain black power suit with a white shirt buttoned up to the neck and no jewellery. She wore the trousers, but warmth and a certain respect was evident between her and Mark and I saw them frequently squeeze hands beneath the table and lock eyes lovingly. I didn't want to dwell on it: I had been a bag of self-pity for too long. Angela was an interesting conversationalist, mostly about business. I didn't mind one bit. She was active on the Credit Union committee and gave up two to three evenings a week to the community's causes. They made a strong couple, and I envied them.

Colm Long had brought a real surprise. I tried hard not to stare at Julia, whom I had seen often in the Credit Union, as she linked him in a 'protect me, please' manner. She looked like she needed reassurance, and from time to time Colm gave it, patting her arm in a fatherly fashion. I was glad he had someone with him but felt a tinge of jealousy.

'Would you get a load of that?' I whispered in Daria's ear. 'Julia Martin? She's ninety if she's a day.'

Daria sniggered. 'What the hell is he playing at?' she said quietly.

I couldn't figure him out and it wasn't from the want of trying. If I had thought I stood a chance of a quick feel in the toilets out back I would have been the first to offer my services free of charge. Tonight he looked rather stunning in a jade green suit, with an immaculate white shirt and colourful tie. What *was* he doing with Julia Martin? This was really scraping the bottom of the barrel. Don't get me wrong. Julia was a nice-looking woman – even if she was a fossilized relic from some architectural dig outside Dublin Corporation. Anyway, it wasn't my place to be judging. At least he'd had the courage to bring someone along. I was just green with envy.

To my left sat lecherous Tom – who had done the pubs earlier and in a hurry, by the look of things. At nine o'clock we were mid-way through our meal and Tom was legless. Always aware of business etiquette he tried to make conversation with Angela, who humoured him but I knew she disliked him. His too-loud false laughter and over-the-top willingness to get the next drinks spoke volumes, and Angela was no fool. She looked like she wanted to have a good time and not be harassed by this idiot. When she eventually changed seats, Tom moved up beside Tweedledee and Tweedledum. That's us, Daria and me. The two spare pricks with silver boppers and no partners, and stuck in what could only be described as a social graveyard.

I eyed Daria and decided she hadn't any excuse whatsoever. She shouldn't have come along without somebody nice. She could have had her pick, but she wasn't the dating type. Her career and her determination to make her mark as a foreigner in Dublin consumed her every waking moment. She felt she had to prove herself. She felt she had to work twice as hard to fit in. It wasn't true, but she believed it. I think she felt she couldn't allow herself the luxury of a boyfriend. She was too frightened. Frankly, I can't say I blamed her.

Irish men would put the fear of God into any woman. They drank like dolphins, gambled passionately, played the field with wild abandon, farted and shamelessly scratched their proverbials in public. Daria was attractive to them, but not in a nice sense. They took her out and treated her like some dressed-up monkey in a cage. I think they expected her to behave like some barbarian half-wit, who howled at the moon and dabbled in witchcraft. She was different and she knew it.

That was not the case with all men, of course, but rather than test the waters even with a toe, she gave the impression that she was a modern independent career girl, who hadn't the time for folly and romance. So Daria spent most of her spare time alone, or haunting me. I had tried to persuade her to ask someone to the party but she resisted. She stated that if she did I would be the only partnerless person there. Noble, but her motive was dodgy. Still, at the end of the day, I was glad we were together. When we had finished the meal, I got stuck into the serious business of getting sloshed. There was nothing else to do and as I looked like a complete eejit anyway (having settled for the old reliable black dress in the end) it seemed appropriate that I behave like one.

We switched our drinks yet again and started lowering

bizarre cocktails. Pretty soon Tom's eyes were roaming over Daria in a frightening fashion, and he seemed to regard her as part of the menu. I didn't really pay much attention to it until Daria began to behave in an uncharacteristic fashion. She had had more than her fair share of drink and wasn't alien to the odd pang of loneliness. Alcohol and loneliness were a deadly mixture.

I ought to have known. I had had experiences in the past when a truly ugly man had looked attractive after ten drinks. Somehow you excuse all manner of awfulness, like bad breath, BO and even evidence to suggest a distinct lack of brain activity. I pondered this while eavesdropping on the conversation taking place between Daria and Tom.

'You know, some girls have said I look like Tom Cruise,' he was slurring into her ear.

Daria smiled at him, all gooey and sweet, a conclusive twitch in her left eye. 'Shid de bed.' She hiccuped.

I looked at Tom and concluded that, as human beings go, he had to be the ultimate write-off.

'You don't bear even a passing resemblance to Tom Cruise,' I blurted out.

Tom wasn't in the least bit upset. He smiled at me. He really believed his own delusions.

'Now if you'd said Tom Waits . . .' I slurped my drink and spilt some on my lap. A puddle was forming there but most people had them so I didn't panic. Daria burst out laughing.

Evidently Tom's confidence had taken a nosedive and now crashed loudly on the floor. 'Hardy-fucking-har,' he sneered at me. 'You're no Rose of Tralee yourself.'

This was true, but being drunk allowed me to dismiss the remark as reality, which I wasn't in at that moment.

Then the night's entertainment made their big entrance.

We were treated to two hours of badly imitated stars. We had Tina Turner, whose wig became displaced so that it looked more like a beard, Bruce Springsteen, who was six feet tall, a shockingly bad Michael Jackson, who had nothing in his vocal cords or his trousers that he could grab on to, a dwarf white Al Green, and then the finale: a female Elvis, who sweated profusely and seemed to think it was perfectly acceptable. When she stopped singing the crowd burst into rapturous applause, prompted only by the overwhelming relief that the ghastly ordeal was over.

Our dancing space was one foot each. If you moved forwards or backwards someone's life was in danger. We stood at our chairs swaying dangerously, bending our knees every few seconds and looking like we needed to go to the toilet.

After a while some slow music allowed us to park our arses back down. Daria and Tom were locked in a drunken embrace, swaying and singing together. Just when I was about to throw my drink over them Colm arrived at my side.

'Hey, Bud.' I nodded in Julia's direction. 'Why don't you pick on someone your own age?'

'Yo, Skinny, why don't you pick on someone – anyone?' He laughed.

'No takers.'

'I don't believe that.' He eyed Tom and Daria, who were looking like they were about to clear the table and make love on it right there and then.

'I know your partner, doesn't she come into the Credit Union every week?' I asked.

He looked temporarily worried. 'Yes. What of it?' He drew himself up on the balls of his feet.

'You should never mix business with pleasure,' I advised.

'You don't know what you're missing, Finn.' He smiled at me cheekily.

I blushed, not knowing what to make of this remark. 'You know, you intrigue me,' I whispered into his ear.

'Intrigue? Is that a compliment?'

'Well, not exactly. It's just, you know, I can't quite figure you out. Like, what's the story, Colm?' I edged closer.

'Story? You've lost me,' he said, peeling back a stray strand of hair that had stuck to my cheek.

'You know, with the grannies, is there some secret I've missed?' I asked.

'Now, Finn, you're misbehaving again. There are no secrets, my darling.'

'Maybe I should try to look older, perhaps grey my hair or get a zimmer frame or something,' I went on.

'*Now* you're being crass.' He wagged a finger back and forth. 'If you are referring to Julia, she hasn't either. Or didn't you notice?'

The swine.

Daria and Tom fell off the chair and landed legs up on the floor.

'Watch him,' Colm said, all of a sudden.

'I'm watching,' I said. I was surprised at his show of concern. Colm often socialized with Tom but he seemed positively uncomfortable with him hanging out of Daria. I pulled her up and plonked her on the seat. She was worse than I thought. She smiled stupidly at me, her boppers crooked and her blouse half undone. 'Hey, go easy on the drink,' I warned her.

'Fock offffff.' She burped loudly. 'I'm enjoying my-ssself.'

Colm pushed his way between her and Tom.

Julia, who seemed to be taking it all in her stride,

stood up, winked at Colm and went to the ladies'. Colm picked up Daria's drink and moved it away. When she went to get it she shouted, 'Where's my fucking drink?'

'You've had enough,' he said seriously.

Drunk as I was, I had noted that Tom O'Hare's arm was now leisurely draped round her shoulder and his hand inching its way towards her chest. I didn't take it seriously at first. If she wanted to have a one-night stand with Tom, so be it, I wasn't going to stop her. Now, though, something in Colm's eyes told me it wouldn't be a wise move and I also noticed Mark Adams watching her disdainfully. A one-night stand was OK, but not in her drunken state. She wouldn't remember anything, and if she did she might not want to.

As luck would have it, she began to turn a greyish colour. Then I saw her gag and dashed to the rescue. I grabbed her arm, pushed through the tables and chairs and we just about made it to the toilet where she threw up as I held her hair. The door opened and I looked round. There was Colm.

'Need a hand?'

'Could do with an extra toilet bowl.' Colm, undaunted by being in a ladies' toilet, pulled at the paper-towel holder and handed me a wad. I dabbed Daria's face and hair.

'Why do women have to get so drunk?' he asked, almost as if he was posing the question to himself.

Daria groaned.

'She's still not used to the Irish drinking standards.' I grinned.

'You mean she's not alcoholic yet?' he asked.

Daria heaved.

'Thanks for helping me – back inside,' I said.

'Thanks for covering my ass when I was in the hair-dresser's the other day,' he said quickly.

'What? how did I cover for you?'

'Well, you did all the work didn't you? Look, you'd want to watch oul Tom. Bit of a goer,' he muttered.

'You're kidding.'

'They're both maggoty drunk,' he said, lifting Daria under the arm.

'You're one to talk,' I murmured.

'Speak for yourself, Skinny. Look at the state of you.'

I didn't have to look. My imagination filled me in pronto. The mental image tortured me.

'Plenty of strong coffee and some Anadin.' He gestured towards Daria, who had slipped into a nice little semi-coma.

'It's a bed she needs,' I decided.

'What if I call a taxi?' he offered.

'Great,' I said.

'I'll come with you if you need help,' he said, jiggling the coins in his jacket pocket.

'What about the granny?'

'Who?' he said, then realized who I meant. He tried to hide a smile. 'She's no problem. Anyway, it's time for the old medication and glass of warm milk. Besides, she loses track of time after midnight,' he quipped. I eyed him suspiciously.

'Alzheimer's,' he added.

'Alzheimer's, is it? Has she a trumpet for the hearing as well?' I threw back.

Colm did his best to keep the grin off his face, but I had won and he let out a muffled chuckle. As much as he tried to pretend he didn't approve of my jokes about his escort he could never resist a good old-fashioned gibe.

'Do you want me to help you or not?' He tried being serious.

'Colm Long, are you up to something?' I asked, my flushed face dancing with glee. Hope springs eternal, they say.

'Like what?' he answered, looking genuinely confused. 'God, can't a guy be nice any more? Besides, I owe you one,' he said.

'My mam told me all about nice guys,' I said dejectedly.

Colm was staring at me like I was a sandwich short of a picnic. 'You haven't got a touch of Alzheimer's yourself, have you?' He pulled out his mobile and dialled a local cab number. I glared at him. Just then, Julia, resplendent in her gold backless dress, tiptoed into the toilet all smiles and gentleness. She kissed Colm on the cheek, a long, loving kiss.

'I'm just calling a taxi, pet,' he purred.

'Pet'. He called her 'pet'. What the hell is wrong with me? It was the alcohol-loneliness twins and I felt jealous again. No one ever called me 'pet'. Shane had never called me 'pet'. I wished someone would call me 'pet'; I'd have paid them just to hear that word. I would really like to be somebody's pet. A poodle or a Persian cat, anything, even a goldfish.

'What's wrong?' Julia asked me, leaning her head sleepily on Colm's shoulder.

'Daria is dead drunk. Tom O'Hare was getting a bit heavy. Colm came to the rescue.' I smiled at her.

She kissed him again, on the ear this time: I could almost see his erection waving at me. 'Is there anything I can do?' she asked. We all looked to Daria, who was snoring her head off.

'Have to get her into a taxi and bypass Mark Adams, if we can. She'd die if she knew he'd seen her in this state,' I thought aloud.

'I'll get the taxi to come round the back entrance,' Colm said. 'Would you mind if I helped?' He turned to Julia.

'No problem. I'm tired too. Just drop me off and I'll call you later.' She winked at him with a cheeky sexy grin. His mouth turned upwards and he responded with that devilish grin. The kind of smile that only exists between lovers. An exchange that said guaranteed pleasure awaited their attention later. I felt awkward. What was I doing thinking he was making a move? For God's sake, how desperate can one get in the fantasy department?

I had a stinking drunk woman hanging out of me and I was sure I looked just like her. A long woollen crochet coat camouflaged my black ensemble, hiding all the bulges, but I could smell vomit on my clothes and wished I had some perfume to dab on my wrists and neck. Colm's delicious smile had made me weak at the knees. The alcohol had planted in me a doomed hope that a miracle might still manifest itself.

# Chapter 8

We managed to slip past the manager and his wife, who were engrossed in a long-drawn-out raffle event. The taxi man was not amused as we dragged the dead body into the back of the car. When he realized it was a woman's, he became slightly more sympathetic. ''Tis a shame to see a young woman in that state,' he tut-tutted. 'This millennium thing has got out of hand. I think I'm going mad meself. Like yer man Van Gogh. I'll be cutting my ear off next or something,'

'Ah, you're right there. Nothing worse than a drunk woman, eh? Wasn't I only saying that a while ago?' said Colm, all responsible and mature.

'Yeah, you were.'

The smell of drink off us all could have killed a horse. One breath between us could have ignited the morning's planes from Dublin to Heathrow. The windows were open in case of an accident as we drove through the open-air asylum that Dublin had become in the early hours of the morning. Colm and I sat in the back, flanking the near dead weight of Daria, who groaned every time we went over a bump.

When we reached the flat, Colm stepped out and seemed to take for granted that he was coming in, which made me nervous; the place was a mess and I distinctly remembered leaving a pair of tights crumpled on the bathroom floor. After we had dumped Daria on the bed and covered her with a duvet, I made us some tea. I peered out through the crack in the door and watched Colm roam about picking things up and putting them down again. I darted in and out of the bedroom and bathroom, gathering odd socks and pants as I went.

I stopped dead in my tracks when I heard Colm tinkling on the old piano. Out of the blue I felt a surge of protectiveness towards it. He was hammering two fingers down on two conflicting keys, making it sound like a bag of cats.

'Hey! Go easy, eh?' I startled him as I stood at the door with two cups of weak tea – I had only one teabag.

'Is it yours? Do you play?' he asked, taking the cup and looking into it as if it might contain an asp.

'Yes and no,' I answered.

'Why own a piano if you can't play? It sounds awfully out of tune too,' he said, giving it a final thump. I covered my ears and ran to put down the lid.

'Sorry,' he said.

'It's OK. It's just . . . Well, it's my dad's, you see. He's passed on and it's . . .' I broke off, lost for words.

'Of sentimental value?' he tried to help.

'Exactly.' I heaved a sigh of relief.

There was an awkward pause. I wanted to change the subject.

'So, what was all that in aid of? I mean, back at the party.' I sipped my tea.

'Sorry?'

'All the good Samaritan stuff.'

'You're very suspicious, Skinny, always looking for an ulterior motive.' He sipped his tea now and tried hard not to grimace.

'That's because I always find one,' I said.

'Is that a fact?' he said heartily. 'What happened to make you so mistrusting?' he probed.

'Experience.' I was annoyed he had been that perceptive.

'I wouldn't like to see Daria getting hurt. I hadn't any ulterior motives. I do care about people, you know,' he said.

I sensed there was more to his actions than he was willing to confide.

'She ought to find herself a decent boyfriend. A fine thing like her.'

How could anyone disagree with him? I wondered did he fancy her himself. If so, I couldn't blame him – I imagined every man would. 'She could have anyone she wanted,' I agreed, manipulating him into thinking he didn't stand a chance with her.

'Does she never date guys?' he asked.

'Now and then. Oh, he's a lucky man who gets her I can tell you.' It came out a bit snottily.

'What about you, Finn? Still grieving that gonk Shane?' he said, without a hint of shame.

'He wasn't that bad.'

'For God's sake, he was a *creature*,' he said, picking up an ashtray. I threw him a packet of cigarettes. 'If you must know, I'm glad we've had a chance for a private chat. You seem to be in the pits lately. I just hope it's not over him,' he said.

'I'm not grieving Shane. I haven't met anyone else, that's all.' I paused.

'Why not? Are you saving yourself for Mr Right or something like that?' He yawned, as if I was a tiresome bug that had just landed on his cheek.

'Is there something wrong with that?' I asked.

'No.'

'You just told me Shane was awful,' I reminded him.

'He is.'

'So? What are you suggesting?'

'Why don't you try looking for Mr Appropriate? He's much more likely to come your way.'

I laughed. Little did he know that at that moment even Mr Completely Fucking Unacceptable was unlikely to materialize.

'Jesus, Colm, I'm fed up with it all. Where are you supposed to go to meet decent people anyway?' I was trying to find out where he went.

'Well, I have been trying to bring you out for lunch but somehow you keep eluding me.' He darted me a sarcastic glance.

'I mean, where are you supposed to go to *meet* someone?' I regretted saying it seconds after it came out.

'Oh, you mean, as in a nice bloke, someone you would date, is that what you mean?' He took it on the chin.

'You know perfectly well what I meant.' I blushed.

'Oh dear, I'm afraid I wouldn't be able to answer that. You're asking the wrong bloke. I'm a bastard, remember?'

'Hey, I never called you a bastard!' I laughed.

'You call every man a bastard.'

'Yeah? Maybe I've done too much complaining lately. I can't help it, Colm, I'm becoming very disillusioned.' I sighed.

'Maybe you're looking in all the wrong places, Skin.' He fidgeted with his ankle.

'I'm not looking at all at the moment,' I told myself more than him. 'Anyway, you don't understand, you're a man and you always have a girlfriend.' I pouted.

'Now you're being a real dumb-ass. I don't always

have a girlfriend. Sometimes I think they're more bother than they're worth.'

'What about Julia? Is it serious?' I tried to squeeze some info out of him while the going was good. I was watching him like a hawk for some hint of vulnerability. I needed to do something with my hands so I fiddled with some Christmas decorations, then decided to water the plants, which was strange as it was the early hours of the morning. I didn't care; it calmed me, brought me back down to earth. I wandered from pot to pot, picking out dead leaves, checking for dampness.

'Julia.' He smiled that gorgeous smile again. His foot did a little dance, as if it had a mind of its own. If I had known him better, it would have suggested a ripple of nervousness. 'Who knows?' he said, revealing nothing.

'She's very nice, Colm,' I said, trying to sound encouraging and friendly.

'She's a cracker,' he agreed, forefinger tapping the side of the mug.

So were Mary and Anne and Colette and Sandra. They were all 'crackers', I remembered, so why didn't he stay with any of them? I was just about to ask when we heard a deep snore from Daria and giggled.

'Is there something about Tom O'Hare that I should know?' I asked suddenly.

'He's a right oul whore,' he said.

'I meant tell me something I don't know,' I sneered.

He was moving around the room now with long strides and stretches. I noticed a couple of grey hairs at his temples, little wisps that looked newly sprouted, recent accolades bestowed upon him. I wanted to tell him that when he stood next to me I had trouble remembering my own name. I prayed rather wistfully that I could stop staring at him, just for a minute.

'What was he at this evening? I mean Daria, and in front of Mark Adams and his wife – the nerve!' I spat.

'He was just being his usual horrible self.'

'Daria was out of her face,' I said.

'I've seen worse,' he replied.

'Yeah, remember last year?' I grinned.

'How could I forget?' He blew smoke towards the ceiling, perfect white circles that disintegrated against the yellowing plaster. Tom O'Hare had made a pass at a member's daughter. It turned out she was only sixteen and there was mighty gossip about it for weeks afterwards. I tried to remember who Colm had been with but couldn't. I had no problem remembering who I was with. Shane had accompanied me and we'd had a good time. My face must have given me away because Colm homed in on it immediately.

'What happened with you and Shane, anyway? I thought it was the romance of the century,' he asked.

'I don't really know,' I answered.

'Well, who ended it?'

'We both did.' I nodded in an effort to convince myself.

I took off my shoes and noticed a graze over my big toe; it had bled slightly from the crucifying high heels I had worn all evening.

'You mean *he* did,' he retorted.

'Huh?' I pretended not to understand. It was the truth, but I didn't want to hear it.

'Hey, Skin, relax, will you? You're not the first person in the world to get dumped, you know.'

*How would you know? You've never stayed with anyone longer than two days.*

Before I could say another word he moved forward and grabbed my right foot.

'What are you doing?' I asked.

'Looking at your toe, if that's OK with you.'

I shut my mouth, fearing he would recoil at the stench.

'Have you a plaster?' he asked.

'In the kitchen press.' My breathing was askew. All he was doing was holding my foot. I wondered were there hormones in there that the scientists hadn't discovered yet. I was awash with sensuality as he rubbed it gently with expert hands.

'If you wore proper shoes, this wouldn't happen,' he said.

I vowed inwardly to wear crippling high heels for ever more. They had done more for me than Opium perfume or a crate of Impulse. 'It's all in the name of fashion,' I confessed.

'You're destroying your feet. You don't see men wearing high heels, do you?' he said.

'Actually—'

'Don't answer that,' he interrupted.

'Men are very fashion-conscious now,' I observed.

'Maybe, but they don't maim themselves.'

'They do.'

'Yeah?'

'Sure.'

'Like?'

'Well, I was having a facial done a while ago and there was this guy having his nose hairs extracted. The tears were running down his cheeks. With each *ping* he winced in agony. Serves him right, I thought. Such vanity! I mean, fucking nose hairs?'

'So, let me get this right. He was vain, so that makes you . . .'

'I'm a woman, for God's sake.'

'What's that supposed to mean? You have some monopoly on the feel-good factor?'

'Well, it's all a bit strange, this trend in men's beauty treatments. Can't even have my hair cut in peace and there's some guy peering out from under his mesh high-light bags. I mean, you have to set limits.'

Colm was rubbing between my toes and thought this hilarious. Then suddenly he stopped laughing. 'What are mesh highlights?' he asked.

'Think of Dessie's hair, but properly done.'

'Maybe I should book myself in for a leg wax,' he remarked.

'Or you could have a massage.'

'Nah. Don't believe in all that. It's all right for the Dessies and Toms,' he decided.

'Oh, butter wouldn't melt in your mouth.'

'What?' he said, clipped, rapid-fire response.

'Oh, come on, sitting there trying to convince me you're different from Tom O'Hare.' I wanted to see if he would rise to the bait.

He dropped my foot, picked up his cup and swirled the tea. Slowly, making large circles.

'What makes you think I'm like him in the first place?' He sounded taken aback.

'You hang around with him, right?' I reminded him.

'I don't actually, Skinny. Still, I can see why you would think that,' he said quietly. He seemed to want to elab-orate but apparently changed his mind.

'I wish you wouldn't call me "Skinny",' I said.

'No?' He sailed past me on a sea of aftershave, put his cup on the draining-board and I heard him rummaging around in the cupboard. Presently he returned. He grabbed my foot again, roughly this time, and wrapped a Mickey Mouse plaster round my big toe. 'Take my advice, will you? Stay away from Tom O'Hare. There's more to him than meets the eye. I don't like hanging around with him. I'm doing the boss a favour and that's all I can tell you, I'm afraid.'

'Colm, you know things aren't good for me and I appreciate your concern, but in my most desperate hour I wouldn't turn to him,' I said confidently.

'I'm glad to hear it. You're worth more than that. You listen to Uncle Colm, OK? So what that you broke up with a goon? Think of it as a learning experience. You'll get over it and meet the right guy in time. To be honest, I'm delighted that gobshite is out of your life. Don't ever sell yourself short. Do you hear me? You've got so much to give. Keep your chin up and forget about him.' He encouraged me.

I wished all my toes were in bits. I was so happy having him before me on one knee attending to my foot. I felt a bit like Cleopatra and bathed in the sacred ritual. When he had finished, he stood up, stretching himself and shrugging his shoulders. He fiddled with his ankle. It wasn't a scratch or a pain. He did that kind of thing a lot I'd noticed, fiddling and fidgeting. He pulled at things for no reason, his clothes, his ears and his hair. I found it amusing. It wasn't as if anything needed adjusting. He must have felt it did. It was a chink in the armour.

I found myself smiling and blushing. Deep down, I loved the way he called me 'Skinny' when I was anything but. Somehow, I could take it from Colm. It wasn't meant as an insult. It was affectionate, just between him and me. If Dessie had ever tried to pull a number like that on me I would have left his nose in a wheelchair. I stole a sideways glance at Colm, who still seemed to be thinking about the question I had posed.

If he didn't move soon the alcohol and loneliness were going to make a fool of me. I was alone in the flat, except for my drunken friend. I was a woman and he was a man. No matter how scrupulous I thought I was, my morality was rapidly abandoning ship. In an effort to distract my thoughts I switched the conversation back to work.

'We've got the interest going on tomorrow,' I said.

'Christ, I'd almost forgotten. Why did you have to remind me?'

'Yeah, and don't go missing like you usually do.' I remembered last year's chaos and how Colm had gone sick, leaving the rest of us under extreme pressure.

'I had the flu.' He buried his hands in his trouser pockets.

'You had in your arse.' I laughed.

'I had so,' he insisted.

'You'd better help out this year, Colm, flu or no flu,' I warned him.

'I will, I will.'

'No disappearing on the night of the AGM either. I don't want Dessie in my face all night. I'm warning you, I'll come looking for you, I promise,' I said.

He gave me that look. No one went looking for Colm and to my knowledge no one had ever been invited to his house. 'Are you the manager now or what?' He moved closer and took my chin in his hand.

'No, but remember, the manager doesn't have to put up with the members, it's us who have to deal with them,' I reminded him. My legs were like jelly and my tummy kept flipping over like a pancake.

'Yes, yes – God, you're like a bloody broken record. I'll be there. I'm always there when you really need me. Finn, you need to learn to trust people.' Colm said.

I looked straight into his eyes. He was serious. I wanted to kiss him badly. I yearned to go to bed with him. But my mind kept telling me how fat I was, how flat-chested, how ugly. I could not bear the thought of him looking at me. I would die of shame.

There was an awkward silence. Colm adjusted his tie. He looked uncertain of what to do next.

'Yes. Well, Skinny, better get to bed, I suppose,' he said, all semblance of frivolity vanished. One minute he was making rampant totty with my big toe, the next he looked fit for a good night's sleep. I pulled myself together as best as I could, stood up and straightened myself out. I tried to behave like nothing had happened.

'Yes. Well, I'd better toddle off to bed too,' I said chirpily, remembering he had Julia to attend to as well. I imagined her splayed erotically across silk sheets, wearing a cute little nothing. No wonder he wanted to go.

'Yes, I suppose you should,' he said. 'On the scale of crap nights where would you put it?' he asked.

I ran my hands down my dress. It was a mass of creases and I was sure my mascara was down on my chin. 'I think I'd have to give it the full ten this year.'

Colm took out his mobile and dialled another taxi. It arrived almost immediately, not giving me a chance to think things through. We said goodbye at the door, amid a brief, awkward cuddle. I wanted to stay there for ever in his warm arms, but the taxi man beeped his horn impatiently. Colm wished me goodnight and left.

Back inside, there was only one thing for it. I hunted out the fistful of sweets hidden in my uniform pocket. When I had devoured them I went looking for my real hit. I found six empty Energyade bottles under my bed. Not a drop left in any of them. I felt really upset with myself. I knew now how desperate I had become.

Here was a man being a friend to me: he had made

a noble gesture, by helping me protect Daria. He looked on me the same way I looked on the residents of the old folks' home down the road. Second, there was a woman in his life. Who the hell did I think I was? Kylie-fucking-Minogue?

I stripped off and stood before the full-length mirror on the back of my wardrobe. I looked fat and ugly. My boobs hung down like two pears and my belly lunged forwards like a Christmas pudding. Yet none of that diminished in me the desire for him to tear off my clothes and fuck my brains out right there and then.

# Chapter 9

By the following weekend I had made up my mind. I was tired of being fat, ugly and useless and I was going to change it. An idea had taken hold with a vice-like grip and I couldn't shake it off. I wondered why it had never occurred to me before. How could I not have thought about having a job done on my breasts? I was rooted to the spot with the sheer logic of it. I could and would have a breast enlargement.

You see, my body and its small breasts had suddenly become my most important asset. When had I stopped seeing it as a vehicle that kept me alive and started regarding it as something that would determine my success as a human being?

I suppose I had always believed that a woman's breasts are like military tanks. They are a trademark of assurance, of confidence, of leadership. In the wars of sexual superiority, the breasts reign supreme.

Every time I saw an ample-bosomed woman I watched her carefully. She would walk with her chest out, purposefully, proud. Her self-esteem seemed to stem from her mountainous mammary glands. They commanded a peculiar respect. They ruled victorious. Women like that knew they were women. And so did everybody else, I thought sadly. Especially men. Which probably explained why I was always mistaken for one, when I went topless on foreign holidays. It also explained why I was frequently flung into the water and used as a surfboard.

I had spent my adolescent years waiting for puberty to provide me with a female form. My weight fluctuated and played mental ping-pong with my confidence. At fourteen, I was near the eleven-stone mark. My friends teased me about it but I always joked back.

'You really ought to get in shape,' they would advise.

'I am in shape,' I would protest. 'I'm round.'

However, the *specifically* circular bits still hadn't introduced themselves. My mother assured me that my breasts would develop. I was a late starter, she would tell me. I waited and worried and waited for the late start that never got past the red flag. I believed that I would just wake up one morning and they would be there. I would wobble and bounce my way to the bathroom and complain that I couldn't tie my shoelaces any more. With my new shape, the rest of me wouldn't look so out of place. My breasts would balance out the other curves.

I thought some more. All my life I had refused to wear a bikini. I had learned to camouflage my impediment by wearing loose garments to draw people's attention away from my body. It ensured that they couldn't tell what kind of a bust I had underneath. I might have been as flat as a breadboard or as voluptuous as Hattie Jacques from the Carry On movies. The not-knowing was mysterious enough to keep them all in the dark.

I never sunbathed and I never, ever allowed the opposite sex to see me naked. I perfected the art of undressing in the dark because I always wore my T-shirt in bed, no matter what. I used to watch my blossoming girlfriends pile themselves into 36C-sized bras and size ten jeans. Oh, how I wanted to be able to pile my flesh into decent-sized cups.

The only thing I ever piled on was makeup, acne cream and pounds of extra flab in the wrong places. I couldn't lose weight – on the contrary I kept finding it. As for the gym, all I had to do was sit on the rowing machine and it sank.

Every now and then, prompted by PMT or sexual loneliness, I made sporadic shifts into the DIY methods of increasing my bustline. I used a variety of creams, lotions and gels, including cocoa butter and aloe vera. I did special weight-lifting exercises. I went on diets that purported to encourage breast-tissue development. I blamed God and threatened to kill myself. And there were the plastic nipple extractors, worn at night to draw them outwards, thereby giving the illusion of larger breasts. After three weeks my nipples ached, and for all the agony endured they still looked like a couple of shrivelled grapes. None of it was worth the effort. It was like setting up deck-chairs on the bow of the *Titanic*. I was doomed.

Now that was going to stop. I had made up my mind.

I scanned the pages of the telephone directory. A moment later my index finger had located the plastic surgery section in the *Yellow Pages*, all four pages of it. I was surprised to see so many advertisements. Smiling faces stared at me, with gleaming white teeth and below them, pert breasts.

I took a swig of Energyade and noticed I had emptied the bottle, the third that morning. It was high time I cut down on it. What kind of a fool would consider a breast augmentation? I asked myself. A *desperate* fool, came the answer, loud and clear. Someone who didn't have any other options. What was the harm in it? I jotted down a lot of phone numbers and slipped them into the front pocket of my bag. While I was rooting about I found some loose Jelly Tots and scoffed them in double-quick time. I licked the sugar off my fingers and thought about phoning Daria, but I knew she'd have a fit at the mere suggestion of surgery. Besides, there was no big deal. I hadn't *really* made a decision. I was just accumulating information, wasn't I? I decided to arm myself with as much as possible before I talked to anybody.

After breakfast I pulled up a chair and started dialling. To my annoyance, none of the receptionists would talk to me: each insisted that it was imperative for me to consult with a resident doctor. They advised me to set up an appointment, told me the consultant would answer my questions, explain the process, the financial requirements. Not one would respond to my probing. After the seventh call, I gave up.

I sat back in the old armchair and bit my nails. I made another cup of tea and took two paracetamol tablets. I had a headache from all the sugar. I chewed my nails some more, then I dialled the first number again.

'Good morning! You're through to the Hussledorf Plastic Surgery Centre! How can I help you?'

'I wish to make an appointment to see a consultant, please.' I had whispered it although there was no one in the flat but me.

'Certainly, madam. May I enquire with regard to what?' the receptionist asked.

'I'm interested in obtaining more information about breast augmentation.' My tongue wrestled with the last word. It was the first time I had ever said it out loud.

'Certainly, madam. There's a waiting list, I'm afraid.' Waiting list? I was shocked. I heard her rustling through the pages of a book. 'Let me see.' She paused. 'Yes, it'll be at least two weeks, Madam, before I can give you an appointment, it being Christmas time and the millennium.'

This millennium thing had gone far enough, I thought. There was no need for ordinary people to start hacking away at themselves for the sake of a hooley. I was different, you see. I really did need an operation, whether the millennium came or not. This was not a Christmas present to myself. It had just so happened that I had stumbled upon the answer to my unsatisfactory situation at this time. I was annoyed at the other mortals who were messing up the line for us more serious cases. My jingle bells and Christmas baubles were a matter of life and death.

'I see.' I sighed, like someone who had an abscess the size of a grapefruit under their back tooth and had just been told that the dentist was holidaying in Haiti for the next ten days.

'I apologize,' she said, with warmth. 'Perhaps if there is a cancellation before your allotted appointment I can call you,' she offered.

'Do you get many cancellations?' I pried, overwhelmed with a sudden sense of fear.

'Sometimes.'

*Relax for God's sake. Think of all the actors or models who had this done!!*

'I see. Well, go ahead, please, make the appointment,' I told her. What harm was there in talking? At least then I would be better equipped to make the right decision. Yes. That was the sensible way to approach it. I would get all the information first and then I would discuss it with Daria. A familiar sense of foreboding came over me. Well, I would just have to explain to Daria yet again that it was all right for her to condemn my plan when she already had her testimony to the Breast Brigade. I wanted to belong now, and it was my choice.

'Fine, Madam, I can fit you in on Monday the twentieth of January. Your consultant will be Dr Eduardo Fajita,' she finished.

Fajita? Sounded like an El Paso dinner kit. Suddenly I didn't feel so sure about it. All I needed was a Mexican maniac moulding my breasts like a lump of mincemeat for a good old-fashioned chilli. Was he one of these psycho butcher boys who went around smelling of tacos and kidney beans with a blood-stained cleaver tucked under his bandanna?

'Can you spell that for me?' I asked, and wrote down the name, address and the appointment time. 'Thank you,' I whispered and put down the receiver.

I knew I had made the right decision. I had known since I was seventeen that it was right – but I hadn't been able to admit it. I hadn't been able to see a way out. I should have done something then, I thought. I didn't want to remember being seventeen. I had tried to obliterate every tiny memory of that awful year and what had happened. At least it was not too late. Recent events had only confirmed what I had known all along: that I would never be a real woman, not a *real-real* woman . . . until I had decent boobs.

*I am seventeen. My mam is calling me to say there is a man at the door to see me. A man? I check my appearance in the mirror and amble downstairs to inspect the stranger. He isn't much to look at. OK, he isn't anything to look at. He has a seventies-style pumpkin head of carrot-red corkscrew curls. His face has more potholes and craters than a slab of Emmental cheese. He is thin and gaunt-looking, with ghostlike eyes, like he has smoked too much hash. His nose is of Roman descent with an arched bridge that struggles to belong. It reminds me of the town roundabout: no matter what direction you approach it from, you have to yield. He is staring at me with a glazed expression.*

*'Are you Fainche?' he shouts at me. He looks at the photo ID in his hand, as if perhaps he had the wrong address.*

*'Yes,' I say quietly.*

*'Fainche O'Farrell?'*

*Perhaps he's blind.*

*'Yes.'*

*He looks at the photo again and his expression changes. For a second I think he looks a little bit disappointed.*

*'I found this.' He produces my purse and photo ID and thrusts them under my nose.*

*'Hey, thanks! I mean, em, thanks for bringing then back to me,' I gush. I'm surprised. He doesn't look like the type who would bother to return such an item, more like someone who professionally confiscated them: the type who would drag you and your bag to the ground and beat you to a pulp for a tube of Chapstick and Rimmel eyeliner.*

*'Must have had a good night,' he adds, displaying a set of half-rotten molars.*

*'Not really,' I confess, jiggling from one foot to the other. The stranger stands there, staring at me, his eyes now dismembering me. 'It's an awful fucking kip, isn't it?' he says.*

*'The club?' I check, in case he is referring to my house.*

*'I had to get a late-night bus back into town,' he says, with disgust. 'I found this on the dance floor, thought you might need the bus pass.'*

*'Thanks, that was very kind of you.' I begin to feel guilty. He has gone to a lot of trouble to return an empty purse.*

*'Is there anywhere I can get a drink round here?' he asks, suddenly changing the subject.*

*'There's O'Riordan's. It's only a five-minute walk from here. Look, why don't I show you where it is? I'll buy you a drink. It's the least I can do for all your trouble,' I chance.*

*'Jeysus, thanks.' He smiles – and I hope he keeps the smiling to a minimum for the rest of the evening.*

*We walk to O'Riordan's in the warm September evening. The flies swarm about his head like the rings orbiting Saturn. Some get lost for ever in the fiery candyfloss.*

*We arrive at O'Riordan's, where the scarlet mane makes a beeline for the bar and orders us drinks. I try to pay for them but he insists.*

*'What's your name?' I ask, my red face glowing like the full moon.*

*'Michael, but me friends call me Mickah,' he says.*

*I stare at the floor. I can't look him in the face, and that is a welcome relief. The soft lighting and trick mirrors aren't doing anything for him. He is still the ugliest-looking bastard I have ever laid eyes on. 'Mickah,' I repeat, but it doesn't sound the same. I decide not to attempt it again.*

*We sip our drinks in silence. I continue staring at the floor, feeling foolish. I relentlessly pull and tug my jacket downwards making sure it covers everything above the knee. I am conscious of my best friend – a roll of flab that lies on my lap – protruding and I can feel the flesh double up. I suck in my stomach.*

*'How often do you go to the club?' he shouts, like a brickie on a building site.*

*I don't know why he's shouting: there's no music, the pub is relatively empty and I'm not displaying a hearing-aid. 'At weekends mostly,' I reply, 'and you?'*

*'Only been there the once. Not my kind of thing, really.' He drains his Harp and lime.*

*I notice he is quite shabbily dressed. I have thrown on my black velvet jacket, a life-saving item that goes everywhere with me. I never take it off, even in summer. I no longer notice the perspiration running down my back – you get used to these things, when you have to, and the jacket serves its purpose well.*

*By now, the alcohol is penetrating my reserve. I drink my third Dubonnet and lemonade and feel a little light-headed. My Dutch courage is nearing the fluency mark. We are talking and even laugh a little. The Titian stranger is suddenly a little attractive. I think, Yeah, he's OK. Harmless, even. Yeah. By the time I've had my fifth he isn't bad-looking at all. By the seventh he's fucking gorgeous and I want to kiss his face off.*

*We decide in our drunken delirium that we will hit the club again, this time together, just for the sheer hell of it. I clutch my bag possessively, in case another ugly bastard finds my name and address. Mickah is in the full swing of it. We dance till our feet ache and lurch precariously through the slow sets. He attempts to kiss me but I can still see his teeth in my mind's eye. I let him have a taste but pull away quickly. We hail a taxi at two in the morning and pile into the back. It's quite a drive home in more ways than one.*

*Not long into the journey, Mickah slips a heavy arm round my shoulders. I don't mind that, as long as he doesn't try to put it round my waist. I sit motionless, holding my tummy in. I can hardly breathe with the effort. His sweaty left hand hovers above my open jacket. My white shirt is unbuttoned at the top and I tremble at the thought of being touched. I close my sleepy eyes.*

*Mickah fiddles around. My nipples are instantly erect, almost reaching out to find his hand and bring it home to rest there. I want him to touch me. I'm willing him to touch me. He goes for it. His hand moves left, then right, then centre again, as if searching. It eventually lands on my nipple. He pinches it. I moan. I hear him sigh, as if disappointed. His hand fiddles some more and then he pulls it away abruptly.*

*Oh, the horror of it. I realize he is searching for my breasts! Only I haven't any! So he's given up. He has assumed that because I have small breasts, I am immune to the pleasure of being fondled. I am so humiliated. I hate myself, I hate my body and wish I could die. Goodbye, Fainche . . . Hello, Finn . . .*

# Chapter 10

For the first time in a long time, I wanted to go the gym. Now I *always went* to the gym, but I actually *felt* like going this time. I was filled with new hope. What if this body problem could be solved after all? I raced upstairs and gathered my kit. I threw in a nice bottle of shower gel, just to get myself feeling good. I could have a long swim and a walk to finish off. All was not lost. I could feel the excitement in my stomach. If I kept up the gym and got myself some new boobs, I just might taper off into a decent-looking babe. There was no reason not to be optimistic. Why couldn't I aspire to being beautiful and sexy too? I walked towards the bus stop.

I haven't felt this bloody good since I left Shane! I'll show him! I'll show Colm! I'll show them all! The next time any man sees me I'll be sporting the top of the range in the silicone market and a trim waistline to boot. Men will be begging me to perform unmentionable sex acts on them. The mere touch of my hand will have them dizzy with desire. I'll be able to buy bras by the skipload.

I'll be able to wear T-shirts, skimpy ones, the type that clings to your torso accentuating every curve. I might even pour myself into a pair of leather jeans. Wait a minute. No need to get tarty. Well, just a little, perhaps. Imagine wearing a button-down blouse with a little piece of lace open at the top, a fleshy valley displayed for all and sundry, inviting to the male eye and erect penis? Oh, I couldn't wait!

As I walked towards the gym, I wanted to run with the euphoria. My step was light and carefree. My mind had entered Happy Town, a place where problems melted into the distance, a place filled with opportunity, mysterious liaisons and illicit affairs. I was going to be free! I was going to be me! At long last I was going to start living! My enthusiasm raced on. Hey, I may even have my nose fixed. My stomach bypassed. My arse sucked out. I might even have my clitoris 'sensitized'. . .

Yippee! I'm alive! I smiled at the water-aerobics teacher whom I normally grunted at. I jumped up on the scales, not caring what insult it threw at me. I had lost another pound, which was self-explanatory. I put it down to the sickness of the previous morning's hang-over. I made a mental note to eat less chocolate and drink more Energyade. I had so much energy that morning I surprised all the regulars. I did a full four lengths of the pool after the aerobics class and visited the sauna, steam room and plunge pool. I ended up showering leisurely for half an hour. I felt damn good.

The thoughts persisted, bringing new ideas, new fantasies. I thought of a bikini, which only the bold and beautiful could wear. I thought of the beaches in Majorca, where I would strut my stuff without a care in the world, my beautiful rear-end the subject of endless discussion among the lifeguards. I imagined nodding at the G-string-clad Spaniards as they stared after me, insane with want. I imagined what it would be like to feel my new breasts bouncing gaily as I walked, how wonderful it would be to watch my chest move up and down.

I thought of all the lovely clothes I had denied myself

down the years. I smiled and smiled, and smiled some more. I had something to aspire to.

I sat at the mirror in the ladies' dressing room and blow-dried my mousy hair. It fell lifelessly on my shoulders. I dreamed of being a blonde, like Marilyn Monroe my lifetime heroine. I would be all bumps and curves, just like her. I would cut down on the Energyade. I could do it now that I had a motive. I pouted my lips and creased my eyelids but I looked nothing like Marilyn. Everything was going to change. I couldn't get a grip on my racing mind. It was like I had already decided my fate. I kept telling myself, 'Wait until you see the consultant. Wait!' But I knew deep down inside that I had already made my choice. It didn't matter what the consultant said to me: if he refused to do me, I would don the surgical gown and do myself.

The excitement of it all! Should I tell anybody? Not yet. Wait! Wait! You must tread carefully! Be patient! Calm down! I can't! I can't! I thought about Mam and how she would disown me. I refused to acknowledge that that had probably happened already. I hadn't been to see her since God knew when. I justified that by telling myself it had been too busy over Christmas and I hadn't the money. The truth was another matter. I just couldn't bear the idea of having to spend a whole weekend in her company, of going home, even for a second. I had come a long way since I had left.

Thinking back, about the only thing I could appreciate about Glenthulagh, my home town, was its rich green grass. It had little else to offer and my father, an old-fashioned fuddy-duddy, didn't understand my desire to explore higher ground.

We didn't live too far outside Dublin, but to me as a kid Dublin might as well have been America. I never got to see this strange exotic city: I only heard about it when Dad returned from some neighbour's house having collected 'the funeral money'.

Known locally as 'the insurance man', or sometimes 'the man from the Liver', he was perfectly happy with the ways of Glenthulagh. He did most of his business locally and enjoyed the one-to-one contact with neighbours. An upstanding member of the community, he was popular, courteous, civil and well-mannered. In those days, people still invited 'the insurance man' in for a cup of tea. My Dad loved his tea, and he loved his job. I can still see him, tall and distinguished, with a jump in his stride and a smile on his lovely face. How the women loved him, and how my Mam hated to see them all weak at the knees at the sight of him. The finest crockery was brought out, the best of the baking, and their aprons were stiff with starch. There was no denying it. My Dad was a fine-looking fellow. He kept the curtains going back and forth in Glenthulagh. I dare say that without his welcome presence in the small community the women (perhaps even the men) might have died of boredom.

Of course, times changed and the 'call-out' side of my Dad's work dwindled. Advancing computer technology increasingly replaced the need for a personal service. He had always been meticulous in his recording of accounts. His little black books were kept safely in a leather briefcase. I often sneaked a look at his pristine writing etched in black ink, denoting amounts and names. It was when the manual transactions were computerized that my Dad died a little death.

No more fine scones and cups of tea. No more gossip. He missed the regular contact with other people. If it hadn't been for his constant involvement with the GAA club as a coach, his only other passion, he would probably have died earlier. Of course, the club fell apart as most of the young ones moved up and out to Dublin where it was all at. Mam always said it was this final loss that killed him.

I can still remember my one and only trip to Dublin with Dad. Once a year he had to check in personally with the head office and return his books for auditing. For some reason, probably due to my persistent begging, he had decided to take me with him. He had huffed and puffed and frowned and mumbled. I wasn't allowed to wander in the city while he did his business in the big building on O'Connell Street. I was so disappointed – I had hoped he would treat me to tea and a cake in Clery's restaurant, or at least let me look in the windows of the big department stores.

He was in such a rush to get back that I didn't get to see anything, but I had known that as soon as I was old enough I would go back there to live. I didn't want the quiet life. I didn't want to end up like Mam. She never liked to travel into the big city either, preferring to devote herself to running the home and the caring for us kids: Padraig, Fearghal and me, of course. I wasn't going to end up like Mam, not for love nor money. Even when I called her now, which wasn't often, all she ever had to tell me was who had died in the town. I knew she would have a nervous breakdown at the thought of me having my breasts enlarged. I mean, you just didn't do that kind of thing.

I thought about Dad and how he would turn in his grave. The mere mention of it would have caused him a heart attack. He never liked to hear about those kinds of things – women's things. Even women's underwear or toiletries. He hated the sight of Mam's tights hanging on the heaters. He nearly had a fit when I washed mine in the sink one day, and I'll never forget the look on Mam's face when I left a box of sanitary towels on top of the cistern. She grabbed them as if they were the devil's spawn before he saw them. Yet it was always OK for the boys to leave their socks lying around. It seemed to me that everything was OK about the boys and I was expected to be one too.

On arriving home to the flat, I collapsed on to the couch, exhausted by my exertion at the gym. I stared long and hard at the piano. I could almost hear its ghostly echoes, its keys longing to be caressed, to be made useful. My stomach churned. Why did I insist on keeping it there? I told myself it was time I grew up, put the past behind me, threw out the piano. As part of the past, it had no place in my life any more. It didn't fit in with my new plans. It had to go.

I got up and made my way to the fridge, grabbed an Energyade and opened it. Then I rooted out the large bar of Cadbury's Fruit and Nut that I had hidden down the back of the sofa. I didn't feel guilty – why should I? I had worked out and I deserved a treat. I had earned it. With my prize possessions beside the couch, I had almost set the scene.

I went to my record collection, lovingly fingered it and wondered what would suit my mood tonight. Would it be the dark, heavy Russians, perhaps a piano concerto by Shostakovich or Prokofiev? No. I paused briefly at Bartók, the Hungarian, but decided he was too difficult for me to concentrate on just now. Rachmaninov? Definitely not!

No. I needed something easy, something surreal, beautiful, and romantic. A Beethoven monumental? Too long, too invigorating. What about Schubert? Too short and sweet for the mood I was in. In the end, I decided on Chopin, my absolute favourite, and no one played Chopin like Arthur Rubinstein. One went hand in hand with the other, as if the composer had written for that pianist alone.

I put the record on my old turntable and the room was immediately filled with softness. I lay down on the couch and closed my eyes, breathing in each note, each achingly beautiful cadence. My fingers were in mid-air, playing the familiar melody. I could feel the composer's pain, his ecstasy, his frustration and his triumph. I was grateful to him because he made me feel all that I couldn't feel for myself.

# Chapter 11

Both Daria and I had endured a long, passionate love affair with good-quality ice-cream. This particular night we were in my flat and having supremely satisfying oral sex with a two-pound tub of rum and raisin. There wasn't enough room for two spoons so when there was a lull and my spoon dawdled for more than a second she would plunge hers in and dig frantically. Her architectural deftness was paying off, and her skill had improved, which forced me to gather speed. We left the African cheetah in the halfpenny place. Sometimes we ate two tubs, depending on the time scale. Our record stood at an unrivalled twenty minutes, although there was a chance we might have broken it. A dozen crocodiles let loose in a child's swimming-pool couldn't challenge us.

On occasions, our gluttony would surpass that of a slip reported at a fully attended Overeaters Anonymous meeting. Tonight, the spoons banged and clattered louder than a 'traditional' session at Slattery's, as we pillaged like Attila the Hun and his barbarian hordes. The audible hollow scratch of cardboard told us that we had reached the bottom of the carton. An orgasmic sigh concluded the rampage and we fell back satiated and as sick as parrots.

For those twenty minutes we had sat in silence watching *When Chefs Go Mental 5*. A series of ad breaks held our interest. A number of products tried to tell me that if I bought them I was guaranteed the kind of sex life only available to those of Olympian gymnast standard. One suggested I was so sexually confused that I might well be attracting lesbians unconsciously. If I wanted to sort it out I had to buy a certain type of mobile phone. Well, at least there was a solution.

According to the television, my life was a sham, echoingly devoid of sex, love, happiness, and general well-being. In short, I was a disgrace to human nature and didn't deserve to take one breath of the Earth's precious oxygen.

If I didn't buy the latest fat-busting video, I was a lonely half-wit and the male species would give me a wide berth.

If I didn't eat the right kind of yoghurt or drink the right kind of milk, there was no point in blaming anyone else when I was at death's door with a fatal calcium deficiency.

How could I justify my inaction if I died leaving my family destitute because I hadn't bothered to get the fully comprehensive insurance that other *less selfish* people had?

And if I was as rancid as a certain perfume suggested, and stank like a refuse bin that had been left full to the brim with old spaghetti Bolognese and parmesan cheese over the holiday period, had I really got the right to feel hard done by?

What kind of a cow was I not to be concerned with the effect I was having on the starving millions and the abused orphanages in Russia because I refused to buy a certain type of black sack?

And I obviously didn't give a fiddler's about the ozone layer and the rainforests because I didn't purchase a certain type of paper. I searched the empty ice-cream carton for a friendly green symbol. There wasn't one.'

I felt like a piece of shite.

And only a gobshite would do without a certain sanitary towel: I was missing out on all those ordinary things a girl should be able to do when she has her period, like bungee-jumping and hang-gliding.

As I contemplated my inability to move with the times I felt exhausted, and guilty for being alive. According to my television, I was doing nothing, going nowhere and not fit to be let out. I looked to Daria, who seemed to be simmering in her own pot of guilt and remorse.

I contemplated telling her, at this vulnerable moment, about my visit to Eduardo Fajita, the Burrito Boy, in the plastic-surgery company. She was intent on another ad that threatened our arses with extinction if we didn't buy *their* toilet roll right *now*.

'Is there any more ice-cream?' I asked, knowing there wasn't. It was an attempt to open up the conversation corridors where truth lurked and hoped for an out.

'No, there is nothing in your cupboards. I just looked,' she said, staring headlong into the abyss.

'Are there any crisps?'

'You know quite well there aren't.'

'Peanuts?'

'No.'

'Cornflakes?'

'No,' she said, this time a little annoyed.

'Is there anything to eat? Anything?' I tried.

'There's some soy sauce,' she said.

'I'm starving.' I wasn't, of course, but I got up to

check in case she was lying. I found a pot of natural yoghurt and some oat flakes in the fridge and I knew it wasn't mine. It wasn't what I wanted but food is food.

'Don't even think about it.' Daria stood at the kitchen doorway.

'You're not going to argue with me over some porridge and rancid yoghurt?' I asked.

'It's for my face,' she said.

'Excuse me?'

'It's for a face mask. I brought them over especially, put them back in the fridge,' she ordered.

'What a waste of decent food,' I tut-tutted.

'It's good for the skin.'

'Your skin is perfect.'

'Now you know why,' she grinned.

I was determined to have the yoghurt. I just wanted it because it was something I could put in my mouth.

'Couldn't you use something else, maybe some Colgate mixed with Parozone?' I suggested.

'Don't be ridiculous.' She snorted and began mixing the yoghurt with the oats in a bowl. Her long legs strode across the room and then she was taking up the whole couch. I was five feet six but Daria was almost six feet. She looked like giraffe with hair and a bowl of porridge plastered on its face.

'Any news?' I was trying to figure out whether it was safe to broach the unspeakable.

'Nothing. I'm so bored.'

'Good, you can make me a cup of tea while you're waiting for your face to crack.'

'Stop making me talk,' she said, through clenched teeth.

'I only asked you to make a cup of tea.'

'I just sat down,' she complained, but it sounded more like, 'A jast shat dan.'

'What did you say?' I bent my head forward.

'A sad a jast shat dan.'

'I can't understand a word you're saying.'

The porridge had dried and she looked like something from *Fright Night*, the final uncut version.

She unravelled her long legs from beneath her bum and waddled into the kitchen. I heard her wash the goo off her face at the sink.

'Have you no milk?' She stood at the door, patting her pretty face dry.

I shrugged my shoulders innocently.

'You have to have milk.' I heard her clattering the cups. I followed her into the kitchenette and lifted up the empty carton. A few drops remained in the bottom and we shared them out like precious Valium tablets.

'You know, I was thinking . . .' she said. When Daria was thinking, it took some time for the thought to make the necessary journey from her head to her mouth. She was careful always to form her sentences strategically. I envied her thoroughness. '. . . about the party,' she said, swirling her Hermesetas in the tea as if she was a paragon of self-discipline with regard to her eating habits, and had forgotten the orgy of a few minutes before.

'What about it?' I asked.

'About Colm Long,' she said thoughtfully.

'Good old Colm,' I quipped.

'He's not such a bad guy, after all,' she mused.

'He's a ride.' I left nothing to the imagination.

'What's a ride?' she asked.

'Don't start, Daria. I've explained it to you a million times,' I said.

'Yeah. But what is it exactly?' she asked.

'God, I don't know. I think it means to ride like a horse.' I was annoyed I didn't understand my own language.

'Ride like a horse?' she repeated.

'Yeah. Sounds thick, really. You know, ride?' I jogged up and down a bit to demonstrate.

'Is that all the Irish can come up with to illustrate the sexual act?' she asked smartly.

'What do you want? A *Black Beauty* video?' I snapped.

'Well, excuse me, but I don't have sex like that,' she said snottily.

'You don't have sex at all,' I replied.

'Perhaps. But I do know there is a vast difference between sex and riding a horse,' she concluded.

'Frankly, I can't see any difference. Up, down, up, down. All that pelvic thrusting and your arse is in bits for days,' I said.

'God, Finn, I wish you'd meet some decent bloke who might teach you the real thing.'

'Well, it won't be Colm. He likes the old ladies. I'll try again in ten years.' I sighed.

'Bet he's a whiz in bed. Shit the bed, Colm! Get it?' She squealed with delight at her own joke. It wasn't that funny. I was always trying to get her to let rip with a good old howl, but all she ever breathed was a mouse-like squeak and even then, she felt she had lost all control.

'Yeah. I'm cracking up.' I yawned. 'Do you fancy him?' I asked nonchalantly, not wanting to appear too interested in her reply.

'Fancy him?'

'Yeah. You know . . . like him or what?'

'No. Yes. I like him. Does that mean the same thing?'

'Jesus . . .'

'Would you . . . you know . . .' I spelt it out.

'Would I have sex with him? No! I just thought that what he did was really nice, you know, at the party.' She paused. 'I think he really likes you, but doesn't know how to approach the matter,' she said.

'Mm,' I nodded, secretly pleased.

'Well, maybe that's all Tom O'Hare is, a drinking buddy. Maybe they're not such good friends after all. Maybe there's more to our Colm than meets the eye,' she replied.

'Tom O'Hare is a dirt bag,' I muttered.

'What's a dirt bag?' she asked.

'Daria!' I moaned.

'I'm just trying to understand. You don't even understand yourselves. It's all "you know" and "yer man" and "herself" and weird words like that,' she said.

'What the hell does "shit the bed" mean, then? That's the weirdest thing I ever heard, or what about "just now", what's that supposed to mean?'

'Just now? In a little bit? Soon?'

'Doesn't make the slightest bit of sense. You're all mad over there.'

'It makes sense to me,' she replied.

'Well, we have our expressions too,' I said.

'The Irish don't have expressions, Finn, they curse. That's all you do. Curse and swear. It's called profanity in cultured countries,' she said.

'I assume you're referring to England. A pack of thugs with an obscene penchant for conquering the world? Hardly cultured,' I snarled.

'If you feel so strongly about it, why don't you go on hunger strike with the IRA?' She shrugged her shoulders.

'I wish,' I moaned.

'A noble cause, Finn. You'd be taking a political stance and at the same time saving Ireland from another famine,' she joked.

'Very funny.' I jabbed her in the ribs. 'Listen, I wanted to talk to you about something.'

'If it's about money, I'm broke,' she cut in.

'No. It's not about money,' I had already figured out that particular problem and how I'd get round it.

'And if it's about my purple dress, no, you can't have it,'

'No. It's not that.'

'Then it has to be about money.'

I cut her off at the kitchen sink. 'It's about these.' I pointed to my chest.

She looked at me like I'd lost my marbles. I pointed again to my chest.

'Finn, I know things are pretty bad at the moment but you're not making a pass at me, are you? Come on, I know you're desperate but, Jeez, shit the bed . . .'

I burst out laughing. 'No, seriously, what do you really think of them?' I said, without thinking.

She stepped back, horrified.

'No! No! I mean, look at them. They're pathetic, right? They're practically non-existent!' She was staring at me, not knowing whether to leg it or call the police.

'I was thinking, you see,' I rushed on, 'that night we were in the pub with the lads and we were talking about plastic surgery—'

That was as far as I got, she was wagging her finger, warning me not to continue but I did. 'Look. Don't panic. Just hear me out.'

She shook her head defiantly and went into the bedroom.

'Will you just wait a frigging minute?' I raised my voice.

She was rooting through my swimming gear. 'I'm putting the earplugs in *now*,' she shouted.

'Put them away, you eejit,' I said.

She shoved them in and they looked like two warts hanging out of her ears. She danced round the room, pretending she couldn't hear me. I pulled them out with two sharp yanks.

'You have to hear me out, Daria. I'm not you and I never will be. I'm miserable about this and if you're my friend you'll at least listen.' She stopped dead and waited.

'Sit down,' I ordered, 'and don't lecture me until I've finished. You can lecture me then, but not before, OK?' I said.

'Right, you big weirdo.' This was Daria at her most uncouth: a big weirdo was the best she could come up with.

'Right.'

'Right. Get on with it.'

I sat down, knowing it wasn't going to work. I could tell her all the facts and what had happened at the plastic-surgery centre but it wouldn't do any good. She wasn't going to agree to it. I knew by her eyes, and I knew why. But I had to tell her everything, even though she wouldn't agree. I had to tell her about the visit and what had happened, building up to what I would have to divulge at the end. No matter what she said, I was having it done. I had made up my mind.

# Chapter 12

When I had arrived in the consultant's room, I had wanted to skip all the pleasantries because the only thing bothering me by then was how I was going to afford the operation. I let the El Paso dinner kit fill me in on the various types of breast augmentation. I didn't really listen; I was waiting for the bombshell – how much it was going to cost.

I was also fascinated by his face. His smile was stuck on like a fridge magnet, starting at the corner of his mouth and ending at an ear-lobe. It had a mind of its own. It sat there, leering at me, ever-constant. If his family had been kidnapped and their legs hacked off with a chainsaw, you'd never have known he was upset. He must offend an awful lot of people at funerals, I thought.

His hair was black, slick and stiff, and his nose had been slapped on and pushed up – it had had its fair share of artificial moulding. His hands, though, gesticulated with an artist's flair, introducing me to the range of wares that he had displayed on the table before me.

The implants were the strangest-looking UFOs I had ever seen. It was hard to believe, looking at those squidgy lumps, that they might find their final resting-place above my ribcage. I picked one up. It felt like a soft toy and I had an urge to hurl it across the room, just to see if it would bounce. The consultant – hereinafter referred to as the Smile – explained that I had two choices. Silicone or saline gel.

Which to choose? They felt and looked the same. I asked him the difference between them and he explained there wasn't any, but in recent years there had been scares about silicone. He went to great lengths to reassure me that it was as safe as houses.

He explained that capsular contraction – I never asked what it was – occurred in about 10 per cent of women and chronic low-grade infection in less than 1 per cent. There was also the possibility of rupture in the shell of the implant. What happens then? I asked. Well, he said, that was where the scares had come from, but there was no medical evidence to support the notion that the substance did any damage if it was released inside the body; it usually just dissolved in the system and Bob's your uncle. I didn't relish the idea of a toxic substance roaming around in my blood.

The saline implants, he said, had their advantages: in the unlikely event of a leak, the solution was easily absorbed and excreted, and they weren't as hard as silicone. But they never looked as realistic as their silicone counterparts, and sometimes could be felt, or even seen, sloshing around under the skin.

No, thanks. I would go for silicone.

The Smile finished off by handing me what is known in the business as a 360cc. It was fucking enormous and would have been a health hazard to those within close vicinity. I told him that I'd had something a little smaller in mind, and that was when it got horrible. The Smile insisted that he couldn't tell accurately what size would suit me unless I peeled off my clothes. So I did.

Oh, God. The humiliation. I waited for him to tell me

I wasn't that bad, he'd seen worse; maybe I should think about what I was doing, I didn't need to go to such drastic lengths. It was hard to tell what he thought. Was he laughing or crying, commiserating or bursting with amusement? His eyes told the truth, and his words confirmed it. If he were in my bra – which he was now – he would have had it done years ago.

He spoke to me softly, as if he understood the enormity of the problem, tut-tutting intermittently. Oh, how he empathized with my lifetime's misery. He nodded, and assured me that I was making the right decision, that I would be grateful to him for giving me a proper body.

Wasn't it a miracle that people like him could save me? Didn't I realize he was an earth angel? A messenger sent from heaven? He told me how I would recall with fondness the day I met the miracle man, the day he put my life back together. By the time he had finished I was bawling my eyes out and on my knees chanting prayers. I was sold. For three thousand five hundred pounds. Cash. No refunds.

The Smile went on to tell me that the operation was painful. I hadn't expected that, although I knew it wouldn't be plain sailing. I was willing to suffer for the miracle he was about to perform on me. No pain, no gain. He suggested I take two to three weeks off work, which I had already guessed I would need. Then we chose the appropriate implant. In the end we settled on the 360cc silicone. (Sounded like a motorbike to me: I'd soon be whizzing round Dublin powered by my new twin engines.) Can the operation be reversed? I asked. Of course, he responded. However – he laughed heartily – it was hardly likely that I would be wanting that, was it? He showed me, with some clever computer graphics, the change that would take place. The 'augmentation mammoplasty' would increase my cup size and lift the breast tissue to give me that much-sought-after pert look. I couldn't take my eyes off the screen. I couldn't wait. I just *could not wait*.

Daria sat with her arms folded, a blank expression dominating her face.

I smiled half-heartedly.

'You've got to be joking, Finn. You're joking, right?' she whispered.

'I'm not joking,' I pleaded, with doggy eyes.

'You can't do this,' she said calmly.

'I can and I will,' I said.

'Who have you told about it?' She wasn't giving up easily.

'No one,' I answered.

'Not even your mother?'

'She's the last person in the world I'd tell. You know that.' Any mention of my mother sent me into a spin.

'Anything could go wrong,' she said, as if I was stupid.

'It's a commonplace operation, for Christ's sake. Look at all the stars, nothing's gone wrong with them,' I said.

'Not yet,' she warned.

'Dolly Parton's had hers since she was in kindergarten. Nothing wrong there,' I tried.

'We don't know that,' she said.

'I think we would. Let's just say the silicone business would crash overnight. We'd have a massive economic depression on our hands if anything went wrong with Dolly's.'

'Finn, her circumstances are slightly different from yours. She has enough money to *buy the silicone industry* if the need arose,' she said.

'Yeah. Jammy bastard,' I mumbled.

I looked around the flat for something to divert my attention but there wasn't much to look at. There was the long stringy couch that we fought over constantly whenever she was here because of her legs. There was a small table, two white garden chairs to sit on, and my piano. Oh, God, I hated the way the piano called to me. I went over to it and rubbed my hand along the top. The thick layer of dust almost made me choke. I hadn't played it in years. When my father had died of a heart attack five years ago, Mam had said I could have it. I took it, but I'd never looked after it. There were grooves and scratches, and the middle C confirmed just how out of tune it was.

I hadn't had the time, money or interest to have it tuned. Besides, as I said, I never played it. One day I was constipated and asked Daria to go to the chemist for me. I wrote out a note for her on the piano and the word 'suppositories' was still etched into the wood. I had also carved my own initials on the left-hand leg when I was very young. I didn't want to think about that. It made me sad that I had neglected it so, and I made another mental note to get rid of the damn thing. Every time I saw it, it put me in a bad mood.

'You're going to do this, aren't you?' She stood up.

She sounded like Mam and I resented it. 'Yes. I *am* going to do it. Nothing you or anyone else has to say is going to stop me.' I stood tall, which was pathetic. I was still half a foot shorter than her.

'You haven't the money,' she tried.

'I work in a Credit Union. I can get a loan,' I responded.

'You'll be in agony.'

'I'm addicted to pain, you know that,' I reminded her.

'You'll have to take all your holidays in one go,' she lashed back.

'I already cleared it with Mark Adams.'

'What? I can't believe you've arranged that without even discussing it with me first. I thought we were going to visit my parents,' she said sadly.

'We're not husband and wife.'

'No, but I thought we were best friends.'

That twisted the knife. Good old-fashioned emotional blackmail. When all else fails it works like a fucking treat.

'You never go to see your parents anyway,' I said.

'I do so. I was there nine months ago. And who are you to talk? When was the last time you visited your mother?' she asked sternly.

I didn't answer.

'You have no excuse. I live overseas,' she went on.

'So do I.'

'Huh?'

'I live on the north side of the Liffey. She's on the south side. That's overseas, as far as I'm concerned,' I joked.

'It's not funny, Finn.' She meant business.

'Hey, quit the lectures about my mam, OK?' I snarled. If she wanted to get on the wrong side of me she was doing a damn good job of it.

'There's absolutely nothing wrong with your breasts. How am I ever going to convince you? You have to learn to love yourself. Beauty is only skin deep—'

'There's everything wrong with my breasts!' I screamed, blowing a fuse in the middle of her sentence. 'I'm flat-chested. There's nothing there, right? I'm not thick, you know! I've heard all this horseshit before. We are supposed to *love ourselves*, believe that beauty comes from the inside and all that *bolloxology* you keep trying to sell me. It doesn't work, you see, because it's not true! How would you know what it's like to have bathroom tiles for boobs? I'm not happy. I'm not complete. It's easy for you to pontificate when you haven't suffered like me!' I roared, pounding my chest like a deranged Mighty Joe Young.

'I've suffered.' She rose up, glaring.

'Oh, spare me!' I laughed at the idea.

'Not only are you flat-chested, but you're blind, dumb and deaf as well! Ask the doctor to perform brain surgery while he's at it!' she flung at me.

'Daria, this thing is ruining my life. I have a dead-end job, no boyfriend and a boring personality. You, on the other hand, have it all. You don't understand what it's like,' I said.

'Big breasts aren't going to change any of that,' she said angrily. 'As for me having it all, Finn, shit the bed, do you think these are going to guarantee me a life of happiness? 'Do you think people look at me and say, "Wow, nice pair of boobs, she has it all sewn up,"' she said harshly.

'For God's sake, your figure and skin and beauty are the envy of every Irish woman, don't you know that?' I laughed.

'Big deal. I'm not a lesbian. It's a man I want!' she yelled.

'Well, why don't you let one take you out?' I screeched.

'They never ask!'

'You never let anyone near you, for Christ's sake.'

'Well, they're not clamouring for my autograph,' she protested.

Daria was so paralysed with fear about her foreign status that she tended to come across as a snob, but she wasn't: she was just shy with the opposite sex. It didn't help that she didn't understand the Irish way, how we slagged each other for a living and meant no harm by it. It was all good clean fun, but to her we were insanely rude and difficult to understand.

I looked at her with her arms folded. She was pouting big-time, her heels dug in. Trying to budge Daria when her mind was made up was like trying to get Dublin Corporation to come out and clear the drains.

'You're making a big mistake,' she grunted.

'Then *let* me, right? Let me make the big mistake. It's all mine to make and at least *I am trying to do something about myself*,' I said sourly. I was seething with anger.

'Meaning?' She turned on me.

'Nothing.' I pouted.

'I don't know why you're treating me like the enemy,' she said, her voice quivering.

*She was the enemy. She had boobs.*

All of a sudden I felt foolish. My reaction had been that of a child who had just found the winning ticket in a Willie Wonka chocolate bar and now someone was trying to get it off me. They could have all the chocolate they wanted but they weren't getting the ticket.

*No one was getting the ticket.*

'I'm sorry,' I said.

She didn't answer.

'About the holiday,' I tried again.

'You're a stubborn bitch.'

I heard her sniffle. Christ, she was crying. 'Daria.' I went over to her and gave her a big hug. 'How can I convince you how much this means to me?' I said, into her thick black hair.

'How can I convince you that you don't need to do it?' she replied. 'You won't change your mind, will you?'

'No.' I wagged my head from side to side.

There was a momentary pause.

'OK, if it's what you really, really want.'

She had surrendered, and I felt awful. She was going to give in just like that? I had expected World War Three to erupt, or at the very least some smashed furniture. I had expected her to tear the flat apart, but she was agreeing with my insanity. I didn't know what to say. She was my best friend and a pain in the ass, but I loved her for accepting that I was going to do what I wanted to do.

We stood there hugging awkwardly and I knew it wouldn't be too long before we would never be able to do it again. Two large busts just wouldn't allow for it.

# Chapter 13

On St Valentine's Day I went in to work early, expectant and hopeful that this year Gabriel Byrne had found out where I lived. There wasn't any question mark over whether he would want me or not. That was a foregone conclusion. I knew that eventually he would tire of the Hollywood babes and want to settle down with a steady Irish girl. Like me. If it didn't happen this year, there was no need to be despondent: it was only a matter of time before he saw sense and came running. It was the waiting that was awful. But I knew all good things come to those who play Ostrich's Arse Up long enough.

I was first in the queue at the bakery and ordered a mountain of pancakes for our lunch so we could heat them in the microwave. I put them into a large carrier-bag and tore off little pieces, stuffing them randomly into my mouth while no one else was looking. I ambled along with the early-morning town traders, enjoying the hustle and bustle. Already the florists were putting together beautiful bouquets and the smell of roses wafted through town. It made me feel all soft and romantic.

I let myself into work and wandered around the offices. I filled my little pink watering-can and checked the plants with my forefinger. I found a box of green staples stuck upright in one pot, and some scrunched-up paper in another. Someone had left a rotting apple core in the creeping ivy. Then I heard a banging on the window and looked up to see Colm smiling in. I wondered how long he had been watching me. The others began to arrive and I let them in. The familiar click of the computers spluttering into action prepared me for another day.

I had tried to get into the swing of St Valentine's Day. As usual Mark Adams had asked me had I any ideas as to how we might mark it. I had suggested we hand out a single rose to the first fifty women who called in. He frowned at first, thinking of the expense, but had finally relented. I was struggling with the roses that had arrived in the early morning when Daria burst through the ladies' room door.

'Shit the bed, he found you at last,' she joked.

'Who? Gabriel?' I laughed.

'Did you tell him about me?' She giggled.

'Of course.' I grinned. 'Yours are in the forty-foot trailer outside, with a skip full of cards. Didn't you see them?' I pricked my finger on a thorn and cursed. 'Where are we going to put these bloody things?'

'I don't know. It was your idea, remember?'

Colm passed by on a wave of newly dabbed-on after-shave. 'What the hell is this?' he queried.

'It's Valentine's Day, did you forget?' I said.

'How could I?' he said sarcastically.

'I don't know what to do with all these. I wish I'd kept my mouth shut,' I said. The doorway to the ladies' was jammed with roses and Daria had already trampled on a few on her way out.

'What did any of our members do to deserve them?' Colm inquired.

'That's not a nice thing to say. Where is your

generosity, your heart? There's not a romantic bone in you,' I said.

'I'm romantic when I want to be,' he said. 'Didn't I tell you I bought us tickets to Paris for the weekend? I'm just popping in here to get them.' He closed the men's toilet door behind him.

I banged on the door after him. 'That's not bloody funny!' I yelled.

The office opened at nine as per usual and I sat at my workstation. It was very quiet, which surprised me. Daria sat beside me and I rapped on the flimsy sheet of Perspex that separated us. I gestured to her to pick up her internal phone.

'Did you do this?' I asked, holding up a bunch of carnations crudely clustered together in a sheet of crumpled paper.

'No,' she said innocently.

'Daria, I know you did. You did the same thing last year. Look at the state of them! Am I to believe someone would insult me with dead carnations tied up in . . . What the hell is this?' I examined the paper. '"Congratulations it's a boy" gift-wrap.'

Daria stared at me vacantly. 'What's wrong with it? It's the thought that counts. At least I didn't do this.' She held up an equally sad-looking bunch of roses, the ones she had trampled on.

'I didn't do that.'

'Finn, the red ribbon is missing off the Christmas tree,' she pointed out.

'So it is,' I remarked. It was still standing in a corner, and its only decoration had been a single red bow at the top. I had tied it round the bottom of the roses. I should have known I'd be snared. We stared at each other in shared empathy and compassion.

'OK. They're not from me. They really are from Gabriel Byrne,' she said, shrugging her shoulders.

'If you say so.' I nodded. 'And you know, of course, that *they* really came from Brad Pitt.' I gestured to the roses.

'Naturally.'

At lunchtime, nothing had arrived for Daria or me but, then, I hadn't expected any surprises. There was always the hope, though, and it was a bit of excitement. I handed out roses to members all morning and some really appreciated the gesture. I enjoyed bringing a smile to their faces. Later I gathered up those that remained, brought them into the canteen and plonked them in the sink. They were looking a bit tired now.

'Do they have to be in here?' Dessie asked.

'I have nowhere else to put them,' I told him.

'I can suggest a place,' Tom said.

'Please don't.'

'Look, there's barely room to move as it is,' Dessie moaned.

'Oh, stop complaining, all of you. Look, I have some nice pancakes for us, if I can just find a clean plate.' I searched through the cupboards but every piece of crockery was piled high in the sink. I set about washing up.

Mark Adams ambled in with his newspaper tucked under his arm. 'I smell food.'

'Pancakes,' Daria said, without raising her head. She was browsing through *Vogue* and *Cosmopolitan*, taking out the free samples as she went along. She had made a meal out of a Shape strawberry yoghurt, spattering little drops on the table.

Colm burst through the doors, whistling.

'What's wrong with you?' Dessie asked.

'I love my job. Move up, gang,' he ordered, and they all shuffled up a space. He plonked a kebab and some chips on the messy table and began to eat.

I put the pancakes in the microwave and waited for the *ping*. I drummed my fingers on the sideboard, as the others whistled, coughed, burped and scratched. The internal phone rang, but no one got up to answer it.

'Don't all kill yourselves,' I muttered. 'Hello? Yes. Who's calling? OK, just a second.' I put the call on hold.

'Colm, are you in or out?' I asked, as I tried to put the pancakes on to the plate.

'That depends. Who is it?' he asked, with his mouth full.

'Jean Moore, something about you fixing her car,' I said.

Everybody started laughing, including Mark Adams.

'What does she want? A jump-start?' Tom said.

I didn't think this was funny. I felt jealous again.

'I'm not in,' Colm replied, trying hard to disguise a grin.

I repeated the message and hung up.

'How do you do it?' Daria asked, without lifting her head.

'I only offered to look over her car for the NCT,' Colm insisted.

'Since when did you know anything about cars?' Dessie asked.

'I know quite a bit, actually. It's common sense mostly.' Colm tried to read some of Daria's magazine over her shoulder.

'Do you mind?' she said, pulling it away from him.

'She could do with a service, that one,' Tom added, as an afterthought.

'Leave it out, will you?' Colm told him.

Eventually I sat down with a bottle of Energyade and took a long swig.

'How many's that today, Finn?' Colm asked.

'It's my first,' I lied. When no one was looking I had wolfed down a bag of M & Ms and a Mars bar in the cash office, washing them down with Energyade. I loved to binge in there. I had to be locked in for security reasons so no one could see me. It was the perfect hide-away.

'Well, did you ladies get anything nice in the post this morning?' he asked.

'Oh, yeah, the usual truckload of flowers blocking the driveway,' Daria said, her voice heavy with sarcasm.

'Don't look at me,' I warded him off.

'Are you sure? Nothing? Not a poem? A card? Some flowers?' he pressed.

'I'm *dead* sure,' I said flatly.

'I got a card,' Dessie piped up.

'Finn sent it,' Tom said.

I gave him a dirty look. He was loving the embarrassment on Dessie's face.

'You sent it?' Dessie scratched his head.

'I know nothing.' I waved my hand playfully.

'Isn't that the nice gesture?' Tom snarled.

'I think it's lovely.' Colm smiled at me.

There was a look of tenderness in his eyes. I felt the blood run to my cheeks.

'Are you going to the Credit Union League this afternoon?' I asked Dessie, diverting his attention.

'Yeah, actually, and now that you mention it, I haven't a clue how to get there. What bus is it?' he asked me.

'I think it's the number fourteen,' I answered, rigging up my CD Walkman. The headphone wires were in a mess and I struggled to unravel them.

'What are you listening to?' Colm asked me.

'Oscar.'

'Oscar who?' he asked.

'Oscar Peterson.' I lifted one earphone so I could hear the conversation.

'Who's he when he's at home?' Tom asked, right on cue.

'He's only the greatest pianist in the world,' I said smugly. I hastened to add that I had a collection of music at home that most of them wouldn't have heard of. I was piano mad and listened to all the greats, classical, contemporary and jazz. Today I was in a jazz mood and had tucked in Oscar. Often I took in a lunchtime concert, but I never dreamed of telling my co-workers.

'It's no wonder you're a weirdo.' He raised his eyebrows.

'She plays, you know,' Daria said.

'I do not!' I yelped.

'Do you play the piano?' Mark Adams asked, incredulous.

'Well, kind of. I used to.'

Colm looked at me curiously. 'I'd love to hear you some day.' He gave me an encouraging smile.

'I really can't play that well.' Suddenly I felt uncomfortable.

'I can play Chopsticks,' Tom mimicked, 'with only two fingers of course.'

'I bet she's brilliant.' Dessie smacked me on the back.

'Me too,' Colm said.

'I don't have any talent. I just like listening, that's all.' I didn't want to be probed any further, even though I loved Colm's interest. Thankfully Dessie got up to leave and put on his coat.

'Number fourteen, you say?' He looked to me for confirmation.

'I'm almost sure. Don't forget we need more pay-in slips, OK?' I reminded him.

'That gobshite couldn't remember a simple instruction,' Tom said, as soon as Dessie had gone out the door.

'What are the bets he'll get a ten and a four instead?' Colm said.

They started laughing.

'Oh, you're all so smart,' I said, but I couldn't help having a giggle myself.

By five o'clock reality was seeping in. Gabriel Byrne had forgotten me again. In fairness to him, he hadn't my address. In fact, he didn't know me but it hadn't stopped the fantasy. I had hoped that someone other than Daria would send me something. I even thought Shane might have had second thoughts and waited for Valentine's Day to surprise me. No joy. It would be different next year, I promised myself. I'd have so many admirers I'd be spoiled for choice.

We closed the doors and set about balancing, which was quickly done as business had been slow. I wasn't in a hurry to get home so I decided to clean the kitchen, in particular the microwave – it was sporting a strange kind of mould. I was sure it had grown since that morning. I washed the cutlery and hung the mugs up so that they would be ready for the morning. I whistled to myself as I wiped the draining-board and threw the kitchen towels into the sink to give them a quick wash. I inspected the poinsettias I had bought at Christmas. They were all dead, except mine. I gathered them together and threw them out. I stored the empty pots in the cupboard. I heard the others leave the office, saying goodbye one by one.

Colm appeared at the door. 'Your Mam was on the phone earlier,' he said, rubbing his chin.

'She was? When?' I asked.

'About a half-hour ago. I told her you'd ring her back.'

'You said the right thing.' I was pleased.

'She just wanted to thank you for the flowers,' he added.

I had sent her a bouquet of lilies, her favourite.

'Right. Thanks, Colm. I didn't particularly want to have a conversation with her.' I wiped my face with the back of a mud-caked hand.

'I know.' He winked.

How? I wondered. I looked at him.

'I'm off now.' He coughed into his hand. 'I left the loan applications on your desk. Can you drop them off to the credit committee?' he asked.

'Colm!' I moaned, but I didn't really mind. I was passing on the way home.

'Sorry, hey, are you OK?'

'Of course, why wouldn't I be?' I lied.

'Just, you know, Valentine's Day and all that crap.'

'I'd already forgotten about it.'

'OK, so just don't forget the applications.'

As if I'd forget.

Then he turned and left the office. My heart sank. For a moment I'd thought he was going to ask me to go for a drink or something.

When the kitchen was clean I donned my coat and went to pick up the applications. Everyone else had left and I was really down in the dumps. The place felt empty and lonely. It was Valentine's night and I was going home to eat frozen pizza, drink gallons of Energyade and watch some stupid soap on the telly. What a bloody disappointment the day had turned out to be but, then, it had always been that way. I lifted the receiver to phone

Mam, dialled half the number but got cold feet and put it down. I decided to call her in the morning.

I went to my desk and turned off the terminal. I gathered the application forms together and filed them alphabetically. It was when the desk had been cleared and I had put the forms aside that I noticed the small box sitting on top of my keyboard.

I opened it eagerly and pulled out the contents. I laid them on the desk, like little jewels. A small block of Cheddar cheese, with a birthday candle stuck in each corner. A bottle of white wine, with a wine-glass and a pink rose. At the bottom of the box was a card. I tore it open and read it: 'To Finn, your very own candlelit wine-and-cheese dinner! Enjoy! Love, Colm.'

'Oh, God.'

I was so touched I burst into uncontrollable tears.

# Chapter 14

I was due to go under the knife on 5 March 2000. I ringed the date in my pocket calendar and immediately began to feel different. It was an extraordinary change in personality. Just knowing that I was going to have the operation gave me a confidence boost next to none. I hadn't felt so good for years. Things that had previously appeared off-limits suddenly became a possibility – and apparently it showed in my demeanour at work to the extent that I was suddenly asked to take on some new tasks. When Tom O'Hare went sick, I was happy to do more than my usual share, and surprised to find that I handled the extra responsibility rather well.

It was our worst time for loan applications and the tables and chairs were overflowing with files that we hadn't had time to put back. I also helped out with new accounts, which were a headache. Due to the government's new laws on money-laundering, a new account demanded endless documentation to verify the holder's identity. I mucked in to clear the backlog, and was happy to do so, if only to pass the time.

We were still being kept busy with the interest going on accounts, and the annual general meeting scheduled for the end of February.

Ever since the night of the party I had taken a greater

interest in Colm Long, but even more so since Valentine's Day. I was so touched by his unique and thoughtful gesture. I made a point of talking to him and even joined him in the canteen at lunchtime. At least when the others were blathering about football results, Colm and I could talk about something else. He hated sporty talk as much as I did, and never went to matches or checked the racing results. Sometimes we all went swimming together. It was the only sport I enjoyed, but the mere mention of it was enough to make Colm scowl. I tried to drag him along but it was pointless.

Colm was a wizard with people: he knew intuitively how to handle anyone, no matter what their background, education or needs, and he dealt easily with customers. Eventually I came to understand a certain timidity in him that I hadn't seen before. For instance, today a little woman had approached Colm's desk. She only ever appeared once a year to have her book updated and always went to Colm. She loved him: he was a fine young chap with a good head on him. She shuffled up to the desk, the top of her head barely visible. Colm could only see her hands. They appeared mysteriously over the desk, like puppets.

'Howya, Colm,' she shouted up to him.

Her book slid under the hatch and landed in his lap.

'Is that you, Mrs Kane?' he asked.

''Tis,' she shouted back.

'Aren't you the brave one venturing out at this time of the year? How are you now, pet?' he asked.

'Not bad, not bad at all, love.'

'Will I update your book for you so, Mrs Kane?'

'Ay. Do that, Colm. Isn't the interest due to go on?'

'It is indeed, Mrs Kane. The lads are out the back unloading the truck as we speak,' he said.

I smiled to myself.

'Sure that's grand, then. I knew it wouldn't do to leave it until tomorrow. Make sure I get me share, Colm, ha?'

'Don't worry, Mrs Kane, I've already put yours aside,' he said.

'And was it all there, Colm?'

''Twas indeed.' He handed her back the book. 'I made sure of it,' he smiled at her.

'Ah, sure you're a grand lad, Colm.'

'A happy new year to you, Mrs Kane. You mind yourself now, won't you?' he said, with genuine concern.

'I will, Colm. God bless you, son.' Mrs Kane hobbled out the door and disappeared for another twelve months.

On the night of the AGM Mark Adams called me into his office. He asked me would I represent the Credit Union in uniform at the meeting, taking care of members, handing out raffle tickets and, arranging seating. Without Tom O'Hare he was badly stuck.

It occurred to me that Tom O'Hare had been absent rather a long time. I couldn't ask Mark what was going on, and trying to get information out of Colm was like squeezing blood out of a stone. I knew something was going on behind the scenes and that Tom O'Hare was no more sick than the man in the moon. Colm assured me I would find out everything in the end. In fact, I was more concerned with Mark's request for me to represent the Credit Union. It frightened me first because I was not used to mixing with people at that sort of event. However, Daria had volunteered to help out too and I thought maybe we could nip down to the pub afterwards.

'Sure, I'll do it,' I said.

Mark Adams eyed me over his computer terminal.

'Great. By the way, are you going to Thailand or something?' he asked

'What?' I said.

He held up my loan application for three thousand five hundred pounds.

'Oh, that.'

'Don't worry. It's approved. Just wanted to let you know.'

'Right,' I said awkwardly.

'So, where are you off to, then?' he asked, his moustache bobbing up and down as he demolished a cheese and coleslaw roll. A shred of carrot dangled from the wiry bush.

'America,' I blurted out.

'Any contacts over there?' he asked.

'Yeah. An aunt,' I said.

'Where?' he asked.

*Oh, fuck you, you nosy bollox.*

'New York?' I tried.

'What part?'

'East side?' My voice wavered.

'Jesus, I have cousins there. Don't go without me giving you their address.'

'That would be great!' I lied.

'She must have plenty of money, living on the east side,' he remarked.

'Who?' I said stupidly.

'Your aunt?' He eyed me suspiciously.

'Yeah. Won the lotto,' I said, knowing it sounded about as truthful as the testimonies given in the Flood tribunal.

Mark Adams stared at me long and hard. 'Better get yourself ready for tonight.' He nodded at the door.

'Right.'

'Finn?' He stopped me again.

*Oh, what now? Can't anyone lie in peace any more?*

'Yes?'

'Is Colm still out there?'

'Yes.'

'Good. Don't let him out of your sight.'

'Right.'

'And keep Dessie away from the members. You know what I mean?' He raised an eyebrow.

'Like, make sure he doesn't have a conversation with one?' I guessed.

'Got it in one. By the way, make sure you're in full uniform, Finn,' he added, as an afterthought.

I scowled at him, offended: I always wore my full uniform and it was always clean and pressed. If I hadn't had a clean uniform, I would have missed work rather than arrive in without it. It was another decision I had made based on school experience: my mother had failed to see how important it was to have the appropriate attire. There was nothing worse than standing out like a sore thumb. I cringed at the memory of what I had been forced to wear and the embarrassment I had suffered.

*I am almost twelve. I have started secondary school and I hate it. I'm not very good at the 'good' things anymore. I can't get a handle on maths or bookkeeping and I rate very poorly in the home-economics class. Mam won't let me use the oven at home. She says it's too expensive. I know that's a load of rubbish because I see her using it to bake scones for Dad. Each Wednesday I come home with a recipe and I know it's pointless to ask her to get me the correct ingredients for the next class. How am I supposed to learn how to bake brown bread if she won't let me practise?*

*'Now, if you were making a lot of scones and a few brown*

*loaves, I would turn on the oven,' she says. 'It would be economical then.'*

*I'm always missing some really important ingredient like baking powder so my stuff comes out flat.*

*Whenever I have a sewing assignment she's just as bad. I can't sew to save my life. Not even a square piece of material that the home-economics teacher gave me to practise on. That teacher hates me and I'm the laughing stock of the class. Look what Finn O'Farrell did wrong today, girls!*

*Mam won't let me use the old sewing-machine. She says the needle is broken. My buttonhole extravaganza looks terrible beside the other girls'. It is all smudged and crumpled. I compare it with others, smooth, clean pieces of material that you have to search to find the stitching. You can't even see the thread on some pieces, it is so neatly done. All Mam gives me is black thread and it looks stupid against the pink material. Big lop-sided blotches. It is mortifying.*

*I'm no good at gymnastics, and hopeless at netball and hurley. I don't want to play any sports, but the head nun says we have to have physical education and only a note from our parents saying we are terminally ill will get us excused. It is not that I mind the gym hall so much. I like the horse and the trampoline. I like trying to do cartwheels and handstands. I even like floor exercises. It's the missing PE gear that really gets me. I asked Mam to get it for me before I started the term, a green jersey with a white Aertex shirt underneath and a short green skirt that wraps round your waist and has sticky tape on the inside. She said it was a waste of money.*

*A T-shirt and shorts would do the job just as good. I suppose they would, but I hadn't bargained for having to wear Padraig's rugby kit. There I am, standing in the gym hall, telling Mrs Moore that I have a really bad pain in my stomach and I can't possibly do PE today. She has heard that story four weeks in a row and isn't having any more of my lip. I am to go and get changed immediately and join the class.*

*I get ready in the toilets, thinking if I collapse she might let me go home. I did a pretty mean corpse in the drama class when we were putting on Hamlet. Just lie still and people will know you're dead. The drama teacher said I had captured the character really well! How did I do that? I was dead, for God's sake. I wonder can I play dead now. I mean, really, really dead.*

*Mrs Moore comes looking for me as predicted. She charges into the toilets shouting out my name. She is a big country-woman and her voice booms under the toilet cubicle. I am still in there trying to figure a way out of this unholy mess.*

*'Finn? Finn? Come out here this minute. You're holding the whole class up as usual,'*

*I can see her soft brown flat shoes tapping impatiently from under the door. I amn't able to muster up the death role again so I open the lock and step out. Mrs Moore, God be good to her, does her best to avert her look of shock as I stand there in all my glory.*

*I have Padraig's shorts on; they are far too small for me, I have his green and white striped knee-length socks on. I turn them down but they look ridiculous no matter what I do with them. His jersey is green and white and has a large number seven on the back and front. It has a V-neck, which almost exposes my chest. I look a sight for sore eyes.*

*'Finn, where is your PE kit?' she asks softly.*

*'I lost it.' She looks at me strangely. 'Well, I didn't actually lose it as much as misplaced it.' A right old Pinocchio I am. I can almost feel my nose growing as I elongate and elaborate the lies.*

*She keeps her stare on me.*

*'OK.' I try another tack. 'I had it ready to be washed after last week and my Mam forgot to wash it so I didn't want to*

*bring it in. It's still dirty. In the laundry bag,' I add, thinking that's pretty good and she'll fall for it.*

*'Is that right, Finn O'Farrell?' She nods and draws on her big Mayo accent.*

*'I swear, Mrs Moore,' I offer.*

*'Finn, you had no PE kit last week,' she reminds me.*

*'Oh,' is all I can manage.*

*'Or the week before that,' she goes on.*

*'Oh.'*

*'Or the week before that, even. In fact I don't recall you ever wearing it.' She wags a finger. She's on to me and I'm running out of tricks. I can't play dead and it seems I can't play Pinocchio either.*

*I am snared.*

*'Would you like to tell me the truth now? In your own good time, of course.' Her voice is a little gentler and more persuasive than before.*

*The hot tears spring to my eyes and my throat aches with wanting to cry. I know they're big fat tears too. I can tell by the pain in my gullet. I feel so humiliated I want to push past her and run away from the school for ever.*

*'I haven't got any PE kit, Mrs Moore.' It is a mere whisper but I know she has heard me.*

*In fact, I know she knows I haven't got any PE kit. It only makes the humiliation worse. I knew this day would come. I can't stop the world turning. I can't stop life happening. I keep my eyes on the floor, feeling guilty and ashamed.*

*'Why not, Finn?'*

*She's being very nice now. It doesn't help the tears one bit. I can't stop them, no matter how hard or soft she is with me. I hate the way tears do that. They take me by surprise and neither man nor child can stand in their way when they decide to come.*

*'My Mam . . .' I falter.*

*I can't say it. I just can't say it.*

*Mrs Moore puts out her hand and takes mine. I think she's going to give me a right oul wallop. Instead she marches me down to the head nun's office, while I cry all the way. I plead and beg with her not to bring me there. I will be murdered for sure. She plonks me down on a chair outside and tells me to wait.*

*After I have sat there for several minutes the head nun comes out and calls me in. 'Fainche,' she says, peering through her thick black-rimmed glasses (she is the only one who still calls me Fainche). She looks me up and down, shaking her head and letting out loud tut-tuts. She takes me into her office.*

*'Sit down, child.'*

*I do as she tells me, wishing Mrs Moore had let me change back into my school uniform. I'm afraid anyone else might see, and then the whole school will start slagging me.*

*Mrs Moore pats my shoulder. Why are they being so kind to me? The head nun picks up her phone and it is then I realize they are calling Mam. Now I'm really in for it. I'll get the back of her hand again for making a show of her and having the head nun on the phone. I deserve a good battering anyway. It's my fault. Everything is my fault . . .*

# Chapter 15

The AGM was held in the local community school two streets away from the Credit Union. Busloads of members began to arrive around seven thirty. Daria and I had set up an entrance table with a list of names and ticked them off as the members left the buses and entered the school hall. The turnout was encouraging, but we knew why: the only point of interest on the evening's agenda was the free raffle at the end. Inside, the chairman and panel of committee members started their talk about the financial figures, interest rates and lending power.

After the committee opened the floor to questions the crowd groaned when a member stood up and complained about the opening hours and the endless queues.

Colm had nipped home to get changed. He assured us he would be back in a jiffy. There was no point in complaining, but in any case the members were keeping us too busy to think about it.

'Dessie? Dessie?' A member waved him over. 'Will they be shitin' out of them much longer?' he asked.

'Won't be long now,' Dessie said, dressed to kill in his only suit, a navy two-piece with a polka-dot tie. His shoes were polished and he looked presentable, if you ignored the two-tone hair, and the missing tooth, which showed when he smiled.

'Put me tickets on the very top, right? The oul telly is banjaxed, could do with a new one, especially one of those big jobs.' The man winked. I guess he thought he was being the soul of discretion but it was as obvious as Dessie's missing tooth that he had never heard of the word.

'Got it.' Dessie gestured back.

The Panasonic flat screen TV had drawn more people than we had catered for. They stood at the back of the hall, exuding rudeness in its purest form, talking loudly and waving their tickets while the committee members droned on about profits and new premises. They didn't notice the little touches I had scattered around the bare hall to make it more welcoming. I had placed little vases of flowers all along the main desk, and water dispensers at every exit. I'd even put out dishes of sweets to keep the kids happy, but they didn't go near them. In the end I ate them myself. Finally the speeches ended with a round of applause and we served tea and sandwiches to the hungry hordes.

'Do you see her?' Dessie pointed to an old fat woman, dressed in threadbare black tracksuit bottoms and white stilettos. She's been to the table three times already. Wouldn't you think she'd realise there's other people here? We won't have enough to go round everyone. It's always the oul ones. Why's that?' he asked.

A small child came up and loaded her plate so high she couldn't carry it all back. 'I hope that one is violently ill.' I sniffed, ramming a Jammie Dodger into my mouth faster than a politician mounting a prostitute.

'Speak for yourself.' He indicated my chomping jaws. My mouth was too full for me to reply.

When the raffle was announced the tables were upended by the stampede that followed. A vacuum of wind and some scuttling spiders were all that was left behind. We began to clear up, and with the three of us it was done in no time. I was dying for a pint. I was also dying to find out where Colm had got to. There wasn't any point in getting angry with him: the work was done. 'Are we going for a drink?' I stretched my arms and legs.

'Why not?' they all agreed, and off we trudged to dirty O'Reilly's on the corner. It's the type of place that stares at you before you even go in. The bar stank like a gorilla cage and the 'lounge' was a place you wouldn't bring your granny into. We didn't care. We wanted a drink. As any Irish person who's worth their porter rings knows, you have to suffer these irksome drawbacks.

Once we had a few down, tongues were loosened (in Dessie's case, flopping) and the effects of intoxication turned the place into Caesar's Palace. We made friends with the locals as if they were relatives lost for an age with whom we were reunited at long last.

'It's an awful kip, isn't it?' I said to Daria.

'I know what a kip is,' she said to herself, sipping her drink.

'I'm proud of you, do you know that?' I shouldered her heartily.

'Hey, watch my drink.'

'Where did Colm get to?' I asked.

'I don't know. He said he was going home to change,' Daria said.

'I've heard that one before.'

'We knew he would do this,' she pointed out.

'Yeah, but it's really unfair of him,' I returned.

'Well, we managed very well, I thought,' she said.

'I'm going to say something to him when I see him,' I barked.

'What for?' Daria asked.

'I just think it's mean, always leaving us to pick up the pieces, and Mark Adams never says a word to him about it,' I said resentfully. I wasn't really angry with Colm: I was disappointed that he hadn't turned up and that I couldn't spend the evening with him.

'Maybe you're right. Maybe you should tell him.'

'Huh?' I was surprised.

She had a sly look about her. I glanced up to see the devil himself sashaying across the floor, all smiles like nothing had happened.

Daria stood up to visit the ladies' and was assaulted by comments from drunken bums who drank all day and ran the government from their bar stools. You know the type: they commanded the Gulf War from the Guinness tap and ended the droughts in Ethiopia with their ten-pence contribution to the poor box on the bar.

'Go on, you good thing!' one shouted after her, and his friends exploded into laughter.

Dessie was chatting to some straggling members who had piled in after the free raffle. They hadn't won anything and felt entitled to lash him out of it. Dessie took it all in his stride, promising to bring to the manager's attention that there were no wheelchair ramps and the grub at the AGM hadn't been fit for human consumption.

Daria returned to a torrent of benign depletions.

'Go on, ye beaut, ye!'

'What's a . . . Forget it.' She sat down, confused.

'Don't worry, girl. It's all positive stuff,' Colm said, laughing.

'You Irish are mad,' she told us.

'At least we know it,' I confirmed.

'Where the hell were you anyway?' She said to Colm, surprising us all.

'I got stuck at home. My mam,' he said, as cool as you like.

'I thought you said she was dead? Was her name Lazarus by any chance?' Dessie guffawed.

Colm gave him a steely glare. It wasn't a very nice thing to say – even if it was the truth. 'Very funny, Des. I meant my Dad. He isn't well,' he said, looking angry now. Colm never mentioned his family and none of us had the courage to quiz him about it. It was a taboo subject. Now the look on his face was enough to ward off any questions. At any mention of Mams and Dads Colm became silent and cold.

Daria threw Dessie a look that would have withered a rose.

'Sorry,' Dessie said quietly.

'It's OK. He's getting old, my father. I don't think he knows what he's doing half the time. Found him wandering around out back. Took me half an hour to convince him that the 1916 Rising was over long ago,' Colm said. We all clubbed in with an emphatic nod. Colm's eyes were filled with anxiety.

I felt for him. 'Is there no one else to look after him?' I asked.

'Only me, Skin, I'm afraid. You know, he hasn't been the same since Mam—' He broke off.

The silence was almost tangible. Colm's face was white and drained, like he had the world on his shoulders.

'Maybe you should have him looked over by a doctor?' I suggested.

Colm looked uncomfortable, as if he regretted having said anything.

'Maybe he needs professional care, like a home for the aged,' Daria suggested.

'I would never do that to him. I would never leave him,' Colm said sharply.

Nobody knew what to say to that.

'Well, maybe I will take him to the doctor,' he added, and sipped his drink eagerly.

'Sounds like a good idea to me.' I tried to be gentle and encouraging.

'Great. Now, can we change the subject, please? Yo. Skinny. What's this rumour about you jet-setting off to New York?' he asked.

I was surprised he knew about it.

'Oh, that. Yeah. New York. Always wanted to go there, I suppose,' I blabbed.

'Going on your own?' he asked.

'Yeah,' I said.

'I'd go, if I had the money,' Daria put in.

'It's going to take you for ever to pay off that loan,' he said.

'Believe me, it will be worth it,' I said, annoyed he knew about it but he would have had to file the promissory notes.

'I want to see lots of photos.' His eyes gleamed, peering over his glass.

*You will, you will.*

'When are you going?' he asked, opening a packet of peanuts and deftly throwing a handful down his throat. It was hard to know if he was deliberately extracting information or just enquiring. Either way, he didn't have to pry so hard.

'March the fifth,' I replied.

'That's next week,' he said.

'Yeah. We should do something to mark the occasion,' Daria put in.

'I've got tickets to see Bill Roberts this Friday,' he threw in. I waited for him to elaborate. He didn't.

'Mark Adams got them from a member. Think he'd rather die than be seen there.' He chuckled.

Bill Roberts was another boy band throwback. I detested him as much as Samantha King or Jennifer Eden.

I looked to Daria. From her expression I could tell she was none the wiser. There was an embarrassing silence.

'I have four,' he said eventually.

Daria eyed me.

'I thought you girls might like a couple. Ion and I are going. You know the bloke who comes in every Friday?' he said, chewing his peanuts. I longed to be one.

'Who?' I played dumb.

'Ion, a guy I worked with in Financial Services. You'll like him,' he said.

'Ion? I know him, I think. I've seen him call in a few times – a tall bloke?' Daria asked.

'That's the one. He's quiet, but a dead nice guy,' Colm said.

'I'm in,' said Daria.

'Me, too,' I said, trying not to appear overly enthusiastic.

'Great,' he said, and leaned sideways to get something out of his back pocket. 'You might as well have the tickets now. I knew you wouldn't want to go with us.'

*The bastard*. My head was wrecked and I badly wanted an Energyade.

'It will be a nice send-off for your trip of a lifetime,' he said.

That was exactly the way I saw it. It *was* the trip of a lifetime and I wondered, on my return, would things ever be the same again?

I had made up my mind about the piano. I would get rid of it before I was incarcerated – but it proved more difficult than I had supposed. For a start, no one would come and pick it up without charging me the earth. I had advertised it in the local paper and shops, hoping some talented kid might need it. I would have given it to them for free, but I had no callers. I obviously couldn't move it myself: it had taken several helpers to get it up there in the first place. I wondered again was I doing the wrong thing. I could almost hear my father grumbling. It was a real spit in the face, a final fling of the mud. But he was dead so it didn't matter any more, I told myself.

A day or so after the AGM I planned my strategy and took a detour across town to McCullough Piggott's music shop in my lunch hour. I stalled for an age outside – I hadn't allowed myself to go in there for some time. When I did, I always came out depressed. Yet this was business and I was determined not to delay, just ask the questions and get out of there as fast as possible. I promised myself I would not look at the beautiful pianos, or breathe in the familiar woody scent of their newness. I promised myself to have single vision and ignore their calling, the smooth keys, the crisp, sharp hammers, and the brilliantly shined brass pedals . . .

I walked to the sales desk where a small, balding man, with a thin strand of hair plastered over his skull and a pencil behind his ear, was whistling to himself. 'Excuse me?'

'Yes, madam, what can I do for you?' He peered through his glasses at me, as if I had somehow wandered into the wrong shop.

'Well, it's about a piano,' I started.

'You want to buy one?' He looked squarely at me.

'No, actually, I want to sell one,' I replied.

'Well, you couldn't have picked a worse time. We're

not in the business of purchasing pianos. How old is it, might I ask?'

'Oh, God, you have me there. Well, my father played it and when he died I kind of inherited it, so it's old, very old.' I was disheartened.

'My dear child, I can assure you if it's as old as that you won't get a price for it. You're better off keeping it,' he said flatly.

'Wouldn't somebody be interested in taking it? You know, like some kid who's broke. Surely someone wants a free piano,' I argued.

'Yes, one would think so, but unfortunately the damn things are expensive to move, and most people don't have room for a piano. Believe me, it's my guess you'll end up paying someone to take it away and even then it will probably end up in a dump,' he said.

'That's kind of sad, don't you think?'

'Sad indeed, but the way of the world today, my child. Do you play? he asked suddenly. I knew why: he had caught me staring dewy-eyed at the snow-white baby grand in the corner. I couldn't take my eyes off it. It was majestically set on a pure white rug, which accentuated its brass pedals. The lid was propped open by a superbly finished brass lever.

'I used to,' I admitted.

'You can have a go, if you like.' He nodded at the instrument.

'I can? You mean you'll let me? Are you sure?' I asked, my stomach rising and falling.

'Sure, no one's here, go ahead. You'll never feel anything like that baby beneath your fingertips. Top of the range, she is.' He smiled at me. Another lover of pianos, I assumed.

'But it's a Steinway,' I gasped. I had never even sat at a Steinway, let alone put my paws on one.

'Yes. All hundred thousand pounds of it.' He grinned.

'No!' I exclaimed.

'Go on,' he urged, seeing my excitement. 'Have a go of her.'

'You sure?' I checked again.

He nodded.

I walked slowly across the room, my heart pounding in my chest. Would I do it? Would I sit down and rest my fingers on the keys? I sat on the magnificently crafted piano stool. My bottom sank into its luxurious silk finish. The legs were beautifully carved, like majestic trees, roots flowing outwards and clinging to Mother Earth. I felt like a queen on a throne. I pulled the stool under me, drawing it closer to the keyboard. Then I allowed my eyes to feast on the glory at my fingertips. I held them above the keys and allowed them to hover there, just for a few seconds. My hands were trembling with a mixture of excitement and nerves. My mouth felt dry, my throat parched, I could not swallow.

I had been thirteen, the last time I had played. I permitted my fingers to touch the keys. I closed my eyes and breathed in the piano's character. Sophisticated, I surmised. I could sense its royalty, its class. It demanded I treat it with respect. My head leaned back, my face rose up and then I heard the first sound emanate from its hammers. A soft *ping* of perfect clarity echoed through the shop. This piano wanted a Schubert impromptu. I could feel it. It ached for someone to play Schubert, and nothing less would do. In a trance, I obeyed. It commanded me to bring forth its greatness. The room filled with sound, I swam with its rhythm, letting the piano dictate. I caressed the keys, feeling its sensitivity, its vulnerability, its tone. I played with the pedals, deepening the mood where asked, then lightening, and to my joy the symphony of sound was intoxicating. I imagined Schubert playing, his face etched with concentration, his nimble fingers penetrating the depths of what was in his head, the notes tumbling out and rushing over one another like a waterfall, like a dam-burst. I imagined him lost in it, and I let myself slip into that world. The world where no one existed, only the music and me. A world where I was not aware of time, space, constraint, schedule. I just was. In that piece of music at that grand piano, I was myself once more.

Tears spliced my eyes. They stung but I did not stall; I gathered speed, feeling my emotions rise to the surface. Let them come, I thought. Let it all come now. It was not a painful cry, but a soothing release, a spiritual homecoming. Slowly, the impromptu came to its finale, the last notes distant and subtle, almost as if a ghost tiptoed along the keys and, when it reached the end of the keyboard, slipped off, vanishing for ever.

There was no sound but my own breathing. How long had I been sitting there, unconscious of anything but what I had just experienced? My fingers wavered a half-inch above the keys, quivering, suspended in time. I didn't want to leave my friend, my long-lost friend. I did not want to say goodbye again. My tears flowed freely as I felt the wrench, the loss, the missed opportunity, and the failure to be what I had wanted to be.

An arm rested gently on my shoulders. At first I thought I was imagining it. I did not know who the arm belonged to, but it felt comfortable there, as if it belonged. I wanted to rest my hand on it. I felt it understood me, as if it knew my very being, the secrets I had buried and the pain interred therein.

My nose was running. I realized where I was. Jesus,

I thought, is the shop full? Are people staring at me like I've gone mad? *Have* I gone mad?

I was afraid to turn round. The old man must have taken pity on me. His arm still rested on my shoulder making me feel strangely safe, secure. He was a stranger, yet he probably knew me better than anyone in that moment. I pulled out a handkerchief and dried my eyes. I blew my nose, still conscious of the old man behind me. I cleared my throat and slowly twisted round on the piano stool to apologize for being stupid. As I did, I came face to face not with the old man but with Colm.

'God, but that's so beautiful . . .' He whispered.

# Chapter 16

'Are you stalking me now?' I lunged at Colm in anger and fear. We were walking back to the Credit Union, me dashing ahead, Colm trying to keep up.

'Of course not! I happened to see you go into the shop and, well, I was nosy, OK? God, but you can play! Christ, you're so good. How long does it take to become that good? Was it years? Why didn't you tell any of us you played that well?' He rattled on with a million questions.

'Why did you have to sneak up on me like that? God, but you give me the creeps sometimes.' I sighed heavily.

'You know that bit at the end, where it tapers off? Wow, I never heard anything like that before. It was like being at a recital at the National Concert Hall. How do you do it? You know, that bit that goes like, lah-di-dah-di-dah-di—'

'I don't want to talk about it, OK?' I was horrified. To think he had been standing there all that time watching me, listening to me!

'Hey, I'm giving you a compliment. What's the matter, for God's sake? Slow down, will you?' He was losing his breath trying to keep up.

'There's nothing wrong with me,' I snapped, 'and thanks for the compliment, but it's a long story and I don't want to bore you with it.'

'You're not boring me, not one bit. I'm fascinated. Jesus, Finn, you're so talented. Christ, if you had been my daughter I would have had you in the best music school in town. I mean—'

'Colm!' I shouted, tears spilling down my face.

He stopped in the middle of the crowds and went to put his arms round me. I pushed him away and kept walking, even faster now.

'What is it? How have I upset you now? I don't understand,' he called after me, in genuine vexation.

I kept walking. I wasn't going to give in. He wasn't going to watch me crying. He wasn't going to make a laughing-stock out of me either, giving me all that talented crap. I wasn't going to be anyone's fool. Not any more. Hot tears kept coming and I kept walking.

'Finn! I think you're great! Did you hear me? I think you're the – you're the best thing since the sliced fucking pan!' he bellowed up the street. I glanced quickly back to catch him smiling at some old dears who were whispering and giggling at him. I wiped away the tears.

When he was out of sight, I stopped and leaned against a wall. I closed my eyes and, to my surprise, a smile came to my lips. I let it have free rein. I jigged about, from one foot to the other, grinning from ear to ear and chewing my lip like a lovesick teenager. I was crying and laughing all at the same time.

There was great excitement at the Bill Roberts concert, although I felt decidedly over-aged at twenty-five. An eight-year-old girl wearing silver boppers danced away in the seat beside me as her mother looked on with a satisfied smile. Perhaps they had bought the tickets thinking they were going to see Daniel O'Donnell. But it wasn't Daniel O'Donnell who was now practically having oral sex with his microphone. I wondered how Irish mothers managed to believe that this was an evening of family entertainment.

Colm had omitted to tell us that the four tickets were for four seats in a row so we ended up sitting beside him and Ion anyway. Ion turned out to be a pleasant surprise and caused a momentary silence when he was introduced to Daria. She couldn't believe her luck.

'Ion, this is Daria Alexandru,' Colm said, pushing the sandy-haired pale-skinned man towards her. He wasn't heart-stoppingly handsome but he wasn't ugly either. He was a bit too tall for me, though. He stooped down almost apologetically, as if he wished he were shorter, and took her hand.

'Nice to meet you, Daria. That's Romanian, isn't it? Daria Alexandru?'

His accent was unfamiliar, but that wasn't a rarity in Dublin any more. You could ramble around Temple Bar and believe you were in London's Piccadilly Circus, there were so many different nationalities living and working in Ireland now. It wasn't perfect English and it had a smack of German to it, guttural and harsh.

What struck me was Daria's frozen expression. I took this to be a good sign as she stared long and hard into the grey eyes of the quiet stranger. I wasn't sure if she had fallen instantly in love with him or just remembered she had left the oven on at home. I broke the silence with a feigned cough and Colm turned to me.

'And this is Finn O'Farrell. Finn, meet Ion Florescu.' I stepped forward and shook his hand. It was damp with nervousness but his smile was warm and I decided I liked him. I was too afraid to ask where he was from because I had never owned a world atlas and wouldn't have known the capitals of Europe, never mind anything more. I made a mental note that he hadn't a humpy back and checked for a clubfoot, just in case Colm had tried to pull a sneaky one. Nope. He was normal. Everything was in place. It was almost annoying.

'Ion did some work experience with me on the financial-services course. He now works for an aviation Credit Union in Swords. Much smaller than ours, of course,' he added.

'Cool,' I said, taking a swig of Energyade.

'How many staff do you have?' Daria asked.

'Two,' he answered.

'Two?' we exclaimed.

'How do you manage with only two staff? What about all the members?' I asked.

'We don't have any,' he explained, shoving his rather large maulers into his jeans pockets.

'What?' I stared at him.

'I'm sorry. Of course we have members – but we never see them. You see, it's all computer work. Postings and loan repayments are done through direct debit, through computer. We don't have an open office. No need to. It's all computerized.'

'Sounds fucking awesome,' I said.

I distinctly saw Daria frown. She was embarrassed. That was when I knew she liked him.

'Wow. No members. Must be great.' She smiled at him for the first time. He smiled back at her and a gentle wind seemed to blow between them.

Taking full advantage of the situation, I sat on Colm's other side, forcing Daria to sit beside Ion and get better acquainted.

'Well, Skinny, are you out of your bad mood?' Colm shouted.

'I wasn't in one to begin with,' I lied.

'You could have fooled me. You're full of surprises,' he said.

'Don't you like surprises?'

'Sure,' he said, 'if you could just give me advance warning, you know, when the next "surprise" is about to be unveiled.'

'I'll try to remember.' I laughed now.

'Aren't you going to explain to me what I did wrong?' he asked.

'You didn't do anything wrong,' I said gently. 'It's a personal thing, OK?'

'Maybe some day you'll tell me,' he probed.

'Maybe.'

'What do you think of Bill Roberts, then?'

'He's a Goddamn midget, for Christ's sake. What do women see in him? I'm mystified.' I shrugged.

'You don't think he's the sexiest man alive?' he asked.

'Who said he was the sexiest man alive? The blind community?'

'Only the female population of the world,' he replied.

'They did?' I said, trying to forget that to me Colm looked just like Bill Roberts.

'What's your type of guy, then, Skinny?' he asked. He was right on cue to surprise me, but I was getting used to him jumping between giddy idiot and serious man.

The mob went berserk as Bill dropped himself into the crowd and he was passed around like a parcel. Pieces of clothing were torn from his back and he was loving every minute of it. If he had passed over me I would have torn out a clump of his hair and hoped it hurt.

'Colm, that is not something I dwell upon,' I told him.

'Let me guess, then. You're the John Wayne type, aren't you? All muscle and scars.' He squeezed my arm gently and fixed me with those dazzling eyes, then lifted three fingers and brushed them against my cheek. My skin tingled and a rivulet of sweat ran down my back. I wasn't ready for *that* kind of surprise. This was no leap from here to there: it was a triathlon long jump. I froze.

Not for the first time I wondered what Colm and I were. Old friends, or something more?

'You're wrong.' I smiled at him, gently pulling myself away. 'I'm more of a Woody Allen girl, if the truth be known.'

Colm stared at me then burst out laughing.

Bill had returned to the stage, minus his clothes, and launched into a romantic ballad. I had a desperate urge to reach out to Colm and touch his hand. I wanted it back on my face. Instead, I watched him tap his knees in time with the melody.

I had made the study of hands a lifetime hobby. His were soft, clean and manly. No signet ring from Mam and Dad on his twenty-first birthday. No watch for graduating. No warts or calluses. No scars from falling off his three-wheeler when he was a toddler, no pins in the joints, no knobbles on the knuckles. Nails even and dirt-free, cut with clippers, I surmised. Hands that told nothing of his past. Only the flick of his fingers as he kept time with the music suggested a rhythm in him that was steady and carefree. The odd sudden movement out of time with the beat hinted that he might have known I was watching.

Daria was still talking with her new friend Ion and I thought what a perfect set-up it was. How could I not hope that friendship would lead to romance? That, in some strange way, the line would become muddled for him too, and Colm would find his feet moving across it like it was the most natural thing in the world. It never occurred to me that he might need a hand. Men were supposed to help *us* across, not the other way round, so I stayed on my side and he stayed on his, wistfully looking over now and then, and always hoping for a miracle. That evening, the miracle seemed close at hand.

I was relieved when after the gig Colm suggested we all go for a drink. It was the perfect ending to a perfect evening. And it was all perfectly destroyed when I saw Julia cross the floor to him. I realized why he was in such good form. I looked at her closely: she could have been my mother. What was it she had that I hadn't? It dawned on me that he had probably arranged to meet her there. As a platonic friend, I couldn't complain or show any signs of jealousy. Dashed again, I thought. I had got my wires crossed. Why did he seem to go out of his way to show interest in me and, just when I was about to give in, do something like this?

I excused myself and joined the long queue at the ladies' toilets. When I came out, I decided it would not be a good idea to join them. I was sulking and I was mad jealous and was not about to let him know that. I sat down on the floor to guzzle my Energyade, hoping they would forget all about me. Unfortunately, the men's toilets were to the right of the ladies' and I was soon looking at Ion's feet.

'Hey,' he said, 'we were looking all over for you. Aren't you coming for a drink?'

'I think I'll take a raincheck,' I said, standing up and smoothing myself down. 'I suddenly feel very tired.'

'Oh, come on. Colm has told me so much about you and we have only just met.' He smiled at me warmly.

A nice guy, I thought.

'Thanks. All the same, if it's OK with you lot, I'd rather go home. Will you tell the others?' I asked, trying to keep my tone calm. I wanted to get out of there as fast as I could.

'If you wish. But wouldn't you like to tell them yourself? After all, they will be worried about you,' he said. My eyes welled up. Fuck it, I did not want him to see this.

'Em, no, honestly, I don't feel well,' I stammered.

'At least let me take you to the exit and get you a taxi. There's hundreds of people queuing up outside already,' he said.

I watched the droves passing, all going the same way, like a swarm of bees, hustling to get through the double doors all at once. Thank God Ion had the sense not to comment on my flooded eyes. I was sure he could see I was upset, but if he did he was kind enough to play my game and pretend nothing was wrong. After all, we didn't know each other.

'OK,' I said, resignedly.

We walked to the doors and Ion stood in line with me. I prayed I would not see Colm and Julia together: it would have been too much. Ion seemed to understand my unspoken sadness. 'I'm very taken with your friend,' he said.

I'm very fond of yours I wanted to say, but declined. 'She's wonderful,' I admitted.

'Look, I know we don't know each other well, but I know Colm very well,' he said. 'I know his behaviour can be a bit strange, but don't pay any real attention to it, OK? He is very fond of you. In fact, he never stops talking about you. I don't know what the story is with him and Julia. Actually I thought that had had its day. I really don't think he had intended to meet her here tonight. Won't you consider changing your mind?'

There was no sign of Colm or Julia so I wasn't convinced. 'No. Honestly. I'll be fine,' I said.

'If you say so,' he said, placing an arm protectively round me as the crowds multiplied.

'How long have you known each other?' I asked.

'Quite a number of years. He really helped me when I first came to Ireland. I did the Credit Union rounds but no one was willing to take me on, until I met Mark Adams. At the time there were no vacancies, but he recommended I do the training course. He was really good to me. I met Colm on the course. He offered to let me stay in his house until I got settled. He was taking a risk, you know. We've been best buddies since. He's a good guy,' he said.

'I didn't know any of that. I thought you were just a distant friend,' I said, surprised.

'Well, now you know,' he said.

'There's so many things I don't know about Colm,' I whispered, almost to myself.

Suddenly Daria appeared at my side, breathless. 'I've been searching the length and breadth of this place looking for you. What are you doing? Don't tell me you're heading home?'

'Yeah. I just feel really tired and, with work tomorrow morning, I thought I'd get an early night,' I waffled. I could see her disapproving glare, but I wasn't thinking of her, only of myself.

'Look,' she whispered in my ear, 'you're taking this the wrong way. I think Julia just turned up at the concert. They hadn't arranged to meet or anything. Can't you think of me for once in your life and not yourself?'

'What do you mean?' I asked. Daria's eyes went over my head to Ion, who was whistling a Bill Roberts tune.

'God! You're actually interested!' I said.

'I didn't say that,' she said.

'You don't have to,' I pointed out.

'Please stay,' Daria begged.

Colm and Julia were crossing the huge foyer. Julia

had her arm in his and they were sharing a joke. I heard her shriek with laughter.

'No way,' I said, tight-lipped. 'You go.'

Daria sighed, but I knew she understood the quandary I was in.

'Go on, it's fine,' I said.

'I feel bad about you going home alone.' Daria bit her lip.

'Don't. Ion is a nice guy and I think he likes you. Go on. I'll be fine,' I urged, and mustered a smile to make her feel more at ease.

I realized miracles were about as fathomable as the existence of a loving God. For too long I had believed that, between God and myself, we could hack anything. I had omitted to acknowledge that I forgot from time to time just who was who . . .

# Chapter 17

In early March 2000 Lolo Ferrari was found dead in her bed. She was thirty-seven. I heard about it from a taxi man, who was engrossed in *Irish News* while he waited for his next customer, which turned out to be me. Until then I had never even heard of Lolo Ferrari. The taxi man spoke of her like she was the girl next door and he had watched her grow up before his very eyes. Like she was public property. Everybody knew Lolo Ferrari. He handed me the newspaper and told me about her while I read. 'Ah, Jeysus, love, you must have heard of oul Lolo?' He laughed.

'No,' I said quietly

'Lolo, sweetheart, you know, the one with the . . .' He drew an imaginary mound on his chest indicating that her fame had something to do with her chest. 'Twenty-two operations she had, a seventy-one-inch bust, and each breast weighed three kilos. That would be the *size of our Joey when he was born. Sure how could you hold one of them in your hands? Imagine! Ha!'*

I'm sure you would have found a way, I thought.

'The lads and meself always wanted to get a photo. You know, with Lolo. To show it to the heads in the pub. That would have them talking, ha? The wife would have a seizure, of course!' He chuckled away.

Lolo's photograph stared up at me. She was a grossly hideous deformity of a human being. Her breasts looked like over-inflated footballs, perched on the top half of her body.

'Had a job done on her nose, mouth and chin too. There wasn't anything original left.' Then he barked into the radio that he was heading across town.

The newspaper told me that Lolo had ranked as one of the top sex stars in Europe. She was a bleached blonde who had spent her entire life trying to become what she perceived to be the perfect woman. The result was a thick-lipped, almond-eyed, humongous-chested wonder of modern science. She was billed as the woman with the biggest breasts in the world. The article made several sick jokes about her, although it was really an obituary. She was cold and dead in her grave and no one seemed to think that mattered much.

'My mother told me I was ugly and stupid,' she had told a reporter. 'She said I was only good for emptying chamber-pots. Actually, I'm like my mother. She thinks she's ugly too.'

The paper said she had hailed from France and resided in Cannes up to her death. Lolo (derived from *'les lolos'*, which is French slang for 'breasts') was a multi-talented woman with more assets than the ones on her chest. She was an accomplished singer and performer and had released a single as well as appearing on *Eurotrash* and romping unashamedly in low-budget hard-core porn movies. The cause of her death was not yet known but a preliminary examination by a local coroner indicated that she had died of natural causes. However, Lolo was believed to have suffered from chronic depression, and might have committed suicide. Nobody knew for sure. It was only speculation.

My stomach lurched.

According to statements made by her husband and manager, Eric Vigne, she had been planning her funeral. She had recently visited an undertaker, picked out a white coffin and asked to be buried with her favourite teddy bear. I blinked back the tears, not understanding why I was upset. I was terrified to examine my feelings because of the journey I was undertaking at that moment, but foreboding washed over me as the taxi man droned on and on about her. He was more interested in discussing the dead woman's breasts, which were rotting as he spoke. There was something indescribably sad about that, irreverent too.

*But who was I to be standing in moral judgement? Was I not on the way to a plastic-surgery clinic to butcher my own body in the same meaningless pursuit of perfection?*

No. *No!* Mustn't think. I asked the taxi man to put his boot to the floor. I was late for an important appointment and my job depended on me being there on time. I asked him to play some music, and he obliged. I stuck the newspaper into the car-door pocket and willed it to stop calling me. I concentrated on the inch-by-inch movement of heavy Dublin traffic and chewed my nails. Thank God Daria had not been able to get the time off to come with me.

I arrived at the Hussledorf Medical Centre at eleven o'clock and was greeted by a series of friendly receptionists all bumping into each other and getting tangled up in each other's breasts. I guessed it came as a perk of the job as they were displaying uniformly abundant cleavages and couldn't all have been born with such bastarding good luck. They might have been the offspring of old Dolly Mixtures, of course, but I doubted it. They chatted to me as if I had arrived for a facial or a manicure, and I behaved accordingly.

I was brought to a very nice ward with three beds. The walls were covered in modern art, a black square with a banana in the middle that was supposed to reveal the world's spiritual mysteries and such. The only thing it revealed to me was that I needed to go to the toilet. I hadn't been able to go for nerves. Now I felt like I could flood Calcutta. I sat awkwardly on the only vacant bed, and gazed at my right-hand companion. She seemed comatose and had tubes going in and out of her chest. I tried not to ask stupid questions, like 'Are you sore?' Every now and then she let a little cry, almost as if the pain was too bad to express.

I did a double take when I looked to my left. I thought Lolo's body had been flown over from France and temporarily set up in the bed beside me. The blonde bombshell's head was barely visible compliments of her massive chest.

*She can't be serious?* I thought. *She cannot seriously be having a boob job?*

The receptionist told me to settle down and change into some nightclothes. I asked could I have a cup of tea as I had been fasting from the night before. She told me I couldn't even have a glass of water before surgery, that it wouldn't be long before the good doctor arrived and I would be trundling to theatre on my way to Happy Diddyland. I wasn't worried. I had a stack of Energyade and chocolate hidden in my overnight bag, waiting to be scoffed later.

I took out my Walkman, and placed my tapes on the locker beside the bed. I couldn't decide who would be right for this place. I studied the selection. Keith Jarrett (too complicated), Earl Hynes (too old), Liberace . . . Liberace? How had he got in there? Anyway, he was too cheerful for a plastic-surgery clinic. I paused at Ray

Charles (a bit too lovey-dovey) then at Jools Holland (too much awe) but when my fingers hit Joe Sample, I knew it would be him, with his sleazy jazzy American type sound. I pulled the curtains round me and undressed, taking one last look at the real me.

I pushed up my breasts, then let them fall again. They drooped like the heads of spring snowdrops. I looked in a small wall mirror at my nipples, which resembled a pair of light switches, and bade them farewell for ever. The fuller breast would make them stand out like bullets and I dreamed of men choking on them. I couldn't wait for the anaesthetic to pull me into that delicious black hole. I prayed for the Smile to make his appearance sooner rather than later, or I would have to make conversation with the headless woman in the bed beside me.

I took out my magazines and my stomach rumbled. I could have eaten the receptionist's leg. I hoped they did nice food.

This is cool! I thought. Warm, comfortable bed, magazines, television with remote, flowers on the bedside locker. Hey, this isn't too bad at all, I convinced myself.

'What are you having done?' a voice asked from the left.

'Excuse me?'

'What are you having done?' the breasts asked again.

'These,' I said, pulling my nightdress over them.

'Enlargement?' she asked.

*No. I'm having a fucking tooth pulled.*

'Yes,' I said, snottily communicating my distaste that she was here when she could be saving third-world countries from starvation with just one of her breasts.

'You too?' I asked, turning the pages of *Vogue*.

'Not likely.' She burst out laughing.

'Oh?' I turned to look at her.

'Jesus, enlarge these? Are you for real, girl?' She was a country girl, pretty but fat, and the boobs didn't help matters. 'I'm having a breast reduction,' she said, as a flicker of worry crossed her furrowed brow.

'Can they do that?' I asked.

'Sure,' she said. 'I wish I looked like you, normal,' she said.

'God, I'm not normal,' I said surprised. 'I'm as flat as a board. It makes me miserable,'

'This is misery,' she said, still holding the offending article, and I had to admit to myself that I would rather have died than walk around looking like a nuclear missile.

'What size are you?' I chanced.

'Thirty-eight H,' she said, sighing.

'Right.' I tried not to look like I had been run over by a JCB.

'I can't take it any more, can't get a bra to fit me – or any other clothes for that matter. Can't sleep properly either – and the slagging! Jesus, I hate it.'

'Slagging? Surely you mean cat whistles and compliments?' I argued.

'Compliments? Listen. Titzilla? Queen Cleavage? "Hey, you, did two Scud missiles hit you in the back or what?" Do they sound like compliments to you?'

I was having trouble stifling a smile and was horrified by my own insensitivity: they were dreadful taunts for anyone to have to endure. I'd thought mine was the only problem, you see. I had never imagined anyone suffering from oversized breasts. I had assumed their life was plain sailing and had envied them.

'What are you going for?' she asked, turning to face

me properly. She had ruddy cheeks, sparkling eyes and lovely long blonde hair.

'Nothing too big. Three hundred and sixty cc, I think.' I was glad now of someone to talk to.

'That's big,' she said.

Not that big, I thought.

'It doesn't sound like it, but under your stretched skin it's going to feel mighty peculiar,' she said.

I tried to look like somebody who had weighed up all the pros and cons and knew exactly what I was doing. 'It's quite small, really,' I said, with assurance.

'I wish you luck.'

I was still reeling at the mathematics of her chest size.

'How do they . . . you know, reduce breasts?' I asked.

She pulled them out and they sat on her ribcage like two Charleville cheeses. 'See here?' She lifted one up and drew an imaginary line round her nipple. 'They make an incision all around here, leaving only the nipple in place. They take out the breast tissue and literally cut half of it away, then stuff the rest back under, pull the skin down over it and stitch it back into place.'

I was green at the thought of it. 'What does the breast tissue look like?' I wondered.

'It's weird, like intestines. It unfolds like layers of uncooked minced beef. It's really disgusting.' She laughed.

Now I felt really sorry for her. No matter how bad I felt about my lack of breast tissue I wouldn't have liked an abattoir of meat to be dragging out of me. 'Well, tell the doctor to hold on to the leftovers. If you give me half of yours we'll both be perfect,' I joked.

The girl laughed.

'I'm Finn.' I smiled at her.

'Patricia.'

'I'm absolutely starving,' I complained.

'Tell me about it.' She leaned back, allowing her breasts to smother her again.

'What time are you down for?' I asked.

'I was meant to be done at nine this morning,' she said, looking at the clock on the wall.

It was now one o'clock and I was also supposed to be on my way to theatre. The nurses flitted in and out, asking about our medical histories, checking whether we were on any medication. They took our pulses and temperatures, and I got the feeling I was in safe hands all round.

At three o'clock, Patricia, and her extended family, were wheeled off to theatre. I bade them a cheerful farewell and sat staring at the wall in abject terror. At four o'clock I heard the familiar screech of the trolley heading in my direction. I was lifted on to it, although I told them I could do it myself. Insurance, they quipped. Right so. On I popped. The trolley-wheeler whistled a merry tune as he manoeuvred me into the lift and out again. Eventually we arrived at the operating theatre. Patricia passed me by as I went in, but she was out cold. *Now I felt scared.*

I was terrified of the pain that lay ahead. I kept thinking about the woman in the bed with all the tubes who moaned every couple of minutes. Suddenly the dream was a reality and I wanted to see Daria's face more than anything else in the world. I lay on my back, staring up at the bright spaceship lights in a flimsy green gown with a string holding the back together.

The Smile arrived.

'How are you?' He peered into my pupils.

'I'm OK,' I warbled.

'Everything's going to be fine,' he said reassuringly.

I extemporized something guttural. Pure fear had rendered me wordless.

'Let me explain what we're going to do,' he said.

I would have preferred him to spare me the details, but as he talked the nurses gathered around and I realized he was explaining it to them as well. *Christ, didn't they know what to do?*

'We cut here and here, at the sub-mammary crease,' he said, raising my arms over my head and pointing below my breasts. He made a mark about five centimetres long on each side with a black felt pen. 'Working through the incision we will lift the breast tissue and skin to create a pocket, yes? The implant will then be positioned behind or underneath the pectoral muscle. We will make that decision when we are in. We will also attach a draining tube for a couple of days. Bleeding may be excessive. Nothing to worry about.' He laughed at me, but I'm sure he didn't mean to.

I nodded, and swallowed my stomach at the same time.

'Then we will suture all along here, bandages will be taped on to protect the stitching and then further gauze bandages will be applied over your breasts to help with healing. Any questions?'

*Yes. Can you please stop smiling at me?*

I shook my head from side to side and pulled the piece of cloth tighter over my breasts. It was a nonsensical reaction for one who, minutes before, had been perfectly willing to have their ribcage sliced open.

'Good,' the Smile said. 'We will now administer an anaesthetic and you will drift off into sleep, yes?' He moved away and the nurses came forward and rigged up the needle on the front of my hand. It didn't hurt and I didn't look. 'You will be very happy woman when you wake.' The Smile patted my nipples like they were legs or arms.

A nurse held my hand aloft and instructed me to count out loud from ten backwards.

'Ten, nine, eight . . . happy woman . . .'

Black.

'Miss O'Farrell?' I heard a voice.

'Miss O'Farrell?' I heard again.

'Miss O'Farrell?' she called loudly.

My throat felt like a rat-infested sewer. 'Yes,' I croaked.

'It's all over, Miss O'Farrell.'

I could feel absolutely nothing, just a faint tightness in the chest area. I was lying on my back and dared not move. I was still in the operating theatre and the glare of the saucer-shaped lights above made my eyes ache.

'Everything went fine. No need to worry. Sleep now,' she ordered.

I wanted to tell her that I loved her deeply, and that I loved my Mammy and my Daddy too and that, in fact, I loved the world and everything about it. Then I realized I was delirious with the drugs and fell into more fragmented dreams.

When I woke again, I knew the drugs had worn off because I hated everybody. I was wide awake and beseeching God to help me with the indescribable pain. It wasn't only in my chest; it ran like a river of lava, bubbling with intense heat, underneath my arms, across my back and even as far down as my abdomen. My breasts in particular felt like they had two burning coals in them. This wasn't the 'dull ache' I had been told about. They throbbed with unrelenting agony.

Weak with the pain and throat dry as a desert, I begged the nurse to administer me some strong painkillers. I went ballistic when she told me I had already received a rather large shot of morphine. It was then I realized the ride I was in for.

I remembered Patricia trying to make conversation with me. I vaguely recalled telling her that she was nothing but a bag of shit, and if she didn't shut her fucking mouth I'd turn up her morphine. I was an awful whiny bitch. I'd had a choice about what to do with my body, but she hadn't asked for breasts like basketballs. I was in so much pain I never even thought to ask her if she was OK.

The next forty-eight hours were spent crying into a soft pillow for my Ma and Da and having no shame about it. It wasn't that I had ever been close to either – in truth, I resented them greatly – yet in those moments nothing appeared more comforting than the thought of being smothered in a mother's strong arms. The fact that I could never have told my mother what I was doing made me feel dreadfully sad. The fact that we now had minimal contact made me well up. The fact that I had refused to let her know me, and that she had stopped trying because of that, made me weep inconsolably. I needed a mother. I had always yearned for my mother, but she had not been available to me because of my father's incessant demands. I simply could not forgive her for that. I had needed her then, I needed her now, and I hated myself because I had to admit it.

If I moved to the left or the right, the pain seared through me like hot knives. So I lay on my back just trying to breathe. As the hours passed, the tightness increased. The Smile visited me a number of times, but I didn't hear what he said and slipped in and out of the mind-blowing agony.

On the third night, Daria arrived with flowers. I burst

into tears before she got to the side of my bed. I was a gibbering wreck. The pain had reduced me to a state of humility not even experienced by the most hardened saint. I grabbed her hand and held it for dear life.

'Easy,' she said, looking frightened by the ghost-like apparition I now presented. 'Easy now,' she said again.

The pain had rendered me speechless. I waved my hand, indicating I would like some water, and she spilt it all over the floor. 'Shit the bed, Finn,' she muttered. She held the half-empty glass to my lips, which were split and dry.

I drank the water. It lubricated my larynx just enough for me to say a few words.

'Christ, are you that sore?' she asked.

'Yes.' I wept, feeling demoralized and stupid.

'Oh, God,' she said.

She pulled the pillows from behind my head in an effort to prop me into a sitting position and soon realized the error of her ways when I screamed.

'Oh, Jesus,' she cried.

'Stop cursing,' I croaked.

'Can't you sit up?' she said.

'No. Hurts too much,' I confided.

'Is it supposed to?' she asked.

I nodded.

'What are those tubes?' she continued, her eyes wide.

'Bleeding, draining,' I whispered.

'I brought you some magazines and some Energyade. When I didn't react, her head went down, she pulled a paper tissue from the bedside table and blew into it. She knew only too well that on a normal day I would have drunk it all in a second, then gone on to eat the bottle, the wrapper and the brown-paper bag it came in.

She put her arms round me gently and cuddled me like a child. We sat there for ages, me too weak to acknowledge anything but the searing pain and her too upset to talk. Eventually she tried half-heartedly to pull away, but I clung to her for dear life.

'Finn, you can let go. Let go of me now, Finn. I have to go home, OK?'

I let go reluctantly. She kissed my forehead. That was the last thing I remembered.

# Chapter 18

When I awoke Daria had gone. The pain had localized itself in my breasts. I pulled myself up into a sitting position and felt grateful for it, even though the effort almost killed me. After another few hours, I managed to get my feet on the floor and walk a few steps with the help of the nurse. 'It gets better,' she reassured me. 'It's all worth it in the end.'

'It better be,' I replied, through clenched teeth.

The sooner I got myself moving around the better. I wanted to get out of there, and fast. I made it to the bathroom hoping to see a vast difference, but I could see nothing at all. My top half was covered with bandages and it was impossible to tell what was underneath. I was a bit disappointed that they didn't jump right out at me.

On day four I was moving around uncomfortably but at least I was moving. I was anxious to talk to the Smile. At six o'clock he arrived with a clatter of papers that he asked me to sign. He told me I could head home soon but someone had to pick me up. I was thrilled to bits.

We walked to a small room not far from the operating theatre and he sat me down. 'How is pain?'

'It's getting better,'

'Good. We check for infection and see how healing is coming along.'

'OK.'

'You must return in ten days so I can remove stitches, yes?'

'OK.'

'We take a look?'

'OK.'

'Don't be nervous. First impressions will be disappointing. There will be bruising and swelling and scars. Will take some months to heal.'

'OK.'

'Sit upright, please.'

'OK.'

The Smile began demummifying me. I watched as, layer by layer, the blood-soaked gauze bandages came away in his hands. He dropped them to the floor. I sat in front of a full-length wall mirror, scarcely daring to breathe. As the last bandage was unwrapped I winced with pain. It had attached itself to the tapes on the stitches and pulled at the flimsy pieces of skin that held my breasts together. I squeezed my eyes shut and offered it up to St Anthony.

'You look now,' the Smile said.

The big moment was upon me.

I opened my eyes . . . and passed out.

What had I really expected to see when I looked into that mirror? I expected to see Samantha King, that's what. So what planet was I on? I hear you ask. I was on the same planet as you, planet Earth. You see, all I had seen was Sam in her video and the rumours. Had she or hadn't she? Had a boob job, I mean. Who cared anyway? The video had more than likely taken days to make. The video did not show the twenty-four hours' hair and makeup preparation beforehand.

If she had had a job done, the video hadn't shown the operation: who wants to see the bandages, the pain, the mutilation, the stitches, the bruising and the swelling? I hadn't seen any of that. I hadn't wanted to. Was I as thick as two short planks? Perhaps, but then again, I don't think so. I bought the dream. I bought the lie. You would have, too, if you had felt like an alien in your own body.

I had slipped out of my skin years before and disowned my very own soul. The new one didn't hold much promise, or so I thought on that fateful day. It wasn't much of a surprise that when I came round from my blackout I was in a state of shock.

My breasts were bigger, all right, but crooked and inflamed. They were black and purple and lumpy. The stitches were crude and uneven, with yellow rims along the incisions. This, coupled with the dried blood, made me look as though I had been skinned alive. No wonder I'd passed out. This was not Samantha King before me: I looked like I had recently been beaten to a pulp. The only thing that kept me together was the Smile's assurance that it was all perfectly normal.

There was nothing in his manner or the nurse's expression to suggest that anything had gone wrong with the operation. I found this practically impossible to believe. This *was* what it looked like. I just couldn't handle it.

After I had drank many glasses of water the Smile managed to extort Daria's phone number from me. I had put her down as next of kin on the admittance forms. He insisted she come to the hospital before he could sign my release. As I was not allowed travel home alone, I had to relent.

While I was waiting I packed my things in silence, uncomfortably conscious of Patricia in the next bed. She had complied with my vicious invective and left me alone. I was sorry for that now – and I understood why women in the middle of labour shouted things like, 'Johnny, you fucking whore's melt, you're nothing but an oul bollox and I rue the day I ever let that thing inside me.'

The pain of the operation had knocked me for six. I had never felt anything like it before and never wanted to again. Patricia lay on her back, quiet as a mouse, and I realized, with shame, that she must have been in terrible pain herself and I hadn't uttered a kind word to her since my own trek through the Garden of Gethsemane. My Calvary had exhausted my capacity for fellowship.

I took Daria's flowers and placed them in a vase on Patricia's bedside locker. I looked down at her face as I arranged them fussily. Her eyes were half open.

'Patricia, are you awake?' I said softly.

She nodded.

'Is there anything I can get you?'

She shook her head.

'I'm really sorry for being such a bitch to you the other day,'

She nodded and I saw she was crying.

'I was in agony and couldn't focus on anything else,' I said, filled with shame.

'It's OK,' she mumbled.

'Are you still sore?' I asked.

She nodded again.

I knelt down beside the bed and pushed her hair off her face. It was wet with perspiration, the type that results from the hard slog of trying to control physical pain.

'Did they take away a lot?' I whispered.

'A couple of pounds from each.' She winced.

I knew that must have been horrific. The removal of any muscle tissue causes massive bleeding and swelling. The Smile had put my implants over the muscles so I hadn't had to deal with that. Patricia had had half of hers hacked away. The thought made me cringe.

'Look, want some advice?' I brought my voice down.

She nodded a third time.

'If they come round with spaghetti Bolognese for dinner, think twice.'

Patricia's face melted and she burst into reluctant laughter.

'Hey, relax or you'll burst your stitches.' I laughed too.

She squeezed my hand in gratitude.

'I wish you all the best, Patricia,' I said, and stood up to leave.

'Thanks, and I wish you all the best, Finn,' she said 'Knock 'em dead with your new boobs.'

'I intend to. Literally,' I said, pushing my voluptuous new shape forwards.

She waved a limp hand at me. I turned away and walked to the door.

Daria arrived by taxi and the ride home was a never-ending nightmare of invading fearful thoughts. No matter how much the Smile had tried to convince me that I would look better in a few weeks, I refused to believe it. My body looked like a scalded cat's and I couldn't believe that the hideous scars would heal.

Over the next days, I followed the doctor's orders to the letter, wearing the prescribed Velcro surgical bra and refusing to look again until my six-week appointment. At first the implants felt strange. My arms had to get used to the extra flesh they pushed against and I had to be careful not to lift anything heavy or bend down in a hurry. I couldn't stop looking down at the mound beneath my chin. I sometimes caught it in the corner of my eye and wondered, What the hell is that? Then I would remember. It's my new breasts.

While I convalesced I decided to change my hair too. Why not go the full monty? First, I booked myself into an upmarket and expensive beauty salon and treated myself to a St Tropez tan. It looked a bit out of place in March but I felt brilliant. Then I went to a top-class stylist in Grafton Street and had my hair highlighted. I had long sun-streaked blonde tresses, just like Samantha King. It took hours to do, the colour, the cutting and the straightening. The end result was a luscious mane of golden hair spilling over my shoulders and it looked natural. I felt beautiful. I was changing it all, and the universe was contributing changes in other areas of my life.

After three weeks the pain had fizzled out leaving just a little pressure and tightness where the stitches had been. I was driven insane with an uncontrollable urge to scratch, especially at night. The itch was indescribable and it took all my strength not to claw at it. The Smile told me it was a sign of healing. Eventually the itching and the pain stopped altogether. The only continued sensation was a burning in my nipples, but he reassured me that that, too, would disappear. I had days when I forgot about the operation but I was still reluctant even to take a peep. I didn't want to pass out again.

At the six-week appointment the Smile undid the Velcro bra and revealed a whole new life to me. I couldn't believe the difference. My breasts were large and round. I was Lara Croft in the flesh. Apart from some small scars, they looked beautiful. I cried with the relief. The heaviness and tightness had gone and they looked almost real. I felt them sway and change position with my body movements. It was a welcome sensation, which I had pined for all my life. The purple and black bruising had disappeared and they now had a milky pallor; my nipples were erect pinnacles of perfection. I wanted to bare them to the public, such was my jubilation. At long last I had arrived.

I celebrated by ordering a new uniform, one that fitted me properly. The new short-sleeved summer shirts were a dream: they were double-breasted with gold buttons and tapered in at the waist. My full bust sat behind the triangular pockets snug as two bugs in a rug. I had won the lotto twice over and the fun was only just beginning. I had one cherished mission to accomplish, and in my lunch hour, I almost ran up Henry Street, such was my urgency.

'Remember me?' I smiled at the silver-haired lady in Arnott's lingerie department.

'Should I?'

'Probably not,' I conceded.

She had undoubtedly experienced hundreds of deformed deranged women just like me, coming in and out of her safe, happy little world.

'I need to be fitted for a bra. *Again*.' I winked with heavy emphasis on the last word.

'Certainly, madam,' she replied, a tiny hint of recognition now in her grey eyes.

We went through to the changing rooms, me grabbing boxes and bags as we went. I stripped off my clothes without having to be asked. The measuring-tape was produced and I let her do her thing. If she noticed the slight swelling and remaining scars she didn't comment.

'You're a thirty-sixC,' she said, somewhat mystified.

'Thirty-sixC,' I echoed proudly, like a child who has just found a rare Pokémon card.

I wasn't happy with one go either. I wanted a second and a third . . . and a fourth.

I drove her insane with endless requests to measure me.

'My dear, I've already told you. You're a thirty-sixC.' She sighed.

'You're sure?' I asked.

'I've done it four times already.'

'Say it again, please,' I begged.

So she did. 'You're a thirty-sixC,' she concluded.

The words were like liquid honey oozing from her pursed lips.

Thirty-sixC.

*Do you hear that, you fucking bastards?*

Thirty-sixC!

The tiny cubicle was crammed with an assortment of boxes containing all the delicious lingerie I had never been able to wear before. I wanted it all. Red, black, white, lace, silk; underwired, backless, plunge. I bought enough to make up for Emmeline Pankhurst's followers, who had burned a century's supply of brassieres in the struggle for female emancipation. I'm sure the assistant suspected I was as mad as a brush. All I was short of asking for was the mirror on the wall: I could not take my eyes off it.

I had a cleavage. A beautiful, perfect cleavage where my breasts met and fell in synchronization. I pushed them up and piled them in, then repeated the whole exercise again, laughing at the ease of it. I molested myself with wild abandon enjoying the soft, plump, goose-pimply texture of my boo-boo-bee-doos. I marched to the checkout desk. I looked to the assistant and beamed at her. I was bursting with joy. She gave me a half-hearted smile, and it was then I noticed she had one hand on the emergency red button under the till.

'Credit card or cash?' she said nervously.

'Cash,' I replied, handing her the remaining hundred and fifty pounds of the Credit Union loan.

'Thank you,' she said, with a look of terror in her eyes.

'No! Thank *you*!' I shouted, over the boxes and bags that all but rendered me invisible.

# Chapter 19

On returning to work I thought about how I had managed to pull this whole thing off and get away with it. I couldn't believe how much things had changed in such a short time. I had struggled through the first three weeks, but Daria had covered up for my strange silent interlude. She had been a tower of strength through those first few weeks, never once jumping on the I-told-you-so bandwagon.

Getting round the endless questions about America was another story, though. I concocted great big whoppers about my trip across the Atlantic and what I had done there. I promised to bring in photographs, but explained I hadn't a penny to my name after the expensive holiday and couldn't get them developed just yet.

There were a few surprises in store for me at work that I hadn't expected. The first was that Daria had been dating the mysterious Ion Florescu. They had struck up quite a friendship while I was convalescing, which explained her softened attitude. She wasn't gushing with intimate details about Ion, or confiding whether the friendship had blossomed into something physical, but I sensed it was a serious relationship and that she had found someone at last who believed her worthy of courtship.

The second surprise was that Tom O'Hare was still ill and it was rumoured that he was leaving. I knew it was more than a rumour: Colm had told me that Tom had been caught mishandling the cash and had been given his notice. At least now I knew why Colm had been hanging around him. Mark Adams had asked him to survey Tom's daily balance and find out what he could. It had taken Colm some time to put two and two together. Tom O'Hare hardly ever balanced and he had handed in one too many difference slips. They always seemed to be on the 'under' side too. The perfect opportunity had arisen while Tom was absent from work. Colm logged on to his computer and checked his figures and dockets. He pored over his paperwork and tally rolls, and soon the discrepancies became clear.

The spin-off was that I was asked to take on even more work, account administration three times a week. I was also asked to sit in on the weekly meeting where loan applications were discussed and got the yea or nay.

I found it rather interesting, weighing up people's credit history, their financial needs, their reasons for taking out a loan. After a couple of weeks of listening I began to know who qualified for one and who didn't. Like most decent Credit Unions, the refusals were practically non-existent: the committee went to great lengths to help those in trouble, and even when a true risk case came up was reluctant to stamp a rejection on it. It brought me into a whole new world.

The loan applications were, to all intent and purposes, the personal details of someone's life. People needed money for happy, sad and sometimes tragic reasons. They were handled with compassion, understanding and sympathy.

I had never realized what a fantastic institution the

Credit Union was and wondered where half of these people would be without it. Indeed, where would I have been without it? Becoming more and more confident as the days passed, I took on my new responsibilities with diligence and a sense of importance. Pretty soon I was being asked for my view on different scenarios and gave it.

What had surprised me most was the smile on Colm Long's face when I arrived back to work. He left a large bottle of Energyade and a glass on my desk with a little note stuck on my computer screen: 'Welcome back, Skinny.' I was taken with the gesture, but I did not want to get my hopes up again. Ever since I'd seen Julia with him at the Bill Roberts concert I had been a bit more reserved. I think I'd expected to fall apart and crawl back into poor-me-no-one-wants-me mode, but I didn't.

Nothing could have been further from the truth. The operation had catapulted me into a warm sea of champagne-bubbly confidence. But I didn't go mad with it: I had to take baby steps. I might have wanted to go topless on my first day at work, but I restrained myself.

The first test came when I wore the new uniform. Shyly I removed the heavy jacket and hung it on the back of my chair. I looked around me coyly. Several pairs of eyes stared back, but no one said anything. There had been many comments about my hair – even some members had said I looked different and really well, but the eerie silence around my new boobs was a little scary. But what had I expected? Was anyone going to say, 'Hey! Nice boob job?' Hardly. Besides, I had always looked like a walking bin-liner. Shapeless, dull-coloured garments had been my choice for ten years. But I couldn't help thinking there was a conspiracy going on. I even got to thinking that Daria was jealous: she said my hair was nice but nothing about the tan. Now, though, I was taking the next daredevil step to emancipate myself. In a way I was grateful that they hadn't fallen into their cash boxes frothing at the mouth: it gave me the confidence to move forward and I began the long walk deep into the forest of fashion fads and designer accessories to find the correct balance between slapper and sexy, sophisticated young woman.

I was a human kite waiting to be let loose in the wind. I wanted to fly. I wanted to do all the things I had thought my flat chest had prevented me doing. I wanted to go bathing in skin-tight bikini tops. I wanted to go water-skiing. I wanted to enter wet T-shirt competitions. It wasn't that I was a slut: I just wanted to know that I could do it. That was all. That I could run with the best of them.

As I had imagined it would, life began to change for me. It was hard to say whether it was the new person who was emerging or whether the operation itself had brought me extra luck. It was a fascinating time. The world was my oyster. I felt proud. I felt confident. I felt like a real woman. I could wear what I wanted. I could eat without guilt and know that I wouldn't look like a boiled egg. I experimented with makeup, hair colour, nail polish, high heels, clingy tops, short skirts and everything that had previously been forbidden territory.

I could walk up Grafton Street in the warm sunny weather and lie down on the grass in Stephen's Green without worrying that some pervert would take me for a boy and try to do business with me at the back of the public toilets. I could sunbathe with the rest of them, knowing I looked normal. I was dealt with swiftly in queues, in restaurants, at taxi ranks and traffic-lights. The newspaper vendor who had never even looked at me began to throw in the odd free magazine. At work I had calls from regular members. And I flirted – boy, did I flirt!

I had a whole new wardrobe, filled with the most outrageous get-ups, and a drawer full of beautiful lingerie. I had suspender belts and basques, stockings and slinky nightwear – but no one to model it for. I felt like a basket of fruit on a hospital bedside locker that no one was going to eat.

I had my favourite haunts, of course, places I went when I needed an ego boost. One of these was the local butcher's. The staff of four young men bent over backwards to help me with my order. I loved to dilly-dally, delay and change my mind just to watch them get tied up in knots. A queue would form behind me and old women would be tutting impatiently.

'I can't quite see those lamb cutlets,' I would complain, bending down over the mirrored counter.

'Will I bag them separately, or will I throw them all together?' The young salesman would wink at me.

'Ah, for the love of Jeysus . . .' someone would moan.

Then there was the bank I went to every Friday. We had an all-year-round Christmas savings club account there. I volunteered to make the weekly visit to deposit the weekly ten-pound contribution from each member of staff.

'Finn, how's it going?' Ed the cashier would enquire.

'Not bad, Ed.' I would beam at him, sporting another skimpy T-shirt that accentuated my shapely physique.

'You're looking very well, these days,' he would say, his eyes bulging with the strain.

'Thanks, Ed. It's very hot out, isn't it?' I would pull my T-shirt out a little and flap it.

'It's hot to be sure,' he would reply, sweat trickling down his white shirt. He would count out the cash, then give me a receipt and a statement.

'That's great, Ed.' I would flash him a smile.

'No problem.' He'd grin back.

One day I chanced my arm to see how far he would go. 'Hey, what's this?' I asked.

'What?'

'This two-pound charge?'

'It's standard,' he replied.

'For what?' I asked innocently.

'For having the account.'

'Hey, we're not money-laundering or anything, just saving for a party,' I remonstrated.

'You never know though, do you?'

'Ed, there's only 350 in the account,' I said flatly.

'Give it here,' he ordered, and hit a few buttons on the computer.

'There's no charges on your account now,' he whispered, handing me the receipt.

'What?' I queried.

'It's cool. Don't worry.' He tapped the side of his nose.

'What if we had direct debits? Credit transfers?'

'Nope.' He smiled idiotically.

'What about Visa and cheques?' I sped along.

'What the hell would you be using them for?'

'The arms-smuggling and drug-dealing?' I grinned.

'No need to worry now. All charges wiped, gone.'

'Ah, Ed, there's no need for you to do that.' I smiled with the innocence of a child.

'No problem. Sure you never use the account for anything else.' He made sense of his irrational impulses.

'Still, that's very nice of you. I don't know how to thank you.' I looked up at him meekly.

'Maybe you'd come out with me some time?' he whispered.

'Sure, Ed.' I gave him a sexy wink.

'Anything else I can do for you?' he drooled.

I took my time trying to think of something else he might be able to give me. 'Well, while we're on the subject, any chance of some sterling without the commission charge?' and on it went. I didn't need any sterling – I wasn't planning to cross so much as O'Connell Bridge. I just couldn't help myself. I couldn't believe his change in attitude towards me, and all because I had big breasts.

Most revelatory were the department-store beauty counters, another of my favourite haunts. I learned that, contrary to popular belief, women do not dress to impress men. They dress to impress women. I loved the outright envy I experienced in the company of those women. They hated me so much that I could almost see the resentment pour out of their nostrils – aged air-hostesses with too much cotton-wool in their fat, drooping cheeks – sitting behind their reeking dominions, in starched white blouses and French cravats, the orange makeup two inches thick on their faces and the fine French plait sitting on the back of their heads like a great turd. Well, I hated them too. All of a sudden I found myself treated like the enemy.

I was the real thing, you see, and, yes, I annoyed the crap out of them. I reminded them of their rapidly approaching old age, inescapable wrinkles and sagging breasts. I had big pert ones. I was a cataclysmic nuclear bomb, and I was standing at their nice, safe, pristine stalls with the noses of my missiles pointed right in their faces. I was the ultimate threat because I was Samantha King in the flesh – an Irish version perhaps, but I was putting it out there.

I felt like there was some secret code among women, an unspoken golden rule that I had broken. I was lower than a rattlesnake's belly because I had dared to be different. Big boobs were reserved for those with privileges: they were only for the rich, famous, talented and exceedingly beautiful. I hadn't any of the latter qualities so I guessed they had surmised I was a fraud.

As far as I was concerned I was entitled to them. I had paid the price financially and physically for the right to flaunt my wares. After all, they were flaunting theirs, but their products came in bottles and jars. Women seemed positively hostile towards me. It was hard to believe that my own kind could turn on me so suddenly. Of course, I put it down to jealousy. I loved wasting their time – I never had any intention of buying anything.

'What's this for?' I would ask, the stiff, cold assistant's perfume overwhelming me.

'That, Madam, is an age-defying cream. It's the latest from Lancôme and it's very expensive,' she would snap.

'How expensive?' I would ask, fiddling with my bra strap as if my weighty chest was a bloody hindrance.

'Forty-nine pounds,' she would reply, through gritted teeth.

'Wow, that *is* expensive.' I would turn the bottle in my hand and smile at her innocently, because I knew she had to smile back. It was her job. I saw the make-up crack, the caked foundation straining to stay put like a tatty pancake and with much the same texture and colour.

One day I had to tell an assistant that she hadn't put it on properly: her body was as white as a vestal virgin's but she had a face like a pockmarked satsuma. 'You need to blend a bit here.' I pointed under my chin.

'Pardon?' she said softly.

'Your foundation, you know, you forgot to blend it into your chin. You must always *blend into the chin*, like this.' I rubbed at my neck, offering a helpful demonstration. The woman was fuming. She couldn't muster a reply, such was her outrage. I was delighted with myself. I had never dared to be so bold and it felt good. I fiddled with a few more bottles, picking up a nice pink one in the shape of a woman's body.

'What's this, then?' I leaned over the counter giving her a full view of my own line in saleable goods.

'That's a moisturizer,' she said flatly.

'I see.' I pulled myself back up and arched my back, rubbing the small of it as if the weight of the world was swinging out in front of me. The assistant's face was green.

'Is Madam interested in purchasing something?' She asked condescendingly.

'Excuse me?' I gave her my deeply offended look.

The assistant manager arrived at my side, his eyes roaming up and down my body. 'Are you being taken care of, miss?' He asked, a twinkle in his eye.

'Oh, why, thank you for asking.' I flirted, winking at him and playing with my bra strap. I leaned towards him. 'Actually, your staff could be a little bit more, well . . . how do you say? Approachable?' I whispered in his ear.

'Do you think so?' He asked, barely listening to my query.

'Perhaps Madam would like to discuss this matter in the comfort of my office?' He suggested, and threw a withering look at the assistant. She was red in the face and there was nothing she could do.

'That sounds like a good idea.' I smiled at him, I flung my hair behind my shoulders and gave the assistant a cheeky once-over.

Then I walked away, grinning over my shoulder, chest out, arse in.

I made them sick with envy.

Life can't get much better than this, I thought.

# Chapter 20

With no holidays left to speak of, I had to make use of the bank-holiday weekends to experiment with my new bod. It was time to test it. I decided my first victim should be a stranger, just in case anything went wrong, like my breast falling off in their hand. I wanted to go to an anonymous nightclub. It was while I was trying to figure out how I could do it that Daria and Colm came up with the answer.

It was the May bank-holiday weekend and we were finishing off the week's balance figures. We were discussing Marcus Myers, who had been in again that day. This time he had found fault with the coffee percolator, a new addition to the office, which Mark Adams had installed at the entrance. The coffee was only warm, there wasn't a spoon in the sugar bowl and the paper cups had no handles, he complained. He had chosen Daria's desk at which to vent his pent-up frustration. It was all her fault. Hadn't she made the coffee? Set it out? She claimed to know nothing about it, so he reprimanded her. She should know: she was staff, was she not?

'If you don't say something to Mark Adams about him then I will. I wouldn't let any man put me down like that,' I said, pasting on a new shocking-pink Rimmel lipstick.

'Really? Since when, Finn?' she challenged me, her voice filled with sarcasm.

'I think Finn is saying you don't *have* to handle it,' Colm said, thumping away with a black ink stamp.

'I wish you'd all back off,' she said.

What the hell was wrong with her? We were only trying to protect her.

Enter Dessie, the Manchurian candidate with the I-Must-Fuck-It-Up computer chip in his brain.

'If I were you, I'd accidentally drop his account book and stand on it. That's what I do when a member really annoys me. I put a lovely black mark on it and hand it back to them.' He laughed, the missing tooth ever prominent.

'God, that's really *scary*, Dessie,' I jeered.

'Yeah? Well, what would you do, then?' he asked.

'I'm thinking,' I answered.

'What about pissing in the coffee percolator? And making sure he had the first cup? I'd spend ages pouring it, and putting the milk in and stirring it all around. He'd drink it too,' Colm put in.

Dessie thought this was hilarious. 'Ye boy, ye!' he yelped, doing a little jig on the filing cabinet with his fingers.

I gave him a withering look and suggested he had his roots done for the summer. His hair had grown so much that the top half of his head was black and the bottom blond. It looked ridiculous.

Colm was still smirking at his own brilliant plan for revenge on Mr Myers. I was thinking about it too. 'I dare you,' I found myself saying. I was getting used to the new, more adventurous, bold me.

'You know quite well you shouldn't dare me. I'll only do it,' Colm said, without looking up.

'Stop egging him on!' Daria shouted, like we were maniacs.

'Just kidding,' I said.

'So was I.' Colm turned to face me and stared at me long and hard.

'Hey, Colm, what's the story with Tom O'Hare? Is he leaving us or what?' Dessie asked.

'I haven't spoken to him recently, but you can pretty much assume he isn't coming back.'

'Did he do something?' Dessie asked.

'He got another job. That's all you need to know,' I jumped in.

Daria shook her head.

Colm's mouth stayed slightly open.

'I thought you two were real buddies?' Dessie looked to Colm.

'Yeah? So did I. Forget about him, Dessie, he was bad news,' Colm said softly. It was the first time I could remember Colm addressing him seriously. I was pleased.

'I'm not thick, you know,' Dessie defended himself. 'Tom O'Hare was a sleeveen of the highest order. I wouldn't have been surprised if he'd masterminded a raid on the Credit Union. That was the type of guy he was, ruthless, secretive and menacingly quiet, a perilous combination at the best of times.'

We were all astounded at this explosion of insight from our Dessie. He stared Colm down, his face flushed with the unexpected exertion.

'I never said you were thick, Dessie. I just wanted to protect you, keep you away from him. He might have used you and I didn't want you to be misled. Tom was a very devious individual,' Colm admitted.

'Yeah, well, good riddance to the dirty pervert. I always hated him,' Daria said.

'You weren't saying that at the Christmas party, if I remember correctly,' I put in.

'Oh, thanks for reminding me. I'd rather you didn't bring that up again.' Daria cringed.

Colm was grinning gleefully.

'What are you so pleased with yourself about?' I asked him, as I took out my pocket mirror and brushed my hair. He just kept hammering the stamp on the black-list post.

'I have tickets to see a trilogy of Beckett's plays in the Project,' he said.

'Never heard of him,' I said, twisting my head this way and that. I loved the way my hair swung from side to side, like Farah Fawcett's in her heyday.

'Are you Irish or what?' Daria looked at me.

Obviously I'd missed something.

'Are you going too?' I asked her. I stood on a chair to water some creeping-ivy plants. While I had been out, no one had bothered to look after them. I decided I couldn't be bothered either and climbed down. It was really only an opportunity to give Colm a full-frontal view of the new me.

'Me and Ion and Colm and Julia,' she answered.

'Nice one,' Dessie said.

*Yeah. Nice one. Nice cosy foursome, y'all.*

'We didn't think you'd be interested.' Colm had picked up the vibes, I thought.

'Hey, it's OK,' I lied.

Daria was twirling her hair, a sure sign of embarrassment.

'We're thinking of going to that new nightclub afterwards, what's it called again? Detroit? he added quickly.

'The Detroit? Wow!' Now I was really peeved.

'Why don't you meet up with us in Temple Bar after

the show. We can all have a drink and then go to the night-club, hah?' He struggled to close the bottom file drawer.

'Kick it!' we all yelled.

He slammed it shut with his Dr Marten's. I glanced at him but his expression gave away nothing. I really wanted to go. I really, *really* wanted to go. But I didn't want to be piggy-in-the-middle with the snogging couples. In the end desperation got the better of me. I decided to tag along because I had nothing else to do and was tired of sitting around by myself.

'That would be great. Great idea. Yeah,' I said. Daria looked decidedly unhappy.

That night, as I got ready in the flat, I spent a long time doing myself up. I put on the Christmas party black dress and surveyed the figure before me in the mirror. I looked pretty Goddamn stunning, and that was a compliment coming from me! I was sex on legs. The sweetheart neckline revealed my bulging cleavage and the plunge bra ensured the volume.

To my amazement, I looked much skinnier and presumed it was because of my bigger breasts. I jumped on the scales for the first time in two months and almost fell off when I saw I had lost ten pounds. I hadn't been able to go to the gym because the doctor had ruled out exercise and I hadn't been watching what I ate, so it was a shock. Then I remembered it shouldn't have been such a surprise, after all. I had been so sick after the operation I was unable to stomach anything for ages. I had lived on bottles of Energyade. I was thrilled. I weighed nine and a half stone, with a thirty-sixC chest, and I looked pretty amazing. I had never looked so good in my life. I preened myself before the mirror, tossing my hair back, posing provocatively.

I arrived at the designated rendezvous at eleven o'clock. As it was a bank-holiday weekend every pub was packed to capacity. I found Daria and Ion in a corner but there was no sign of Colm and Julia, and I was disappointed. Daria and her beau were engrossed in conversation.

'Hi, gang,' I said, looking around for Colm.

'Hello, Finn.' Ion smiled.

'What are you having?' Daria asked.

'Anyone,' I answered.

'To drink, Finn, shit the bed,' Daria mumbled.

'Sorry. A gin and tonic. I'll have a gin and tonic. Make it a double,' I said, as I saw Colm coming towards us with only one glass in his hand.

'What's the story?' I asked Daria quickly.

'With what?' she asked, looking disparagingly at my dress, big hair, high heels and extravagant makeup.

'Where's the granny?' I whispered.

'She was at the play,' Daria replied.

'What the hell does he see in her?' I was asking myself, really.

'Well, she's educated.' Daria was grinning at Ion, who had mooched up with another round of drinks. I detected a slight brusqueness in her reply, but didn't care. I was there for one reason and one reason only.

Before I could ask anything else, Colm arrived over. 'Hi,' he said, beaming.

'Where's Julia?' I blurted, unable to control myself.

'Gone home. The Detroit wouldn't be her scene.' He shrugged.

*Yeah. You have to be under fifty to get in.*

I resisted the urge to jump up and down and start clapping. Instead I changed the subject. 'How was Brackett?'

'Beckett.'

'That's what I said. Brackett.'

'You're a disgrace.'

'I never claimed to be a culture vulture.'

'Everyone knows Beckett.'

'I don't. What's the big deal?'

'I really enjoyed it,' Ion said. 'We never got to see such shows back home.'

'What was the name of the play?' I asked.

'*Waiting for Godot*, that's G-O-D-O-T.' Daria spelt it out.

'Can't be much of a playwright if he can't spell,' I quipped. They all thought this was hilarious.

I wasn't capable of making an informed judgement about any Irish artist, let alone their work. But Ion was. He could make a decent comment about almost anything. He was an educated intellectual and I wondered how he had managed this, since he hailed from war-torn Romania. I was embarrassed that someone from such a faraway land knew more about our playwrights than I. And Romania had been known throughout history for producing sporting champions, Olympic contestants, not educated young men like Ion.

Daria had told me that Ion had attended the famous Brasov University, about a hundred miles from his home in Bucharest. She had explained to me about the *lei*, the worthless Romanian currency, and how his parents had scrimped and saved to get him in. Through a series of black-market exchanges for sterling and dollars they'd had him enrolled and he had been one of the lucky few to graduate. Ion was an interesting specimen and I could see why she was attracted to him.

I did know some other things about Ion. I knew that he was still a non-member of the EU. He was still a refugee, an illegal immigrant. It was something we didn't discuss in great detail. Lately Daria had seemed less willing to discuss private things with me, but in Ion's company she shone, and I was glad of that. They were becoming increasingly close. In some ways, I was a little jealous of the indefinable bond between them. Something sacred and private that I knew I wasn't part of.

Right now, though, I didn't care. Julia wasn't there. Colm was. I was a single woman and he was a single man. My mind raced with the simple mathematics and, after adding two and two, I came up with sixty-nine. I didn't want to waste a minute. After a couple of rushed drinks we were admitted to the nightclub and settled at a small table with four chairs. It was the perfect setting for my subtle game of seduction.

I made a big fuss over taking off my jacket. I did it slowly, tantalizingly. For the first time ever, I saw Colm's eyes flicker. The discreet lapse was so short and sweet I even wondered if I had imagined it. He took my jacket like the perfect gentleman and hung it on the back of my seat. I was totally exposed.

'You look . . . nice,' he said, camouflaging the ripple in his steely reserve.

'Thank you,' I said, breathless at the thought of his hands so near me. I wondered for the fiftieth time what they would feel like on my breasts. Was he the grabbing type or the sensual Don Juan who stroked and caressed? I curbed my lustful thoughts. I reminded myself that I had already settled on who I was going to sleep with first, and it wasn't Colm.

I reflected on my life over the last two months while I sank my teeth into a good half-bottle of gin and an assortment of alcopops. Things were going well, I decided. The job was looking up and I appeared to be getting a lot of extra attention elsewhere. I had new friends. The milkman gave me a cheeky whistle every morning. The bus driver had stopped to let me on even when I wasn't at the designated stop. Winks, nudges and raised eyebrows had become the norm. People were trying to get to know me. Even strangers. Like the ones I was noticing now in the nightclub.

It wasn't in my imagination. I marvelled as I watched them slip, trip, stumble and slobber their way past our table to the toilet every ten seconds. I knew exactly what they were doing. One might say their interest was fanned and further encouraged by my deliberate provocation. But they bought it! I saw them make asides to friends. Heads turned and penises did more than their fair share of twitching. I was the talk of the dance-floor and I revelled in it.

If Colm noticed the ongoing competition he never let his face show it. I continued to dance with every Tom, Dick and Harry. I hardly sat down at all. I was whirled and jostled and flung about, and I was having a ball. All the time I was getting drunker and drunker. I was not sure if it was alcohol or my new-found confidence that had convinced me, once and for all, that Colm fancied me. As with everything else I had managed to justify the unjustifiable.

I was tired of the never-ending struggle between my waning sense of morality and sexual attraction. Colm fancies me, I told myself. It's as simple as that. He wants me. I wasn't capable of identifying the first pangs of love. Until now I had dealt with my feelings using logic. I didn't understand that that was no use when it came to the language of the heart. And I didn't realize the terrible mistake I was about to make. I was building the foundations of a relationship with Colm – but I was starting with the roof. I hadn't learned that you had to build upwards, not from the top down.

I was aware that he was watching me from the sidelines and made full use of the opportunity to show off my new figure. I shot him the odd dazzling smile and he seemed magnetically drawn to me. I was calling him without using words and he responded like a moth to a flame. I saw him cross the floor, slowly making his way through the entourage of men who surrounded me. A break came in the music and it slowed down. He moved in quickly.

'Looks like I almost need an appointment to dance with you,' he murmured. He placed his hands on my hips and I felt them burn through to my skin. Mini grenades exploded along my spinal cord.

'Flattery will get you nowhere.' I gave a big, toothy grin.

'Remember I said earlier that you looked nice?' he crooned into my ear.

'Yeah?'

'I take it back,'

'What?'

'You look. . .amazing,' he said, as his left hand tickled the nape of my neck.

I arched my back, embarrassed by how my body was betraying me with shameless shudders and jolts. I closed my eyes and envisaged him behind me, a fistful of hair in his hands, wrenching my head backwards and devouring my neck. I could feel the tension in his arms. They warmed me, as if I was a slice of bread in a toaster. I was cosy and safe. There was no turning back. I had made up my mind. 'You look pretty good yourself,' I remarked.

'Well, I made the effort.' He smiled.

It had been no effort, I thought. He always looked lovely. 'How are things with Julia?' I asked.

'Oh, we're just good friends,' he said.

I laughed. 'Friends, eh?'

'Yes. I don't get involved, Skin. You know that,' he said.

'You spend a lot of time with her all the same,' I observed.

'I spend a lot of time with you too.' He pulled back to look me straight in the eye.

I wished he hadn't done that because I was drunk and delirious at being in his arms. 'Yes. That kind of confuses me.'

'As I said before, you're always looking for a dodgy motive.' He brushed his hair against my forehead.

His face was so close to mine now, eyes reading eyes, messages hurling through the air, begging to be picked up. 'You are absolutely ravishing,' he whispered.

'You flatter me,' I whispered back.

'You know quite well I can't keep my hands to myself when it comes to a beautiful woman.' He chuckled.

*'Is that what I am? Am I a beautiful woman?'* I blurted. I was desperate to hear him say 'yes'.

He tilted his head, a quizzical look on his face. He was struggling. I pulled him closer to me, not daring to wonder where my courage was coming from. His lips were within inches of mine. He smelt of pine trees.

'I don't know how to answer that,' he said.

'I do,' I said, and placed a forefinger on his lips.

Then I lunged forward and kissed him hard. He let me. I could feel the heat of his body race into mine. I wrapped my arms round him and he squeezed me so close I thought I would lose my breath. His body was rigid with desire. I could feel the hardness of his erection against my thigh. I thought I had left my body and gone to heaven. Seconds passed. Then, without warning, he pulled away.

'Look I—' He seemed to wrestle with his inability to express his feelings.

'What? What's wrong, Colm? Why won't you tell me?' I pleaded.

He leaned his forehead against mine again, eyes closed.

Then he peeled me off him, uncurling my arms from round his neck. 'I can't,' he mumbled. 'I'm sorry. I can't explain.'

'Is it Julia? Or Mary? Or that Karen who keeps coming in with her two-pound lodgement just to see you? Or perhaps it's the blonde-haired one sitting over there who's been watching you all night. Which one is it? Is it them all, maybe? Or is it me? It's me, isn't it? There's something wrong with me. What's wrong with me, Colm, huh?' I was panicking and when I do that I'm unable to shut my mouth.

'I'm sorry,' he repeated, and walked away, leaving me swaying on the dance-floor, humiliated and foolish.

I had never been able to take rejection. I always dealt with it in the wrong way. This case was no exception. Instead of concluding that I had been disgraced enough, I chose to make it worse for myself. How dare he? I was beautiful, exotic, any man would want me! Who did he think he was, turning me down? The knife-edged verbalisms were launched with vicious accuracy.

'You're a bastard, do you know that? A fucking bastard!' I screamed after him. The daggers were designed to slice him in two, thrown in desperation. It was a pathetic attempt at saving face, but now I had not only put my foot in it, I had immersed my whole body.

Like every other attempt in my life to get even, it boomeranged, slashing a gaping hole in my heart.

The last thing I remember about that night was a slow descent into oblivion. I know that I'd turned the consumption of a half-bottle of gin into a full one within half an hour. I vaguely recall Daria and Ion holding me up against a wall. I have no idea where I was, what time it was or what happened next. I'd been on a mission to drink myself to death.

I would hazard a guess that I verbally abused every man I saw ten times over. From past experience, I assumed that I had passed through the throng like Typhoon Tessie, hurling insults at anything that smelt of aftershave and leaving a trail of destruction behind me. One thing was for sure: I don't remember the bouncer on the door handing me any complimentary tickets. I don't remember anyone saying; 'Please call again!' Somehow the words 'Get out the fuck, ye head-case' were probably more in line with the truth. Sure I couldn't remember what I'd done, and it would have been fine by me to remain in denial, only Daria had a different idea in mind.

# Chapter 21

When she called the next day, her face said it all. 'As long as I live I'm never bringing you out with me again,' she growled.

'Stop.' I groaned, arse in the toilet and head in the sink.

'No. I won't stop. Was it not enough to throw yourself around like a whore? Oh, no. You had to talk like one, too. You embarrassed me in front of Ion. You embarrassed Colm. But when you started to strip . . . God, I can't bear to think about it. You had us all barred for life, you know.' She threw up her hands in fury.

'I started to strip?' I repeated.

'You behaved like some professional porn queen, pulling at your boobs and throwing your ass into everyone's face. One of those guys thought you were a lap-dancer and offered to pay for your services.'

'Did I really strip? I didn't! I couldn't have! Don't tell me I did the lap-dancing – you're joking. Please say you're joking,' I begged, between violent retches.

'Oh, you did it, all right. You behaved like a right bloody tart. Dancing about on the tables and tearing your clothes off, all those thugs egging you on. Listen, Finn, if you don't get your act together no one is going to want to know you. Do you know what I mean?' She said angrily.

'You mean Colm won't want to know me. Please, don't tell me he saw me doing all that,' I moaned.

'Him and the rest of the world.'

'I was drunk and things got a little bit out of hand, that's all.' I sighed.

'Your behaviour lately is outrageous.' She wasn't letting me off the hook.

I struck back. 'Oh, fuck off. I don't need this from you.'

'*Fuck off,*' she mimicked. 'Is that it? Is that all you can come up with – *fuck off*? Oh, well done, Finn. You're an original. A few dirty curses and you're on top of it all, eh?'

'What the hell do you want me to say?' I shouted back.

'Can't you take responsibility for anything you said or did? Aren't you sorry, for God's sake?' She was exasperated.

'No. What have I got to be sorry for? He led me on. The bastard,' I spat.

'Stop cursing! I cannot bear to hear that word. Whatever happened to make you use such foul language? It's disgusting. *You*'re disgusting, Finn! Going around in those smutty clothes with about ten inches of makeup on you – and that hair! It's – it's— You look like something out of *Charlie's Angels*.' Daria's face twisted with revulsion.

I blew a fuse. I had had it with the sermons from Mount Daria. 'Disgusting, am I? I'll give you disgusting! Watch my lips. Bastard! Bastard!' I screamed, into her face.

'You're insane, do you know that? No wonder he didn't want you. You know, you've changed so much since you had that operation, and I don't like who you're becoming,' I was stunned into silence. 'You were OK as yourself, Finn. Now you've turned into some bimbo who thinks her boobs are going to find her love,' she said, through gritted teeth. 'Get it into your thick head, will you? You don't need to be anyone or anything else but yourself. It's as simple as that,'

I trembled before her like a baby, lips quivering like jelly, on the verge of tears. I didn't need her turning on me as well. I was hurt enough. She marched to the door.

'Where are you going?' I asked.

'I'm fucking off, like you asked,' she shouted. She opened the door, walked out and slammed it so hard that my eardrums reverberated.

Alone at last. What was new? What futile expectations had I now? None. It was his fault and I couldn't understand why Daria couldn't see it that way. How was I supposed to react to such outright rejection? A fool would have known I had a big thing for Colm. Oh, he bloody knew, all right. He had played with me. He had led me up the garden path. It was a game to him, and he knew I was big into him. I was sure he knew it, and he had still played hardball with me.

I stood in the middle of the room feeling grossly inadequate because I didn't know what was going on any more. I didn't know who I was. I didn't know what to be, who to be, how to behave. I had run out of role models and I had run out of answers. My life was supposed to have changed for the better. I hadn't expected any setbacks. I hadn't allowed for teething problems and minor hiccups.

I'd had it all worked out, all sorted. My new breasts were going to change everything. And they were doing that, but nothing was turning out *exactly* the way I'd foreseen it.

I began to take responsibility for the fact that I hadn't really thought things through. It became painfully obvious that I had made a mistake of the same magnitude as God trusting Judas with his bank account. I had just lost my best friend and the only man I had ever respected, and I worked with them both. There was no way out of this one. I had to go to work: I was in hock to a considerable sum of money and couldn't leave. Had I a choice, I would have taken the first flight out to the remotest island I could find.

It was a little too late for weighing up the advantages and disadvantages but I did it anyway. I scrambled through various pathetic scenarios where I might just salvage the sinking ship, but deep down I knew that God Himself couldn't have extricated me from the situation I was facing. I had to walk the plank.

The disastrous row with Daria was nothing compared to facing work. It was like having your mother find you in bed with the boy next door. I dreaded having to face Colm. I couldn't bear to look him in the eyes. I just couldn't understand him: I was sure I had read the signs properly, and just when I had taken a leap of faith, shown some vulnerability, he had walked off on me. I should have been able to predict his next move but I was so overwhelmed with worrying about how I would cope that I had forgotten his middle name: Houdini. He had the knack of disappearing at the right moment down to a fine art, and that was exactly what he did. He went sick. It was very convenient for us all.

I went about my daily work in a haze. I dodged Daria successfully for the best part of the day. We were so busy, and I was dead grateful for it. I welled up several times at the cash counter and had to leave it to go the toilet.

I found myself making really stupid mistakes, repeating transactions, omitting to fill out forms and I even handed a member an extra hundred pounds. Thankfully, they pointed out the mistake and returned the cash immediately. Still, it was no surprise that I was out of balance a sizeable sum at the end of the day. I didn't care too much.

Daria was quiet and moody. She wasn't exactly ignoring me but she wasn't inviting me round to tea either. I felt lonely and misjudged. What upset me most was what Colm had been up to. OK, I had made the move, but had he really been that innocent? I had never been a controlled person – always the opposite in fact, exploding like a firework at a moment's notice. I wanted to be more reserved, but I realized now that it was pointless to try to change what was an integral part of my nature. I felt hurt for being judged so harshly.

If he had wanted to keep our friendship strictly platonic, why hadn't he said so? Why had he made that gesture on Valentine's Day and thrown me those looks? Why had he shared lunch with me, followed me into McCullough Piggott's and told me I was the greatest thing since the sliced pan? Why did he constantly flirt with me and, as soon as we got close, back off? I couldn't let go of the feeling I'd had when I held him. Had it been my imagination? The tautness of his body, the urgency of the look in his eyes, the way his arms held me. Why had he come to the nightclub instead of going home with his so-called girlfriend? Had it all been in my imagination?

I had too many questions and no answers. Perhaps my pride couldn't handle the idea that he just didn't care. But he could at least have let me down gently, not flung me aside in the middle of a dance-floor. I always seemed to be the one left with the grief.

The more I thought about it the more I banged hell out of the calculator. I was angry, sick and tired, but underneath all that I was deeply hurt. I stole sneaky glances at Daria. She was doing a very good job of being engrossed in the day's filing stack. Her left leg jiggled up and down under the desk. It was the only betrayal that all was not well in the Daria Alexandru Happy Holiday Camp.

Just as we were closing the doors on the business day, Mark Adams called me into his office. What now? I thought. The day had been so difficult. I was worn out with the pain in my cheeks from the pasted-on smile when I had felt like breaking down.

'Close over the door,' he said.

I did so and sat down with a thump.

'Are you OK?' he said, raising an eyebrow in my direction.

'I've never been better.'

'Well, I have some news for you that might cheer you up.'

'I could do with that.' I yawned.

'We had a brief meeting during the week with the Irish League of Credit Unions. They brought a breakdown of figures for the membership count with them. We were amazed to see it had risen from ten thousand to just under fifteen thousand within the last twelve-month period.' He smiled.

'That doesn't surprise me,' I said.

'Why's that?' he asked.

'I can personally vouch for the new members. It's mostly me who has processed their new accounts and I couldn't get over the amount of them, especially since Christmas,' I replied.

'Yes, well, there's been an influx of foreigners with

this Celtic Tiger thing. The problem is, Finn, we haven't enough staff to cover.' He scratched his moustache.

'I know,' I said.

'You do?'

'I'm out there every day, Mark. It's hectic busy and not just at weekends. It's all the time,' I told him.

'Well, Tom O'Hare has left us, as you have probably guessed. Even with Dessie and Colm, staff levels won't cover the extra work so we have been allotted two more casual positions to help out,' he said.

'That's great, about time.' I coughed.

'As you also know, the position for assistant loans manager is now advertised on the noticeboard,' he went on.

'Yeah,' I said, bored.

'I want you to apply for it.'

'*What?*' I exclaimed.

'You heard me. I want you to apply for the job. I have been watching your work performance and closely monitoring your progress. You have surprised us all, Finn. You're a bit of a whiz with the administration and, to be honest, that's what the job is mostly. Paperwork, paperwork and more paperwork.'

'You want me to apply for assistant loans manager?' I had to check just in case he thought I was someone else.

'Sure do.' He nodded.

'But what about Daria?' I asked.

'I'm hoping to make her assistant manager, my right-hand man – or woman, I should say.' He was wrestling with a mountain of fax paper.

'Have you spoken to her yet?'

'Nope. Wanted to talk to you first. What do you think?'

'I don't know what to say.'

'I'm not saying you have the job, understand? I'm just telling you to apply for it.' He winked at me.

'Right.' I understood perfectly.

'Good. Off you toddle. And, Finn?'

'Yeah?'

'Keep it under your hat. I'm thinking of poor old Dessie, you know.'

'Sure.'

I sat there, staring at the floor, biting my lip.

Mark Adams leaned forward. 'Finn?'

'What?'

'I thought you'd be happy,' he said.

'I am,' I said, and tears poured from my eyes.

All I could think of was how little anything mattered unless I could share it with Daria and Colm. I had the figure I had longed for all my life. I had men dancing attention on me wherever I went. I had a promotion in the offing. I had it all, and yet I had nothing.

The following week was the worst in my life. I went to work, cried in the toilets, went home, cried in my bed, and got up to do the same thing again the next day. It wasn't that Daria and I weren't speaking. We had to talk in work. But somehow that made it worse. I felt like she had to tolerate me, that if she had had a choice she wouldn't have bothered. The deathly silence, the empty chair and desk where Colm usually sat made me ache with regret. I wanted to ask Daria had she seen him, had she spoken to him, had he even phoned her?

I was angry he had taken the easy way out. It seemed almost more disrespectful, as if I wasn't worth facing up to. It was a personal attack on my very existence. I didn't see Julia come or go as she usually did, and that was odd. But what difference did it make at this stage anyway?

Daria was pleasant enough, but no more. I missed, her and Colm, the jokes, the taunts, the slagging of members, the little phone calls. My heart was breaking. The only thing that kept me going was the possibility of my promotion. Daria didn't mention it and that hurt too. I knew she had to be aware of it. I watched her arrive for her interview. She was dressed to kill and exuded an air of supreme confidence. I said a little prayer for her, although I knew she didn't need it.

At the end of the week Mark Adams called me in again and told me he wanted me to handle a loan application as a try-out. We had a small but comfortable interviewing room behind the open-plan office and emergency loan applications were seen in there. I didn't feel ready for it. 'Mark, I don't know the process. I know how to read the application forms, but I don't know how to conduct an interview,'

'You'll have to learn, Finn, and there's only one way to do it. You go in there with your pen and paper and you take down the details. Get all the financial stuff – you know, proof of earnings, income ceiling, repayment requirements, amounts and methods, you know the deal. It's really very simple. You don't have to give the answer. That's my job. Take down all the information and bring it in to me,' he said. I knew by his tone that it was one of those days. To put up resistance would send him into a rage. As it was, his moustache was twitching furiously, so I gathered my faculties and walked into the interviewing room alone.

'Hello, Finn,' said a voice, as I closed the door with my back to the occupant.

I turned round, my stomach rising and falling in panic. 'Shane!' I said.

# Chapter 22

'You look incredible your hair, it's . . . beautiful,' he said. His voice was filled with genuine surprise.

I was weighing up the situation. Perhaps I could get someone else to do this. But who? Daria was busy and Colm was still out. Besides, I couldn't have approached either of them for obvious reasons.

'Thanks,' I mumbled, pulling out the chair. I sat down to face him and noticed his eyes roam downwards to the cleavage I had gained since we split up. They rested there for some minutes. I was mortified. I was used to men looking at me by now, but Shane was a different matter. I prayed hard that he had the sense to make no comment.

'How have you been?' he asked.

'Very well, actually,' I lied. 'Things have never been better. I'm up for promotion as assistant loans manager. That's why I was asked to see you.' I rustled papers with an air of importance.

'I'm sorry. Had I known you were doing it I wouldn't have . . .' He trailed off.

'It's OK,' I said.

He looked pretty awful, but the ponytail was gone, I was glad to see: it had never suited him. He had grown it in a time when all Irish men decided they would have the new-age look. Not everyone suited it, and most ended up looking like the rear end of a donkey. Shane had looked more like a Connemara pony. Now he wore his hair short, tight and behind his ears. I recalled that day at the bus stop and how bad I had felt about myself. How the tables had turned. I resisted the urge to play some power games. Thank God it wasn't up to me to decide whether or not to OK the loan. I would have rejected his application without even reading it.

He jiggled about, seeming positively agitated. I waited for him to say he'd changed his mind and that he'd come back another day, but he didn't, so I knew he had to be in bad way to endure the humiliation. He looked pitiful, really, and I felt sorry for him. It must have taken great courage for him to sit there and let me play with his life. Sometimes when members approached the Credit Union, it was their last port of call. They had usually done the rounds of banks, building societies and, in some cases, loan sharks. He must be in a tight spot, I surmised.

'Right. Let's start,' I said.

'Are you seeing anyone?' he blurted.

'What?' I peered over the white form in my hand.

'I was just wondering. Are you seeing anyone?' he repeated, with a cheeky grin this time.

'Are you?' I replied.

'No.'

'Me neither. Give me your wages slip,' I commanded.

'I miss you,' he said, handing me a mangled piece of paper.

'God almighty, what did you do with this? Leave it in the seat of your pants and put it through the washing-machine?'

He burst out laughing. 'Having a bad day, Finn?' he asked.

'No. I'm having a great day. Can't you tell?'

'Why don't you let me take you for a drink after work? I owe you an apology,' he said sheepishly.

'Shane, it was a long time ago, I've forgotten all about it,' I said. But I hadn't forgotten anything. That was my problem.

'It's been six months and twelve days,' he told me.

I was surprised. 'You've been counting?' I eyed him over the computer terminal. So far I hadn't been able to turn it on. All of a sudden I couldn't remember the combination code.

'I've thought about it a lot. I was very cruel to you,' he said.

It seemed a genuine enough remark. 'You weren't cruel, just insufferable. Mostly.' I smiled.

He grinned. 'Hey, you were no saint either,' he said.

Didn't I know it? Well, I was beginning to. Only small beginnings, mind you. I knew my mouth was my worst enemy and I was trying to learn how to keep it shut before it landed me in more trouble.

'Nothing made you happy, Finn. Nothing was enough. If I was all over you like a rash, you hated it. If I didn't pay you enough attention, you hated it. I could never win,' he said.

I thought about that. It was a pretty heavy burden to have asked anyone to carry, even if he was a moron of the highest calibre.

'I wasn't that bad,' I squeaked.

'See? You're doing it even now.'

'What?'

'You know. Am I this? Am I that? Always looking for reassurance. You drove me crazy. You drove *yourself* crazy,' he said.

He had that bit right.

I defended myself: 'I've always been insecure, you know that.'

'Hey, that may be so, but I'm an innocent man. I didn't make you that way. You were always making me pay for something I didn't do,' he said.

He was right, of course – but, bugger it, I wasn't admitting to it.

'I'm not perfect.' I couldn't come up with anything else.

'Let me take you for a drink,' he said again.

I was mulling it over. What did he want? Perhaps he was lonely. Perhaps he had noticed the new bod and was curious to see more. Whatever his motive, he couldn't have picked a better day to play with my dodgy ego. I was lonely and sad, and tired fighting both. 'Shane, by the looks of your application form, you won't have the bus fare home,' I said, scanning the pages.

'Shite,' he moaned.

'I'll see what I can do. Can't you add on something here? A social-welfare payment or something?' I asked.

'My dad gives me a portion of his pension for housekeeping, but I can't put that down as income,' he said.

'I just did. It's income, right?'

'Right.'

'I can't promise anything,' I warned, as I got up to see Mark Adams.

'You can. Even if the loan is turned down, you can promise to have a drink with me.'

He was persistent, I had to give him that.

I got Mark Adams to process the loan there and then, and prided myself on my ability to make a case. I wasn't as bad with people as I'd thought and, having weighed up Shane's application form, I saw I had come up with the right answer before Mark Adams confirmed it.

Leaving the office was a blatantly theatrical affair. Daria and Dessie were filing so I played it up to the best of my ability. I was determined to rattle Colm. Sooner or later they were bound to let the cat out of the bag. Yes, sooner or later he would hear about it through the grapevine. I could bet my money on Dessie opening his big mouth. Shane was perfect emotional target material. I wanted to hurt Colm back. I wanted revenge. I wanted to see him suffer. It never occurred to me to go and talk to him. Oh, no. That was for the movies, where real people did real things. I had hardened. I had a new set of rules and I was going to stick to them. Never give in, never apologize, and never *ever* admit you were wrong.

So I slipped my arm in Shane's, making sure the others saw me. I let out ridiculous belts of feigned laughter whenever he said anything. It was over the top and, like all my great plans for revenge, it backfired. Daria fiddled at her desk with some papers and never raised her head once. We walked out the door and I slammed it hard behind me, leaving her in no doubt that we were going. Had I a loudspeaker on my person, I would have made use of it: 'WE ARE GOING FOR A DRINK SOMEWHERE. ISN'T THAT RIGHT, SHANE?'

I might have even spelt it out, or drawn some pictures on a piece of cardboard to get the message across. But Daria was cooler than the Howth Junction Dart station on a March morning. No dice. She didn't flinch.

In the pub, I watched the door like a hawk. I was fool enough to believe that Colm would arrive. I tried to pretend I was interested in Shane's conversation – nothing had changed: it varied between Leeds United and MTV, MTV and Leeds United, and I thought what a fucking boring asshole he was compared to Colm. Sadness welled up in me and I drank to drown it.

By eleven o'clock I was well on and there was no sign of Colm. I knew he didn't know where I was, let alone want to be with me. Shane was being very familiar and I found myself laughing at his stupid jokes. I was as lonely as a lost puppy and I couldn't tell anyone. I couldn't admit to my mistakes. I had gone too far. I had to see it through to the bitter end.

It had started with me doing one thing wrong, which had led to a succession of others. That was the way I had lived my life, jumping from one disaster to the next. After a while the bad things had become normal, even appeared to be right. As did this little rendezvous in the pub. My old friend Justification was back, with his side-kick Anger along for the ride. Together they came up with the worst plan yet.

We rolled out of the pub into the darkness and moved with the evening crowds. I had already made up my mind before Shane asked.

'Are you bringing me home, Finn?' he slurred, throwing an arm round my shoulders, his drunken eyes unable to tear themselves from my new body beautiful.

'Why not?' I slurred back.

We staggered home to my flat, a bottle of cheap white wine tucked discreetly under his jacket. We fell in the door, laughing. I was in the mood now. I'd been thinking about sex for so long that I wondered was everything in good working order. I had successfully eradicated Colm's face from the present moment. I wanted sex and I wanted it now.

I went about it like you plan the weekly shopping. I checked Shane against the mental list I had been carrying for weeks.

Was he the candidate? Yes. Shane was the perfect guinea pig. Instantly forgettable sexually and emotionally non-threatening. In a zillion years, I would never have to worry about being hurt by him because I didn't give a damn about him. I was happy to let him be the first. I had no respect for him and was looking down on him even now.

What a turn-around. I sneered at him in my head like some prima donna. I felt in complete control. Victorious. I had always been the underdog, the begging, needy, insecure child. Now the tables had turned: he was begging for me and I was enjoying every minute of it. I opened the wine and poured us some in two dirty, chipped mugs. That was deliberate. If it had been Colm I would have used glasses. It's not Colm, I reminded myself. *It's not Colm.* This is not a romantic adventure. This is an experiment. No drawn-out foreplay. No sensuals, just the basics. A feel of the old how's-your-father and a slap on the old bottom, *and absolutely no kissing whatsoever.*

I gulped the wine in a hurry, wanting to get on with the task in hand. Shane sat beside me on the battered couch. Indeed, we had made love on it quite often. It seemed the right place to start. I threw my legs over his and he moved closer to me. I responded by cuddling up a bit more. His arms were round me and it felt nice to have a man hold me. My insides were warm from the alcohol and I closed my eyes to enhance the feelings.

Shane went to kiss me and, rather than reject him, I buried my head in his shoulder hoping he would take it for the whopping hint it was meant to be.

He went straight for it and began to unbutton my blouse. My heart was thumping. I had been wondering for months what would they feel like in someone else's hands. Would they feel real?

'Finn, what have you done?' Shane whispered, as he undid my bra and stared.

'A job,' I whispered. There: it was out. I couldn't lie about it to him and I didn't care what he thought. As it turned out, he thought a lot.

'My God, it's amazing. They look incredible I mean, *you* look incredible,' he said, stunned by the vision before him. I'm sure he thought all his birthdays had come at once. What more could a man ask for? He held one in his hand and marvelled at its beauty.

'What does it feel like?' I asked.

'Beautiful – absolutely beautiful,' he said, his breath rushing in and out with excitement.

It felt beautiful. *I* felt beautiful. I felt like a real woman. I leaned back and let him play, and it was wonderful to be an object of desire, to have that womanly control, to have a man beside himself with want. I was ready for this. I had waited, and now I was glad it was Shane whose head was nuzzled into my chest. He kissed my breasts, little fluttery light kisses at first, then circled my nipples with his tongue – I saw them harden in response. I couldn't wait for him to take one in his mouth. I wanted to know what it felt like.

I opened my eyes to tell him to do just that, then realized with horror that he already had: he was biting and sucking them and I could feel nothing. My nipples were numb.

It never ceases to amaze me how men can make love to you and be unaware that they are doing nothing to arouse you. Is it that they *do* know and don't give a shit, or a case of too much shampoo advertising and they don't know the difference between a real orgasm and a fake one? Should we tell them that their lovemaking skills are more akin to that of a brief struggle with a stubborn splinter?

There I was, all gloriously sexy, poised on the brink of nothingness. Shane was doing his best but his best was usually pretty awful – his foreplay had always been about as exciting as my last smear test. I imagined he was putting greater effort into it than usual. That was because I was worth it now, you see. I had breasts he could do something with – although it would have been nice to feel it. As I hadn't been manhandling my nipples I hadn't noticed the numbness before. Anyway, I did my best Sharon Stone impression and it worked. When it was all over I rushed him out of the flat telling him how wonderful he was, please call soon, no, there's nothing wrong, I had to get up for work and needed some sleep. He had worn me out. (He loved that one.) I was bunched.

I didn't feel guilty, just a little scared. I had a look in the mirror just to check everything was OK. They looked fine, but my nipples were still stiff and erect. I thought that strange. The surrounding area was stiff and numb too. There wasn't any swelling, they just felt rock hard like they do when I'm on the verge of orgasm, only I wasn't on the verge of orgasm and I wondered what the hell was going on.

Even taking into account the small amount of arousal I had felt, it had never taken them two hours to return to normal. I wandered round the flat, biting my nails. I tried everything to distract myself. I ate a whole box of cornflakes and drank several bottles of Energyade. Then I went to the toilet and threw up – my crutch wasn't working any more.

I sat at the piano, staring at the closed lid. I still hadn't got rid of it. I rubbed my hand along the mahogany, the scratches that had accumulated over the years. I wanted to take a quick peek inside. My hand slowly reached upwards, but then, just as suddenly, it stopped in mid-air and I found I couldn't go there . . . not again . . .

I would only see Colm's beautiful face looking at me.

*I am just about to turn fourteen. I play my Dad's piano every day. I can't help being drawn to it. I can't play properly but it doesn't stop me trying to figure out keys and notes. I can play most songs. I hear the music in my ear, hit whatever note ties in with it and suddenly I can play any tune I put my mind to. I wait until Mam has gone out. Sunday mornings are the best times to practise.*

*They all go to mass, you see, Mam, Dad and the boys. I always pretend to go to evening mass but I don't. I hide out in the back lane and sing songs to myself. Sometimes, if I get some money, I buy myself some sweets. They are my favourite times, away from this horrible house, away from Mam. She hates me playing the piano. I was certain I had outwitted her with my big plan but she won again.*

*I think I know this piano inside out. I love to open the top and watch the little hammers pounding off the harp sound-board inside. The tones seem louder when I do this, but Dad gives out to me and always makes me close it. The minute they go out I open it again. My feet can touch the pedals now: the left one makes the sound louder, the right is the soft pedal and the middle one keeps the note prolonged. The sustaining pedal, I think it's called.*

*I was hoping to find out today what all those strange words meant. I often look at the sheet music on the stand in front of me but I can't understand what the words mean.* Allegro, forte, adagio, allegretto. *Then there are all the notes: crochets, quavers (sounds like my favourite crisps!) minims and semi-breves. What the hell are they supposed to mean and why can't the words be in English so I can understand them?*

*That's the problem, you see. I want to learn music but I can't read the musty dog-earned music sheets my Dad has in the stool. I need to go to lessons and I asked Mam could she find me a teacher, but she says it's too expensive and I would have to have talent for it to be worthwhile. I know that's rubbish. It's because of Dad. He doesn't want to fork out the money for such a stupid pastime. Now, if it was for hurling or hockey, even . . . Maybe Mam really believes I haven't any talent. If so, I wish someone would explain to me why I hear music in my head all day?*

*I wasn't going to be put off easily. I got myself a paper round that pays me a small sum of money each week. I have been saving it up and today I went for my first piano lesson. It was hard trying to find a tutor who lived nearby but I got lucky and heard about one from Mrs Brown, our maths teacher. She was sick and tired of having to follow me to the school hall and drag me back to class. I can always be found between classes tinkling away on the battered old piano there. It's not as bad as the one we have at home and at least it's in tune. She mentioned Herb Cooke. I thought, Cool. He'll do. He had a weird enough name and he sounded mysterious. Maybe he played with some of the greats?*

*I was so excited today that I couldn't concentrate in school. I was worse trying to finish my ecker. I just couldn't keep my mind on the job at all. Mam hovered around me clucking away to herself as she peeled potatoes for the chip pan. I wasn't going to tell her. Not in a million years. Not that she cared what I did. I knew if I told her she'd laugh at me.*

*I arrived at Herb Cooke's address. It was a corner house tucked safely away at the end of a cul-de-sac. He wasn't what I had expected: a tall, gangly man with thick-rimmed glasses and a spotty face. I was dubious about his ability to teach piano. He looked more like a science teacher to me. He brought me inside and I noticed the metronome on the lid of the piano.*

*I had always wanted one, even though I had a good sense of delivery with my own style. He gave it a whack as he was talking to me. He seemed agitated and I thought, Oh, God, I picked a right weirdo. I was about to leave when he sat down to play a bit for me first. His left hand was an animal. It pawed the keys effortlessly. He looked so gawky and awkward, his back hunched over the keyboard. But, Christ, was he good or what? I felt like such an imbecile for judging him. Oscar Peterson, move over!*

*This guy's fingers pressed the keys with precision and sharpness and he never once looked at what he was playing. He closed his eyes and let his fingers roam, and they roamed and caressed and tortured at times. He did this fast honky-tonk piece and told me all about Keith Emerson, a hero of his. I had never heard of him but I decided there and then I was going to play honky-tonk piano for the rest of my life and nothing else.*

*When he stopped and asked me to show him what I could do I felt inadequate beyond belief. How was I supposed to play 'Danny Boy' after that? And, anyway, I could only play in the key of C. I felt utterly hopeless as I banged out my solo piece. It sounded crap after him. He stood behind me, his giraffe's neck leaning over my shoulder. It made me even more nervous and I made several stupid mistakes because of it. He kept telling me it was OK, keep going. Not to worry. I was doing fine. I felt like such an eejit.*

*When I had finished, he showed me some music manuscripts. He asked me could I read any music.*

*'No,' I answered.*

*'Well, it's going to be a really hard slog for you.' He sighed heavily.*

*'I'm prepared to work hard,' I tried.*

*'I'm sure you are. That's not what concerns me.' He took off his glasses and gestured for me to sit down on the couch.*

*He leaned against the piano, his long fingers flopping downwards. I sat down.*

*'You see, you have a natural ear for music,' he said.*

*I smiled.*

*'How long have you been playing?' he asked.*

*'Since I can remember,' I replied.*

*'By ear?'*

*'Yes.'*

*'No lessons, no music reading?'*

*'No,' I said. I was pleased with myself and proud of the fact.*

*'Yes. That's the big problem here,' he said.*

*'What do you mean?' I was confused: he had just told me I had a natural ear for music. I was thrilled somebody had said it. It was something I knew anyway but I'd needed to hear confirmation.*

*'Well, how old are you now?' He blew on his glasses and cleaned them with the end of his shirtsleeve.*

*'Fourteen,' I said.*

*'Jeez. If you had come to me when you started I might have been able to train you. Let's see. You've probably been playing the piano all wrong for about eight years, right?'*

*'I suppose so,' I said.*

*'Your fingers are completely misplaced. In fact you've bent your forefinger and thumb.'*

*'I have?'*

*'Yes. It's a pity.' He put his glasses back on.*

*'I'm afraid I can't help you.' He leaned forwards.*

*'What do you mean? I can change the way I play, that's why I'm here, to learn to play properly,' I argued.*

*'Yes. I understand that, but it's not possible at this stage to change your ways. You would have to start from scratch, like learning how to read "Twinkle Twinkle Little Star" and things like that. In my experience, when someone has been*

*playing by ear as long as you have it's impossible to retrain them. You would inevitably end up taking the easy option and just start to play what you hear instead of what you're supposed to be reading. Do you understand? The frustration would be overwhelming for you and for any teacher. It's too late, darling. I'm sorry. As I said, if you had come to me earlier . . .'*

*I'm never going to play the piano again.*

*Mam was right. I have no talent. It's time for me to stop playing Wendy in my own production of* Peter Pan. *It's time to grow up.*

# Chapter 23

The morning after Shane, I arose feeling tired and anxious. I stared into the mirror again and the great nipple *erectus* was still evident. I put on my bra and they peeped through the lace like they would in cold weather conditions. They stood out like two giant Jelly Tots. While they had been sexy-looking last night, I didn't want to go around during the day with two cows' udders pushing through my blouse.

By midday I had begun to panic. The numbness was spreading – or was I imagining it? I kept darting in and out of the toilet to take a look. One breast looked bigger than the other . . . or did it? I touched one and then the other, then did it again. There was a definite swelling under my arm. It felt achy and uncomfortable, maybe that was why one looked bigger than the other. The familiar purple hue around the areola was fading. It had become a pale yellow. The skin was taut and stretched and, if anything, the whole breast was becoming firmer, tighter and even a bit painful. Or was it? I couldn't decide.

This wasn't supposed to be happening. I was sick with worry and fear. I hobbled around at work trying to behave normally and wondering what I should do. I threw beseeching glances Daria's way but she didn't notice – and I couldn't get Colm out of my head. He had arrived back at work and behaved like nothing had happened. I was surprised and upset that he didn't show any signs of wanting to patch up.

Of all the days he had chosen to come back, he couldn't have picked a worse one. At lunchtime, I tried to break the ice by having mine indoors. I sat in the canteen but no one joined me. That wasn't unusual, we couldn't all lunch together, but I checked the roster on the noticeboard and Colm was off at the same time as me. I tried to finish a soggy salad roll but the food wedged in my throat and I went to the bin to throw up. Colm barged through the door with a Kylemore bag just in time to see me hovering over it, hair held back in my hands.

It seemed to me he never saw me any other way. I was always making a fool of myself one way or another. He hung about awkwardly, not knowing what to do.

'Skinny? What's the story?' he asked, cool as a cucumber, his voice soft and low.

'I'm fine,' I choked.

'That's weird. I thought you were about to vomit,' he quipped.

I glared at him.

'I was about to make some tea. Want some?' he asked, his left foot tapping wildly on the black and white tiles. He was scared to make conversation with me in case I savaged him with my vicious tongue. I could tell by the giveaway manic foot-tapping.

'I'm not sure.' I groaned, the salad roll still interacting with my tummy like a roller-coaster ride in Funderland. He must have taken that response as a 'yes' because he put the kettle on. There was a bit of a squeeze as it was beside the sink and I moved clumsily, walking into the table behind me. He dropped the kettle lead into the sink full of dirty dishes. We collided and clattered against the furniture like Laurel and Hardy, a pair of goons not knowing how to behave.

'Shite,' he clipped, under his breath.

I didn't know what to say. I was half laughing, half angry, yet desperate for him to talk to me. He fiddled some more. He grabbed a tea-towel and tried to tear open his lunch at the same time. He was mighty nervous. I couldn't blame him.

'How are you, Finn? You look very pale,' he said, unwrapping some pancakes.

'What?' I asked, my stomach still reeling.

'I said, how are you?' He turned to face me. He was trying. His awkwardness was sweet.

I hid my smile when a sugary pancake plopped on to the floor and he blushed. 'Colm, you're wrecking the place,' I told him.

He smiled. The type of smile that only came with reconciliation. The type of smile someone gives when they have been exonerated. I could almost hear the breath of relief rush from his lungs. 'It's my job, don't you remember?' he said.

'No. It's my job to wreck everything,' I said, and I got up to leave. I saw Colm's hand reach out to stop me.

'Look, can we talk . . .' he tried.

'Don't,' I blubbered. It was the last thing I wanted to say. I wanted to say the opposite, but I was sure I would start bawling-crying and make a fool of myself. Anyhow, I wasn't letting him off the hook entirely. I was still very hurt. He pulled back, mortified.

Dessie barged in. Nothing new about Dessie bolloxing everything up. Only this time, for the first time ever in my life, I was grateful to him. He gave me the perfect excuse to leave. He skidded on the pancake and uttered a few niceties. 'Fuck me, what was that?' He grabbed a chair as he slid past.

It's probably some silicone, I thought. Either that or my oozing confidence has finally found a way out of my arse. I left Colm standing there, an incredulous look on his gorgeous face. He juggled several cups, a torn pancake, a tea-towel and half a salad roll with great difficulty and looked so vulnerable I wanted to kiss his head.

I hadn't deliberately set out to make him feel bad. I was a walking disaster so I reckoned the best thing to do was keep walking. So that was what I did. I had tired of throwing myself at people and was learning that it had the exact opposite effect to the one I wanted. People got bored and walked away from me.

Back in the offices I daydreamed the afternoon away. A typical summer day, it was very quiet and only the odd member came in, usually with a straightforward payment. When the good weather came (which isn't very often in Ireland) the population vanished up its own arse. Whole cities were cleared within minutes. It was the rare visitation of the sun that made everybody go mad. The next day (because we usually only got one day) we would arrive back to work like skin cancer victims, lobster-red scalded bodies, delighted with the new tan. If good weather lasted more than two days it was upgraded to a heatwave.

I thought about approaching Daria but she was like the Antichrist reincarnated and it didn't take a brain surgeon to figure out why. Marcus Myers was at her desk, driving her insane with endless stupid questions. I sat quietly at the far end of the office pretending to be busy with cash.

Daria was trying to placate him but she was losing the run of herself. This was most unlike her and I wondered what the hell was wrong. She was becoming hostile, even rude, and had lost her usually contrite and patient manner. This glitch in the Daria calm was like manna from heaven for Mr Myers. This was what he had been waiting for. He was a cute one. He had known if he kept at her, she would crack some day, and this was the day.

But she really shouldn't break out of character so near to securing her position as assistant manager of the Credit Union. A mistake might have fatal consequences. It was almost as if Mr Myers knew it, and he was pushing out the conversation towards landmine territory and none of us knew where the bombs were hidden.

'All I'm asking, dear, is that you display the opening times correctly. I can't see that sign on the window. Nobody could. You would need X-ray glasses to see the opening times,' he whinged.

'Well, nobody else thinks so,' Daria cut him down. 'In fact, we haven't had any complaints at all.' She picked up a small white square of paper and held it up to the screen. 'We also slipped this into the inside of your book. It says clearly what the opening hours are.' She slid the book back across the hatch.

He noticed it was an angry gesture and made the best of it. 'Don't you throw that at me,' he said indignantly.

'I didn't throw it,' Daria replied, through clenched teeth.

'Yes, you did,' he insisted.

Dessie arrived over. 'It's the arse-bandit again. This time she's really going to give it to him. I can feel it in my waters,' he muttered.

'Somebody better do something,' I said.

'I'm not going to stop her. Nothing would please me more than to see that idiot—'

'Dessie, shut your face,' I ordered him. I wanted to hear what was going on. It wasn't very pleasant.

'You're insolence is unacceptable. Doesn't your training include some basic tutoring in customer relations?' Mr Myers's voice rose.

Daria's face was purple with rage and he was loving every minute of it.

'Yes. As a matter of fact it's the foundation of our training courses. However, I am not trained to deal with extreme bad manners. It's not part of the curriculum. Frankly, we don't expect to have to deal with rudeness on this level,' she snapped.

*Uh-oh.*

Colm passed behind me slowly. I knew he was listening and thinking the same thing as me: Somebody had better stop this before it gets ugly. He stood a few feet away from me, flicking through a Lever Arch folder, calmly surveying the pages with his ears pricked. I glanced at him and he glanced back knowingly. I wondered should I move or would he do it.

Marcus Myers leaned heavily into the hatch, his voice dropping to a menacing whisper: '*Why don't you get on the boat and go back to where you came from?*' he hissed.

That was it. I couldn't listen to any more. I pushed back my chair, but just as I was about to intercede Colm laid a heavy hand on my shoulder. He pushed me down rather firmly. I looked up and realized why.

Mark Adams was behind Daria, his hand on her back, moustache twitching like a trapped mouse and the veins throbbing in his neck with anger.

'She didn't get a boat. She caught a plane. Just like you,'

he said. The heaviness of his words fell on the man with a resounding thud.

'What?' Mr Myers stuttered, his face flushed beetroot.

'I presume you're referring to Daria's nationality, that she's Romanian,' Mark Adams went on.

'I wasn't referring to anything.' Mr Myers had toppled. Face to face with another man he didn't seem so threatening, especially when it was the manager himself.

'I heard you. I hate to have to inform you of your ignorance but not every Romanian arrives on a *boat*,' Mark Adams barked, almost spitting the last word into his face.

'I don't agree with all these foreigners pouring into Ireland, especially when *our own* are being excluded in the employment market,' Mr Myers fought back.

Daria's mouth hung open. She sat wide-eyed and flushed throughout the exchange.

'"*Our own*", you say? Come, now, Mr Myers, you're not Irish! You're Scottish! You're a foreigner and you work here. Isn't that right? What difference is there between you and this lady?' Mark laughed at him.

'I've been living here for over a decade,' he defended himself.

'So has Daria.' Mark Adams leaned forward.

'I am an Irish citizen,' he stammered.

'So is she,' Mark Adams retorted.

'Then I have made a mistake.' Mr Myers looked rattled now.

'You certainly have. A very big one.' Now Mark Adams took the man's account book and slowly tore it in two. He handed the pieces back to him via the hatch.

'Now. Get. Out. Of. My. Offices. And. Don't. Ever. Come. Back,' he said, lowering his voice and speaking each word clearly and separately. I grasped now why he had become a manager. I would never have been able to handle that with such suave sophistication. Not with a million years' training. Mark Adams patted Daria on the back and gave her a thumbs-up. Then, as quickly as he had arrived, he walked calmly back into his office as if nothing had happened.

'Jeysus,' Dessie exclaimed.

I had to pinch myself to make sure I wasn't hallucinating. I wanted to finish the job off properly and get out there and smack Mr Myers's head against the wall. Daria looked pale and shocked. Colm had disappeared. I stood up and walked over to her desk. I didn't care about our recent fall-out. I was calling a ceasefire, whether she was ready or not.

'Daria.' I stood at her desk. 'Mark Adams knew all along, eh?'

'Yeah.'

'Christ, that was some scene. I've waited a lifetime for the boss to do something about him,' I said nervously.

'I'm still in shock,' Daria said.

'You know, none of us could care less if you were half Eskimo, half Cantonese with Australian outback descendants, don't you?' I said.

She nodded, looking like she was going to cry.

'You're the best friend I've ever had,' I said. The words were out before I could stop them. For once in my life, they were the right ones. I had been spontaneous and it paid off.

'Thanks,' she said, eyes welling.

I threw myself at her and hugged her until she had no breath left inside. 'Let me go, will you?' she begged, half laughing.

'Jeysus, give it over, girls.' Dessie squirmed.

Without warning I grabbed him and plonked a huge wet kiss on his quivering lips.

'Fuck off out of that, will you?' He pulled back, mortified.

'Go on, you loved it,' I teased him.

We stood together, wallowing in our glorious victory as Mr Myers shuffled towards the door. We waited for him to leave for the last time so we could applaud, but out of the blue Colm was beside him. I watched him take the shaken Mr Myers by the arm and whisper something in his ear. What the hell was he at? I looked over to Daria. She shrugged her shoulders, none the wiser.

'What's he doing?' Dessie asked.

We all took our stare back to Colm at the entrance. He was still talking to Mr Myers.

'Relax now, Mr Myers. You shouldn't leave in such a state. Here, let me help you,' he shouted, at the top of his voice. He sat him down in a chair at the door and Mr Myers fanned himself with his hat.

Colm reached over to the coffee percolator, which hadn't been used for days, and poured a very murky-looking cup of liquid into a white paper cup. I looked to Daria again. Her mouth was turning upwards.

'Now, drink this and you'll be as right as rain,' Colm instructed.

Mr Myers took the paper cup and brought it to his lips. Daria and I stared on, our mouths agape.

'Take your time now. That's it, drink the whole lot down. It will do you the power of good, it will,' he went on.

*'Fucking Nora.'* Dessie snorted.

'Thank you, son, the rest of the staff here should take a leaf out of your book. You're very kind, young man.' Mr Myers sipped, his hands still shaking from the challenge he had endured minutes before.

'You're very welcome, it's my pleasure.' Colm smiled

at him, the epitome of customer-relations management. He turned to us and winked. The cheeky fuck. Daria put her head on her desk, shoulders hunched, desperately fighting off the urge to get hysterical.

'He didn't,' I uttered.

'He did. Shit the bed, he did it,' Daria whispered.

It was then, and only then, that I realized I was hopelessly in love with him.

# Chapter 24

Daria and I sat face to face in Eddie Rocket's. We hadn't been there for months and the sight of her black tresses flopping into her milkshake made me feel like I was home again. The conversation was rushed, although we had all the time in the world to catch up. I remembered I hadn't shown any interest in her personal life since I'd had the operation and I asked her lots of questions about Ion.

I felt guilty about everything. What was worse, I still wanted to talk about Colm more than anything else. After all that had happened, I was still immersed in my own selfishness: I had never taken her relationship with Ion seriously.

'Are you sleeping with him?' I asked bluntly, wrestling with the top of Energyade bottle. I was really trying to cut down this time and had had only two so far that day.

'Yes.' She laughed.

'Any good?'

'Good? He's the best. A ride? Isn't that what you'd call him?'

'Are you in love with him?'

'Yes,'

'Then he's not a ride.'

'He's not?'

'No. A ride is someone you just have sex with. You can't have a relationship with a ride.'

'Oh?'

'Yeah.'

'What is he then?'

'He's a fine thing,'

'A fine thing?'

'Yeah,'

'I guess it helps that he's from the home turf?'

'Home turf?'

'Irish expression.'

'Right.'

'He's from your side of the planet, isn't he?'

'I have to say I'm ashamed I know so little about my own home. My parents emigrated long before Ceausescu was overthrown. I've had to ask Ion everything. But I'm glad they left when they did. They got out at the right time but many of our relatives stayed behind and suffered. I grew up in London knowing little about my country until I met Ion. I feel guilty when I listen to him tell me the full horror of what we left there.'

'Seems like such a decent bloke, you jammy tart.'

'Finn, your mouth?'

'What I'm trying to say is I guess you were meant to cross paths.'

'Yes. You were destined to cross paths too.'

'Who with?'

'Colm.'

'We didn't so much cross paths as accidentally pee in each other's garden.'

'It's the same thing. It doesn't matter how it happens. Only that it happens.'

'It *does* matter how it happens. Especially when you mess it up as badly as I did. I behaved like a stray dog.'

'How poetic. You've a mouth like a disposal unit.'

'A sewer.'

'Sorry, a sewer,' she corrected herself.

'I miss him,' I whispered.

'I can't believe what he did today.' Daria laughed.

I laughed too. I was so Goddamn proud of him. 'You'd never think he had it in him.'

'What's the verdict, then?'

'What do you mean?'

'You know. Is Colm a ride or a fine thing?'

'A ride.'

'Are you sure about that?' she asked.

'OK. He's a ride and a fine thing. A rare specimen.'

'So what you're saying is, you'd love to sleep with him but you're in love with him so you can't?'

'Hey, it's no surprise Mark Adams chose you to be assistant manager,' I joked, envying her sharp perception.

'Do I get any extra points for figuring out what Shane is? Is he a ride or a fine thing?' she pushed.

'Neither.'

There was a long pause as I tried to come up with a change of subject.

'I know you slept with him,' she said.

'It didn't mean anything.' I shrugged my shoulders.

'Thank God for that. You know, Finn, you have to learn to wait for the good stuff. Nothing worthwhile comes easily. I mean, think about it, what's the point in eating hamburger when you can have steak at home?'

'I get the point, but what you don't understand is that I'm starving. Colm didn't want me. I threw myself at him and he walked away. Besides, he's always got someone else swinging out of him.'

'How much do you want him?'

I wondered about that. 'I think I'd have his baby, then I'd have to marry him.'

'Would you marry him?'

'That's like asking is Paisley a Protestant.'

'So you would.'

'Marry him?'

'Yes. Marry him.'

'You better believe it. Of course, I'd have to be surgically removed from his underpants after the ceremony.'

'You're really in love with him. You just can't say it without swearing.'

'Fuck it. You're right.'

'He's in love with you too.'

'Wrong. Dead wrong.'

'*He is.*'

'Sure. I can tell every time he runs in the opposite direction when he sees me coming.'

'He does that because you terrify him.'

'I haven't gone near him, for God's sake.'

'Precisely.'

'He rejected me outright.'

'He didn't know what to do! You scared him.'

'Is he a man or a mouse?'

'Finn, you're not much better.'

That was true. I was swimming in my shoes every time I knew he was near by.

'I miss him so much.' I sighed.

'Look, this can all be sorted out. He misses you too,' she said assuredly.

'How do you know?' I asked.

'Ion, of course, Colm hasn't stopped asking about you,' she said.

'Why is he with Julia, then?' I asked.

'Ion says it's to do with his mother. Ever since he

lost her, he hasn't been the same. I think he finds it hard to trust. Let's be honest about it. He never gets involved with anyone, not seriously. And Julia? Isn't she a little too old for him? She's an easy touch, makes him feel safe. That's a relationship that's going nowhere and Ion says that's exactly what suited Colm. Something not so serious, something that wouldn't involve real commitment. Then you came along and ruined it all,' she said.

'Are you serious? Did he really tell Ion he was missing me or is this one of your theories?' I asked.

'Ion trusts me. Everything he told me is the truth,' she confirmed.

I wasn't listening too well. Suddenly I was feeling the familiar soft ache under my arm again. I brought my hand to it.

'What's the matter?' Daria asked.

'Nothing.'

'There's something wrong.'

I didn't answer.

'There is, isn't there?' she probed.

'I'm having some problems,' I admitted.

'Problems?'

'Some pain and a small matter of numbness in my nipples,'

*'What? Since when?'*

'I'm not sure if it's anything to be concerned about.'

'You look uncomfortable. Have you been examining yourself like you're supposed to?' she asked.

I went quiet. Then I admitted, 'I'm afraid to look.' I beseeched her with my eyes: I needed to know that she wouldn't go berserk on me.

'What do you mean?' she asked, in a high-pitched squeak.

'I'm not sure what's wrong, but something is. I've been terrified to touch myself,' I confided.

'Let's go home and take a look,' she suggested.

I felt guilty again. Here I was presenting myself with more problems an hour after making up with her. I was becoming a bloody nuisance and was even getting on my own wick. We walked home, talking about the job and the changes that were going to take place in the near future. I told her how proud I was of her becoming assistant manager. She deserved it, and I knew she would make an excellent boss. Mark Adams's faith in her was evident: his support in the office that day must finally have put to rest any fears she might have had about her career.

I felt embarrassed to undress before her. She hadn't seen the beauty I had beheld some weeks previously. All Daria had ever witnessed was bruises and disfiguration. I wanted to prove to her that it was OK. But it wasn't and I had to face the truth that my naïveté had come full circle. In the darkness of the flat I exposed my body for her inspection. What had started out as numbness had gradually turned into a soft dull ache in the armpits that was steadily increasing in intensity. In fact, within twenty-four hours, something drastic had taken place. As I hadn't examined myself properly I wasn't prepared for Daria's reaction.

'What? What is it?'

'I think you better look for yourself,' she answered, her voice filled with foreboding.

My wardrobe had a full-length mirror attached to the inside of the door. I opened it. 'Oh, Jesus,' I cried.

Daria peered over my shoulder, her giraffe legs setting her a foot above my shoulders.

I pinched the puckered purple skin under my arm. The whole area was badly swollen and ached to touch.

'Oh, God,' Daria said.

'What am I going to do?' I stuttered.

'Calm down now. Think,' she urged.

'I'll have to call the Smile,' I said.

'What?' She was still staring at me in the mirror.

'I'll have to call the doctor,' I said, terror in my voice.

Daria let out a long sigh. 'What's he going to do?'

'I don't know. Have you any better suggestions?'

'Finn, *think* first.'

'*I am thinking*,' I said, exasperated.

'Let's talk this through.'

'Talk what through, for God's sake? Look at me! Where do you think we are? On the set of *ER*? I have to contact the plastic surgeon immediately,' I cried.

'He's just going to patch you up again. I wish you'd listen to me,' she shouted back.

'Don't say it,' I warned. 'Just don't say, "I told you so," right?'

'I wasn't going to say anything. I don't *know* what to say. I'm dumbstruck,' she said, putting her hand on my shoulder.

We both stood staring at the battered torso before us. If I had looked ugly before the operation, it was nothing compared to the sight I beheld now. I wanted to die with humiliation and fear. What if he couldn't do anything for me?

I stood in the centre of the room, Daria staring at me, speechless. It dawned on me that she was about as useful as an ashtray on a motorbike She couldn't help me. She couldn't perform miracles on the spot. She hadn't any answers and she didn't know what to do. I was responsible for this monstrosity and I would have to deal with it accordingly. I went straight to the telephone and dialled the plastic-surgery clinic's emergency mobile number.

I got through to the Smile almost immediately. He was no different on the phone than he was in person. He was still smiling: I could hear it down the line. My voice was quivering as tears gushed down my cheeks. He expressed no concern when I told him what was happening, simply instructed me to make an appointment to see him the next morning. Daria offered to make excuses for me at the Credit Union in case I had to miss work.

We sat on the battered couch, me holding my breasts feeling demoralized and small, her hugging me. 'It will be OK,' she reassured me, but we both knew that it wouldn't. Nothing would be OK and nothing would ever be the same again.

I had experienced the awesome power of the human body when it knows something is wrong. I had messed with the man upstairs. I had interfered with His perfect handiwork and my body was rebelling.

It was after ten p.m. before I could persuade Daria to leave. I reassured her over and over that I would be OK. I had to promise her several times that I would contact her the next day as soon as I'd seen the doctor. Ordinarily I would have begged her to stay, but this time I couldn't wait for her to go. I had something to do and I had to do it now. It couldn't wait.

I'm not sure what anyone would have thought if they had known that I had pulled up Colm's account information on the computer screen and written down his address. As a member of staff I had access to all that information. There wasn't time for moral rights or wrongs. After what Daria had confided, via Ion, I had to talk to him before I went back to the clinic.

# Chapter 25

Colm didn't live far from the Credit Union. I wondered why, after all this time, it had not dawned on me to do this before. But I sensed he wouldn't thank me for the visit: he had never invited any of us round.

I trudged up the small row of corporation houses until I found number twenty-four. I had a bundle of printouts under my arm. The backlog of filing was as high as Croagh Patrick and I suggested to Mark Adams that we all take some home with us and at least get it into alphabetic order. This gave me the permission to arrive unannounced. After all, had Colm not thrown a sickie, we wouldn't have been so far behind in our work.

It was about time he was made to take on a little extra responsibility, I told myself, as I pushed open a rusty old gate that hung on one hinge. The garden, if you could call it that, was a mass of tangled foliage. It looked more like a forest. The grass was at least two feet high and it was wild with dock leaves and nettles. More giant weeds had sprung up along the front wall. It reminded me of the wildness of Glenthulagh and I felt a twinge of guilt. I wondered how Mam was.

The house didn't look much better. The windows were especially bleak: the paint had peeled off and dirt clung to the panes. The gutters were clogged with leaves and debris. Bits of old machinery, paint pots, dead plants and plastic shopping-bags had cuddled up to the gate with the help of the east wind. An empty dog kennel lay upside-down in the alleyway. Window-boxes of withered pansies, unpruned rose bushes and a cobble-stoned patio lay neglected, and there was an overgrown rockery at the bottom of the garden. I would have had a fine time restoring it – it was the kind of thing that kept me occupied for hours back home.

The bell didn't work: I pushed it twice, then saw the severed cord running behind the door. I banged on it instead. No one answered and I felt uncomfortable. I had pulled out my notebook to double-check I had the right address when suddenly the door opened a few inches and an elderly man peered out.

'Oh, hello.' I smiled. 'I'm looking for Colm.'

The man peered at me for a few seconds. Then he slammed the door rather rudely. Right, I thought. That's that. I went to move off. The place was giving me the creeps anyway. Just then the door flung open. The man was peering out again. I took this as an invitation to enter, so I did. I stood in the hall in front of whom I guessed had to be Mr Long, Colm's father. He didn't look anything like him, though. He was a pale man with fair hair, thinning on top, and he was at least six feet tall. If he was Colm's father he couldn't have been more than fifty but he looked like he had seen at least another decade. He was a shocking sight, dirty, unshaven. He stank too, a sickly mixture of sweat and alcohol. He wore a pair of dark trousers, the knees out of shape, what had probably been a white vest and an old cardigan thrown over it. He had on a pair of slippers. The toes were torn and tatty-looking, as if a dog had chewed them. The whole house smelt of dogs. I expected to see a mutt come bounding out of nowhere.

'I'm a work colleague of Colm's,' I started.

The man just looked at me.

'My name is Finn,' I went on nervously.

Still he said nothing.

'I came to drop off some work for him. Is he in?' I asked.

He stared right through me. I wasn't sure if he had heard a word I said. He seemed not to understand anything. It almost appeared as if he didn't care to understand either. He had a faraway look in his eyes, expressionless, vacant. He shuffled from one foot to the other, and looked at me as if he was trying to figure out who I was. It was then I realized the man wasn't all there. Something was missing. His eyes mirrored a complete absence of life within.

He moved to the stairs and gestured me to follow. I did so reluctantly. The house was as bad inside as it was out, dirty, yellowed, musty wallpaper, threadbare carpets and that awful stale smell of dogs, alcohol and closed windows. At the top of the stairs, the man opened a door and led me in. I hadn't a clue where I was and there was no sign of Colm. I smiled at the man and he smiled back, an inane empty gesture. His lips moved but his eyes were dead. Then he turned and left me.

I was standing in Colm's room. It was easy to know it was his: evidence of him was strewn all over the place. I felt like I had been let loose inside Aladdin's cave. I was afraid his father was standing outside, but I heard a door close downstairs. I peeked out. Nobody was there. What the hell was I supposed to do now?

Colm's room was a mess too, but it had some order to it. I left down the huge wad of papers and wondered what to do next. Perhaps it would be best just to leave.

Who was I kidding? I had been invited to snoop round in the bedroom of the object of my affection. No woman in their right mind would pass up an opportunity like that. My breathing had quickened and I was excited. I wondered how much time I had before Colm returned from wherever he was.

His bedroom was a treasure trove of information. I set about gathering it as fast as I could. I wandered around touching his personal items. I could smell his aftershave on his clothes, most of which lay in a heap on the bed. The only thing that hung in his wardrobe was his work suit, immaculate as always. My maternal instincts got into gear. I took a pair of crumpled jeans and folded them properly. I checked the insides to see what size he was. Thirty-two-inch waist, 32 inch leg. It was nice to be so close to him without having to rattle and shake with nerves as I did in the presence of the genuine article. This way, I could enjoy him.

I ran my hands over his pillow. I could breathe in his essence. I imagined his head on it. I wanted to lie down on the bed, lay my head on that pillow and plunge my hands into his dreams. Instead I laid my cheek in the dent he had made and inhaled the memory.

Then I noticed his books. At first I thought there might be a hundred or so, and was surprised: I never saw Colm read anything. When I moved closer, I found there were more behind them, hundreds upon hundreds. He had made a crude bookcase out of bricks, one on top of the other. A dash of colour on one showed that he had probably intended to paint them but given up. I liked the bricks the way they were. He had probably thought the same. I smiled. We weren't as different from each other as we had imagined. I picked up a couple of the books and read the titles. *Marilyn Monroe*, *Jimi Hendrix* and *Malcolm X*, an interesting selection. Then I found books about George Best and Jack Charlton and, frankly, I was intrigued. Most were biography or autobiography, a lot of stuff about football. The intrigue turned to bafflement.

Even more interesting were the bookmarks, all resting somewhere around the middle. He hadn't finished any of them. Odd as be damned, I thought.

I wandered about the room picking up this and that, and found more evidence of the same thing. A half-constructed Airfix model, a half-finished two-thousand-piece jigsaw puzzle. Just like Colm: nothing added up; nothing was ever finished. Many fits and starts and good intentions, but nothing finalised.

The more I observed, the closer I felt to him. I wanted to understand Colm. I thought it best to give up poking around – I was invading his privacy. I picked up my coat and was about to leave when something else caught my attention. Huddled carefully under a set of old full-length curtains were several cardboard boxes. I opened one and almost gasped when I saw what was inside. I had expected to see the greatest pornographic collection ever, but I lifted out a trophy, then another. Inscribed on each were Colm's name, a date, and what it was for. Football. I drew a deep breath, but Colm hated sports? At least, that was what he had told all of us. It didn't add up, the books, the hidden accolades. Some of the trophies were heavy, and they all dated back to the 1980s. The last one I could see was for 1990. He had won 'man of the match'. For whom, I wondered. A dark horse or what? Black Beauty hadn't a patch on him.

There were some smaller boxes too. I pulled them out gently – I felt they were sacred articles, even if he didn't.

They were full of medals, all for football. No wonder he had such awful knees, I thought. He must have been good, though. It made me want to cry. Why had he hidden all this from me? Why had he abandoned something that was obviously a gift? Why all the secrecy? It felt eerie. I connected with something vague yet instantly familiar in myself.

I fondled the medals, then decided I was overstepping the mark. I was taking advantage of his absence, and if he had done this to me I would be very upset. I couldn't imagine Colm poking through my personal belongings. He would never have done such a thing. All of a sudden I felt guilty. I wanted to get out of there. I put them all back. Except the last box.

It was wrapped carefully with a satin ribbon. A pretty box with shells stuck on it, a child's box. I couldn't resist it. I listened for a moment, but the house was silent. I undid the ribbon, my hand shaking. I found a photograph inside, a torn photograph. Someone had put it back together crudely with brown masking tape, but I could still make out the face. Instantly I recognised the beauty, the smile and the eyes. It was unmistakable. It had to be his mother. There was also a letter to him, dated 1997. It was signed 'Mam'. That was only three years ago. She might have died since. But he had always talked about her like she had been dead for many years. That was weird. What had happened to make him do that? I wanted to know the truth. I wanted to know him.

'What the fuck do you think you're doing?' I hadn't heard him enter the room, but I didn't have to look behind me to know that he was furious and that I was up to my neck in it. I stood up and turned to face him. He was white in the face, eyes ablaze.

'I'm sorry,' I tried.

'Who let you in here?' He grabbed the box off me.

'Your Dad, I think . . . I came to give you—' I tried.

'Please leave immediately.' He ushered me towards the door.

'Look, wait, we need to talk.'

He grabbed my arm and pulled me towards the door.

'Colm, you're hurting my arm,' I beseeched him. He was livid. He wasn't listening. He wasn't aware of what he was doing.

I struggled to set myself free of his grip but he was strong. 'Don't make me do this,' he raged at me.

'Look, calm down, will you? Let go of my arm and I'll leave.' I sniffled. He looked from me to his hand, which was holding my arm in a vice-like grip. He let it go abruptly.

'You've no right to go snooping around my room,' he hissed.

'I know. I didn't mean to. Your Dad brought me up here and I didn't know if you were in or not and I just found myself—' I faltered.

'Just found yourself being fucking nosy? he jeered.

'I'm sorry.' I felt ashamed. I wanted to explain that I wasn't being nosy, just curious about him. I wanted to get closer to him.

'You know, you have no sense of boundaries,' he said. His beautiful green eyes had turned a steely grey.

'What?' I didn't understand.

'You don't seem to know where you end and I begin. You take liberties like it's perfectly acceptable. You're like a fucking terrorist taking people hostage.'

My face burned. If he was referring to the nightclub I thought it was a horrible assault on my already deflated ego. 'I was only trying to get to know you.' I gulped.

'If that was the case all you had to do was ask.'

'I'm not perfect,' I said. 'I made a mistake. I thought you were interested in me,' I tried to stay calm.

'I am interested in you, but you make things really difficult,' he threw back. 'Anytime I try to hold an intelligent conversation with you, you back off. I got tired of trying.'

'And you don't think you behave the exact same way, Colm? You don't think that you move one step forwards and then ten back?'

'Is this a game of chess, Finn? I move, you move, checkmate?' he roared.

'I beg your pardon!' I shouted now. 'Who do you think you are? Richard Gere from *An Officer and a Gentleman*? Look at your own behaviour. One minute you're all over me, the next you're off with someone else. What was I to think? If you wanted us to be just friends you should have bloody said so instead of humiliating me beyond belief. You don't even seem to be able to decide who you want to be with. At least I'm not running around with some old bastard that I don't care about just for the sake of it.'

'It's none of your business who I'm with,' he said coldly. He was right, of course, but it hurt to hear him pushing me out like I didn't matter.

'Of course it's none of my business, but I will tell you what *is* my business. If you want to behave like Rudolph Valentino, do it with someone else, because you know what? I can't take it. I took it seriously. I took you seriously.' I was quaking inside.

'I took you seriously too. I don't see you like I see the others. You wouldn't understand.' He brushed past me and began moving all his boxes back behind the curtains.

'Well, you could have fooled me! Am I stupid now?

Is that what you're saying? Not only am I a terrorist but I'm a thick shite as well?'

'Yes. As a matter of fact sometimes I think you are. If you just for once opened your eyes—' He didn't get any further than that: I was incensed.

'Well, excuse me for being human!' I shouted. 'At least I had the guts to tell someone the truth about myself, you know what I mean? What's so wrong with that? I wanted you and I thought you wanted me too. So I took a chance. Don't tell me you didn't lead me on, Colm, that it was all in my imagination.' I threw my coat on his bed.

'No. It wasn't all in your imagination, but I have a little problem with what you call the truth,' he said. 'Since when did you become honest, Finn? Yesterday or was it just a minute ago? Like when the big bad wolf fell down the chimney and found his arse in the boiling water.'

'I don't know what you're on about. But don't make yourself out to be in Mother Teresa's little black book. At least I haven't buried my mother while she's still alive. What a lousy thing to tell any of us. What a horrible thing to say about your own mother! You told me she was dead! You've told me so many lies about yourself I don't know who you are any more.'

'You don't need to know anything about my mother, right?' he yelled.

'Why not?' I roared.

'Because I don't know a fucking thing about yours! You could have told me she was dead too and I would have believed you. You never go near her so she might as well be!' he charged on.

'Don't you speak to me like that.' I had started to cry now, really cry. 'I don't particularly like talking about my mother, OK? I never lied about her either. I was honest at least.'

'Honest? Skinny, you wouldn't know honesty if Billy Joel appeared in the flesh in your bedroom and sang the Goddamn song in your face. You know what I mean? Look at yourself. I never thought I would see the day you'd stoop so low as to have those fucking ridiculous implants put in.'

My stomach curdled. I thought I'd die on the spot. My breath left my body. I felt myself melt and crumble into tiny pieces. I opened my mouth to answer him back but nothing came.

I picked up my coat and held it protectively against my chest. 'I bet you didn't complain when Julia had one shoved in your mouth,' I said coldly.

He froze.

I knew all about Julia's boob job. In fact, the whole Credit Union knew about it yet it wasn't discussed openly. She didn't care to keep secrets, not even that she was dating a man half her age. Did he really think I didn't know about her operation. He sure as hell did! What was he going to say now?

'Look, I . . .' He pushed his fingers back through his hair. His foot was tapping wildly. 'Finn, I didn't mean it that way. I'm sorry, forgive me.' He stood in my way.

'Fuck you,' I spat. I walked out, slamming the door behind me. The tears were streaming down my face. I paused at the bottom of the stairs.

'Finn? Finn, wait! I'm sorry,' Colm called after me.

Mr Long was in the hallway, walking around in circles talking to himself. Colm's bedroom door closed. I could hear him thrashing about upstairs. My breasts ached from all the shouting. I drew my arm up to them, but I wasn't thinking about the pain there. It was the pain in my breaking heart that hurt most.

# Chapter 26

The next morning, I was back in the plastic-surgery clinic. I was in a good deal of pain now and it wasn't all physical. My world was falling apart. For the first time in my life, I knew it. Instead of being able to shove it all into some far recess of my puny brain it was all out there for me to see.

I thought it ironic that the pain had centred itself in the heart region. I was sure my heart was actually breaking, that I could feel it. And I could see the error of my ways: my vanity stared back at me in the shape of disfigurement I had inflicted on myself. Sure, the Smile had carried out the operation but I had instructed him to. Now I had to pay for the consequences of my actions. It wasn't going to cost me any money, but my soul was on the block and negotiations weren't looking too hot.

I wondered was God punishing me. Had He, in fact, deflated my heart? Had He had to go to such lengths to get my attention? Was it the only way He could intervene in my emotional suicide? Was He going to have to strike me dead before I understood that I was, in fact, very much alive? That I wasn't the horror I believed myself to be. That I counted, I mattered, that my breasts were only a part of me. They had a purpose and I had misconstrued their role in my life. I had thrown the baby out with the bath water.

I sat on a leather couch in the interviewing room rocking backwards and forwards, for the first time ever feeling protective towards my own physical well being. A piece of me had gone missing. The grief at its loss was surfacing. I drew my arms round my chest in a loving embrace. I dreaded the thought of another spectator, pulling and tugging at me. I wasn't dead. I was still alive. I wanted to feel what that was like again. I wondered what it would feel like to treat myself like a decent human being?

I had begun to feel dehumanized now, like some laboratory specimen. I thought back to Lolo Ferrari, how debilitated she must have felt by the constant pressure to show her boobs for the boys. If her death had been suicide I could understand it now.

How lonely she must have felt and how ugly she must have thought she was to butcher every single God-given physical attribute. I had seen some photos of Lolo long before she had had any operations done. I had been shocked by just how lovely she was *before* the knife had cut it all away. Her breasts were already big and beautiful and she was a very good-looking woman.

The Smile came to see me in the same interviewing room where he had unveiled the new me only a few months previously. I went through the same procedure and undressed in a dazed ritual. I couldn't get Colm's words out of my head. They cut to the bone.

'What?' I stared up at the doctor. He was talking ninety to the dozen. I hadn't been listening to a word.

'See here. We will have to carry out a capsulotomy,' he was saying. 'This problem started with contracture.'

'A what?'

'It's when the capsule around the implant begins to harden,' he continued pulling at the nipple as if it was the teat of a used condom. I felt like a prostitute.

'Have you had any loss of sensation in this area?' he asked.

'Yes.'

'Had you called me earlier I could have fixed it,' he said.

'What has happened?' I asked.

'Implant has ruptured. Sorry. We'll have to replace it now, I'm afraid,' he said.

'Right now?' I was terrified. All I could think of was the pain – and where had the implant gone? Was it floating around in my stomach, because it certainly felt like it, or was it the great big lump that was now wedged in my throat? I covered my eyes with my hands and began to sob.

The Smile carried on with his notes, smiling, smiling, smiling. I hated him so much, yet I needed him to fix me. He had the power to transform me and I had given him that power. I didn't have a choice, or so I felt.

'What are you going to do with me?' I asked, like a child.

'I will have to survey damage first,' he said, with no emotion whatsoever. He behaved like he was chopping off the top of a boiled egg at breakfast time.

'What damage?' I rushed.

'How long has pain been under arm?'

'About forty-eight hours,' I answered.

'About forty-eight hours, yes?'

'Yes.'

'This could mean it has been longer.'

'What?'

'The implant may have ruptured some days ago.'

'Why didn't I feel it?'

'It would take some days. See here, the silicone has begun to gather.'

He prodded under my swollen arm.

'Christ!' I uttered. 'So this silicone stuff is swimming around my body?'

'Can't tell until I go in,' he said matter-of-factly.

'What if I don't replace the implant?' I found myself asking all of a sudden. 'What would happen then?'

'I would have to remove the other,' he answered, looking a bit wary.

'Is there a problem with that?'

'No. If that's what you want,' he said, eyebrows raising and injecting doubt into my already petrified mind.

'What if it was what I want? What would be the results?'

'Well . . .' He chewed a black biro. 'Your skin has been stretched heavily with the implants. I'm obliged to inform you that your breasts won't look the way they did before.'

'What?' I blurted. 'I thought a reversal of the operation was a simple procedure.'

'It is,' he said coldly.

'But you can't guarantee it will look OK?'

'I'm afraid not. I would strongly advise you to go for another implant. These problems are common enough. It can be fixed.' He eyed me like I was an imbecile.

'What are the chances of it happening again? That the next implant won't burst? That I won't get infected or have hardened nipples?' I almost shouted.

'Every woman is different. As I explained to you before, some women experience no problems at all. There is no way to tell how the body will react to foreign substances.'

I sat with my head between my knees and tried to conjure up some logic. This was difficult as I had been living in an illusion all of my life. The first stirrings of reality were being awakened in the form of a strange substance called silicone that was invading *my* body. I had put it there, yet I couldn't remove it without putting it back in again. It seemed absurd and a cruel twist of fate. I was suddenly consumed with guilt. It felt a bit like the irony of the billion abortions carried out in room A; while in room B another woman struggles her whole life trying to conceive and cannot and only God knows why.

How many times would I have to go through with this? Was it going to be a constant source of worry and tension? Was I going to spend the rest of my life in and out of plastic surgery and end up looking like Jar Jar Binks from *Star Wars*? I was beginning to see that, despite the best of intentions, not everything in life could be *forced* to work out properly. My breasts were refusing to co-operate. My body was rejecting my head. It was telling me something. As the doctor droned on about anaesthetics, prosthetics and saline implants my mind wandered aimlessly in and out of the myriad truths that were assaulting my conscience.

'You must decide now,' he was saying, tapping his fingers lightly on the side of his nice safe, steady office desk.

'I don't have any choice,' I whispered.

'Are you sure?'

'Do what you have to do,' I said.

You can't treat measles with makeup, they say. It doesn't work. I discovered this as I sat with my back to the wall, staring out into the future. What did it hold now? I had run out of tears. I held my chest with crossed arms, terrified that if I let go, my heart would fall out.

* * *

Seven days after the operation I saw all the damage. The silicone, mercifully, had gathered mostly in my ribcage. It had been scraped out and I had been stitched back together with new implants in place. I still wasn't sure I wanted new ones. For the moment I had made a decision not to make a decision about whether I would leave them in permanently.

I huddled myself in the silence of it all and found Fainche. Like the prodigal daughter returned home, I could hear her familiar voice in the wind in the trees outside. I could hear her distant tinkling on the piano, like an echo in a dream. She was calling me like a fretful child who had lost her mother. Only she wasn't my daughter, she was me. It was Fainche calling me, begging me to take her home. So I stopped and I listened and I heard . . .

*I am sixteen, I am in bed with the flu and I'm in an awful lot of trouble. I seem to cause nothing but trouble lately. No matter what I do it causes a row between Mam and Dad. Mind you, I'm not surprised it was a real humdinger this time. It was a bit naïve of me to think I could get away with kissing a boy down the back lane. I have no freedom. Dad is like a stalker, following me around, waiting to catch me out.*

*I swear he hides out, biding his time, now that he has nothing better to do. It's not as if it's abnormal at my age to kiss a boy. All the girls are doing it. I don't see why he has to carry on like I've had full sex. It was just an innocent kiss and my Dad was on us like a maniac. He must have been watching us a good while. He dragged me up the lane screaming at the top of his voice for the entire world to hear: 'You'll be the death of your mother!'*

*My mother couldn't have cared less what I was doing. She was busy baking for his retirement party at the GAA club.*

*I was grounded good and proper. My Dad answers the door*

*to my friends and sends them away while I'm in Coventry up here. I swear he gets pleasure out of keeping me from them – and Mam. At least I'm off school and don't have to do any study. I genuinely developed the flu. I probably got it off Billy, the boy I was kissing, because my Dad called to his parents and he was in bed sick too. Oh, the humiliation! Why does he have to embarrass me like that?*

*I don't mind being sick. I love it. It's the only time Mam gets to look after me properly and Dad doesn't interfere. She always makes a real fuss over me. She brings me chicken soup and toast and . . . Energyade. Ever since I was a little thing she has insisted on buying it. Even at sixteen, she forces me to drink a glass of it. She says it's good for me and that it will make me healthy and strong. We never get to taste anything other than water or tea usually, so I don't mind drinking it. It's lovely and sweet. When I feel sad or lonely, I often go to the local shop and buy some for myself, but I wouldn't tell Mam: she'd think it very silly of me.*

*I love hearing her footsteps coming up the stairs. I can hear the cutlery rattling on the old tin tray. Dad can't say a thing because I'm sick and she stays with me for ages. I think she wants to get away from Dad as much as I do. I don't even know why I call him 'Dad'. He's not my real Dad and he has always let me know this in his way. Mam confirmed this for me when I was fifteen but she needn't have. I knew already. Mam and I have great talks in my room when I'm ill. Mam potters around the room, tidying up and polishing, fixing the bedclothes. I feel like a little girl again when she does that. Things were a lot happier when it was just Mam and I, even though we had no money.*

*As a toddler, I remember sitting on her lap in the big garden, making daisy chains and hanging them round her neck. She used to laugh and we'd roll down the hill clinging to each other. The daisy chains would break, I would start to cry and Mam would cuddle me close. I can still smell the bleach on her hands and the scent of the lavender she used to put in our clothes drawers. I suppose she feels she did the right thing by marrying Dad. I can't blame her for making that decision.*

*He used to call to the boarding-house to collect insurance money from the Sisters of Charity. Mam used to make him his tea. It must have been hard for her being a disgraced woman. We had nowhere else to stay and if it wasn't for the nuns' kindness we would have been homeless. She never told me all of what happened, how she got pregnant out of wedlock and ended up on her own raising me. I don't even know who my real Dad is. Mam said it was a one-night stand and that my real Dad wasn't interested in helping us. I often wondered, was he musical? Had he played the piano? I certainly hadn't got the music buzz from Mam.*

*I guess she saw my stepdad as a way out, a chance to find her way into a society that rejects misfits and fallen angels. As a married woman, a woman with status, she would be accepted into the community. It's no wonder she jumped at the chance when he showed an interest in her and finally offered his hand. I dare say the nuns were glad to see the back of us too.*

*Now I watch Mam as she glides round the room, humming because she is free to be near me, free to show me her love. I guess my stepdad felt he had taken on a great responsibility. He certainly never liked me. When Padraig and Fearghal were born, they were the apple of his eye. He only ever had time for the boys. Girls are no use, especially those who are not your own. I think my stepdad has spent his life trying to ignore the fact that I exist, and Mam has tried her best to live in his world.*

*He never stops reminding her of how lucky she is, as if that gives him permission to make me suffer. I know Mam has her own guilt. She cries at night. I hear her often. I know she must feel remorse and regret. But it doesn't have to be this way. She doesn't have to sell her daughter's soul for a home. I would have been happier with the nuns and at least I would have had her exclusive love.*

*We have a decent house to live in, and I know how much that means to Mam, but what a price we have paid for it. I am sure she thought it was the right thing to do by me, that I would have a chance of a decent upbringing and an education. I wish I could tell her that I would give it all up just so we could be ourselves again . . .*

# Chapter 27

I suddenly understood how Beethoven wrote the most rapturous of melodies yet was deaf, how the voiceless and mute could write the most passionate poetry. I also understood why the great artists needed no idyllic setting to produce a masterpiece of detail with a simple piece of broken chalk. I understood how they painted rich landscapes, rolling mountains and green meadows from nothing more than a vivid imagination. They had developed a sixth sense with their impairment. I had had to have my sight taken away, too, before I could see. I was blinded by self-absorption. As soon as I understood this, my new eyes opened and I was back inside Fainche.

She felt strange at first. She was surly and morose. I brought my arms round her and cuddled her, for no amount of words were ever going to make up for the brutality I had unleashed on her. I had abandoned her, abused and ridiculed her.

I had spent my entire life believing that acceptance had to come from the outside, that somebody would come along and hand it to me on a silver platter. Then I would be free. I had craved my mother's approval. I had yearned for my stepfather's love and acknowledgement. I was a girl and he didn't want a girl. I took it into my heart and held it there. It wasn't his fault, it wasn't even my mother's, she had only done what she thought was right for us both. My mother wanted what he wanted. I wanted what they wanted, so I strove to fulfil their long-held wishes, their dreams.

I made myself the patent of their deep-seated ambitions. I behaved like a boy, I tried to be a boy and of course, in the end, I truly believed *I was a boy*.

In this abandonment of self, I compromised that which is most sacred: my soul. It knocked around my life like a spectre. I caught glimpses of its shadow when I was mysteriously called to open the lid of the piano. I heard it play the hammers on the soundboard. I felt it when I touched the ivory keys, or when I ran my hand absently over the brass music stand. I could smell it when I breathed in the scent of polish on old wood, or listened to my tapes.

And where was Colm's soul? Out haunting. Hanging out with mine. I'd held it in my hand when I stumbled on his talent for football. I touched it when I picked up the trophies he had hidden away. I heard it when he raged at me for discovering it. I sensed it in his eyes, in his fury. Not only had I detected it, I had then gone on to do the unforgivable. *I had taken it out of the box*. I knew how much that had hurt him. Neither of us had been careful enough: we hadn't thought to seal the boxes. We had left them open only a tiny gap, but it was big enough for someone to get a hand in. Maybe we had done it deliberately.

In exploring Colm's secrets I had been forced to explore my own. I had locked out my creativity in my futile search for love and acceptance. I had been waiting for permission to be myself. But all along I had had the answer inside me. The key was in a lock on the inside, not the outside. I just hadn't figured out how to use it and now it felt like the lock had rusted over. Nobody was going to let me out. I had to do it myself. I had to call a stand-off, reach an agreement, and negotiate a peace treaty with Fainche. At first she argued.

Fair enough, I reasoned. If I were you I wouldn't pay any attention to me either, but we both have to live in this carcass of a body. We can be enemies and fight to the bitter end or we can come together and be a team. Together we can grow our hair long with big fat curls. We can get our ears pierced and wear gypsy bandannas and do salsa dancing when we see Will Smith on MTV.

We can take classes if you want! It's OK if you want to wear inappropriate clothes, seventies makeup and go barefoot when you leave the garbage out! Just think, we can binge on family-sized packets of crisps, whole blocks of Neapolitan ice-cream and gallons of Energyade. We can visit the Bahamas, drink coconut milk from a shell and do the hula-hula in nothing but a grass skirt. We can go naked, for all I care. We can even pick our toenails and pull our knickers out from between the cheeks of our arse in public. I won't bat an eyelid. Oh . . . and by the way, you and I can play the piano as badly and as childishly as we wish . . . What do you say? I cajoled.

She was speechless with the relief of being acknowledged after all those years of silence and I respected that. She curled up and cried on my shoulder. It was the crying of a river so deep that the rapids threatened to drown us both. But we held on. She clung to me and I to her as we raced through the grieving of a million deaths and separations.

It wasn't possible for me to see what the final outcome would be. The physical pain had initially been as bad as it had been after the first operation but somehow I endured it with more humility this time because I felt I deserved it. In some ways it was welcome. As sore as the emptying of my implants was, it didn't compare to the pain of the emptying of my own spirit. That was an operation in itself and I had no anaesthetic to ease the constant ache. There was nothing to do but hold myself in it and hope that it didn't overwhelm me.

Daria arrived at the hospital. She was quiet and nervous, a red rose drooping in her hand. 'Hi,' she said, smiling.

'For me?' I asked, looking at the rose. I put out my hand and touched its velvety petals. Even with its prickly thorns it exuded its own unique beauty. Just like a human being, I thought. 'Thanks,' I croaked.

'Oh, it's not from me.' She sat down on the bed. The covers pulled at the dressings on my chest and I flinched. 'Sorry,' she said.

'It's OK. It's a lot better today.'

She handed me the rose and I took it eagerly. 'Who is it from?' I asked.

'Colm.' She flicked her black tresses behind her shoulders.

*'What?'*

'There's another forty or so outside. The nurse is trying to find a vase big enough to put them in.'

'Daria, this isn't the time to make jokes,' I said.

'I'm not joking,' she replied.

My lip was quivering.

'He knows everything. I told him,' she said quietly.

'Oh, God, that's all I need.'

'He wouldn't leave me alone, kept asking where you were.'

'Bloody hell. That's it, then, isn't it? He'll never lay eyes on me again.'

'You're wrong there. He's outside,'

*'What?'*

'He's outside.'

*'You let him come here?'*

'He insisted.'

'I can't let him see me like this, I can't!'

'Yes, you can, and you must.'

'Are you crazy?' I barked.

'This is the way it is.'

'It wasn't meant to be this way!' I wept.

'Finn. He doesn't care.'

'Oh, God.'

'Let him come in.'

'No! I'm too ashamed,' I pleaded, hot tears pouring down my cheeks. She was a tower of strength. She wiped my face with a tissue, smiling all the time like there was nothing wrong.

'Listen to me now, Finn. Just listen up. Swallow your pride. A man doesn't show up at a plastic-surgery clinic to pay his last respects, you know. He's out of his mind with worry and he wants to talk to you. That is not the behaviour of a man who doesn't want you. Do you hear me?' Her voice was low, but firm and comforting.

I sat up in the bed, trying desperately to cover myself and realized how stupid I was being. There wasn't any way I could hide myself now. 'I'm so embarrassed.'

There was nowhere to hide, nowhere to run, no false personality to cushion the humiliation. Yet Colm was waiting outside. What the hell were we going to say to each other? I thought of all the romantic nights I had planned, the seductive plots I had painstakingly drawn up. A fat lot of good they were now. I had always imagined me being in bed and he would just get in and make passionate love to me. I was in bed now, scarred and mutilated, and the irony was almost too much to bear. Daria stood up.

'Wait, Daria, don't go,' I pleaded.

'No.' She put her hand on mine. 'Trust me. It will be fine.' She walked to the door.

Then I saw a man's figure just outside and, very quietly, he stepped into the room. I couldn't lift my head to meet his eyes, I just couldn't. I couldn't get out of the bed and walk away. I couldn't hide the massive bandaging around my chest. I couldn't disguise the fact that I was in a bed in a plastic-surgery clinic. I couldn't hide the fact that my nightclothes were granny-type pyjamas and not some slinky chiffon see-through ensemble. I couldn't disguise my blotchy eyes because I had no makeup on.

I couldn't do anything about my hair, which was dirty and knotted. I hadn't been able to have a bath recently and I hadn't even brushed my teeth. I wanted to curl up and die. You see, it wasn't just Colm. In facing him, I was about to face them all, all the men who had hurt me. I heard their ghostly footsteps hovering around me and I knew that to get rid of them once and for all I was going to have to let them in. In seeing Colm they would be banished for ever and I would be able to integrate Fainche and Finn. At last I would be the complete me.

# Chapter 28

Colm stood awkwardly his hand on the door.

'Yo, Skin,' he whispered, afraid to come any closer.

'Colm,' I said, eyes downcast.

'Is it OK to come in?' he asked, taking a faltering step closer to the bed.

'Do I have a choice?' I asked.

'No, actually.' He shuffled over.

I could see his shoes as they approached the bed. When he stood still his left foot was pounding the floor faster than Michael Flatley's in his most memorable performance. I was relieved: it told me he was as nervous as I was. I felt the bed dip as he sat on it.

'Hi,' he said, lowering his head. He tried to make contact with my eyes, but I couldn't look up and I couldn't speak. 'Right,' he said to himself, rubbing his chin.

I twisted the rose in my hand. I felt the thorns prick my skin and it wasn't as painful as I'd thought it would be. I was reassured by this small symbolic gesture from Mother Earth. The silence between us was deafening. He twisted and turned on the edge of the bed, not knowing what to say or do. I bit my lip until I could almost taste blood. Colm hummed a tune. I recognized it. It was 'I'm Stone In Love With You'. I smiled to myself. He just kept humming and I knew he was still looking at me, asking me to meet his eyes.

I chanced an upward glance but found once I had raised my head I couldn't get it to go back down again. Like a kid in a toyshop, I was sucked in. I couldn't tear away my eyes. His aftershave filled the room. 'What is it called, that aftershave?' I asked.

'Pi,' he said looking surprised at such a trivial question in what were extremely difficult moments.

'As in chicken pie or pork pie?' I queried, thinking it a bit of an odd name for a man's aftershave. It didn't smell like sausages.

'No, dope. Pi, as in the symbol.' He drew three fingers over his left hand and tried to demonstrate, then dropped his hands abruptly.

'It's nice,' I remarked, knowing it was the dumbest thing I had ever said. He eyed me suspiciously. We both went to speak together.

'Listen I just want to . . .' he started.

'Look, Colm . . .' I tried.

'You go first,' he said quietly.

'Is there some particular reason why you called to see me?' I asked.

'Yes.'

'Well, then, you speak,' I invited him.

'Are you sure you're going to listen?' He probed me with his intense stare.

'Well, I don't have anything urgent to attend to,' I said, opening my arms out and staring down at my chest.

We both half laughed.

'That was a pretty expensive trip,' he started.

'Excuse me?' I twirled the corner of a pillow until it almost tore off in my hand.

'America. Cost you, didn't it?' He smiled. I hated his honesty as much as I pined for it.

'Yes. Well. I won't be going there again.'

'I suppose not.'

'It cost me a lot more than money, you know.'

'Gambling only pays when you're winning,' he quipped. 'Sorry.' He shrugged his shoulders and fiddled with his left sock.

There was an awkward silence.

'Look. I can't tell you how sorry I am for what I said about your breast implants,' he said. 'It came out all wrong. It wasn't what I meant to say. It was nasty.' He cleared his throat.

Well, that was something, but I wasn't going to say it for him. I wasn't going to do his dirty work. I wasn't going to put the right words in his mouth. He would have to search his own heart and find them.

'I should have explained but, you know, it's easier to put your head in the sand and hope it will all work itself out. I'm not perfect,' he whispered.

'Yes, I understand,' I replied. 'The strange thing is, Colm, I always assumed you were perfect. Isn't that weird? I really thought that.'

'Oh, Skinny, you're a laugh a minute!' He was in genuine stitches. 'You're wrong. You're so dead wrong! I'm not perfect.' His eyes found me and I locked mine into position. The foot was meandering and had taken on a life of its own now. It was flapping faster than Gene Kelly running up and down the walls in *Singing In the Rain*.

'You're wrong, Finn,' he repeated, quieter now. 'Everybody has something. Some people learn how to disguise their imperfections well.'

'Yeah. And sometimes they stand out like two Goddamn flashlights. Sometimes it's real bloody obvious.' I pointed to my chest.

'OK, so what you're saying is, if a flaw is not immediately obvious to the naked eye it doesn't exist. Is that it?' He frowned, looking disappointed that I could be so short-sighted and narrow-minded.

'I hadn't thought about it that way,' I admitted.

'I know,' he said.

'Why did you do it, Colm? Why did you lie to me? Your mother? About the football?' I asked boldly.

'I lied because . . . I thought the truth wasn't good enough,' he said.

I hadn't a word to say to that.

'Look, think about it. Why did you do this to yourself?' he said, pointing a finger at me.

'I suppose I felt I had to. I suppose I felt the truth about me wasn't good enough either.'

'Exactly. I thought that too. I thought I had to do certain things as well. I thought I had to keep myself aloof. I thought I had to be an island. I thought I had to protect myself at all costs. If I let people get close, really get to know me? Well, then, they would find out all that I'm not,' he said softly.

'Is that why you rejected me?' I asked, intrigued.

'Yes. I felt I had to,' he insisted.

'Why?' I asked.

'Because of my past experiences, I found it impossible to trust women.'

'OK, but you didn't have to reject me like that. All you had to do was tell me straight. You should have told me we were only friends and that Julia was the important one,' I rattled on, tears forming in my eyes.

'Yes. If I was a perfect guy I would have handled it differently, but I'm not, you see. I couldn't tell you anything. I hadn't the balls. Don't you understand? I was afraid.' He was struggling.

'You couldn't? Or wouldn't? Did I not deserve to be told the truth?' I cried.

'Yes, of course you did.' He bit his lip. 'You deserve the lot. The whole shooting gallery! How could I have told you about her? How could I have told you how I felt about you when I was certain I'd mess it up? It isn't what it seems. With Julia . . .' He paused.

'Oh, please. Don't do this. It sounds all too familiar. Next thing you'll be telling me she's your wife and that she doesn't understand you or some other equally pathetic made-up piece of rubbish.'

'Will you wait?' he implored.

But I wouldn't. 'It's this, isn't it?' I pointed to the bandages. I didn't care – what was there left to be modest about? It was all smashed, destroyed, broken into little bits.

'No!' he persisted. 'No, no, no! It was never that. But you'll never believe me, no matter what I say, will you? You have this idea firmly cemented in your head.' He pointed his forefinger at his temple to ram home the point. 'You've got this idea that the only important thing about you is your breasts. For Christ's sake! The only person obsessed with them is you! I never noticed anything wrong with them. I never took note of them at all! I was only ever interested in *you*, but you were too preoccupied with your body to notice.' He folded his arms.

It was one – all. I didn't know how to proceed.

'Well, if I'm not the problem, what is?' I cried, tears streaming down my face.

'It's me!' he yelled, pounding his fist on his chest. 'Can you stop thinking about yourself long enough just to let that thought in, just a tiny *teensy-weensy* bit, just let it mooch on in there, slip in sideways or something?

Just give it a chance, can you do that?' he said, exasperated.

'Don't talk to me like I'm an asshole,' I cried.

'I'm sorry, let me try again.'

I bit my lip in silence.

'Julia's not important,' he choked.

'Well, how am I expected to believe that when every time I turn my head she's in your bloody face?' I argued.

'She doesn't mean anything to me. She's a prostitute, OK? She's a high-class hooker, right?'

*'Excuse me? What did you just say?'*

'She's a prostitute,' he said lowering his head.

'A prostitute? Christ, please tell me you're kidding, right?' I was shocked.

'I wish I was. I wish I could lie to you, but it's the truth. I thought it was the right thing to do. It suited me. It was easier, OK? That way I didn't have to worry about making a balls of things with a real woman. No commitment, no emotional involvement. That way I didn't get hurt and no one else did either.'

I didn't understand how he could be with a prostitute and not me. 'Well, that speaks in volumes, doesn't it? I mean about what you think of me. What made you think I wouldn't be hurt when you walked away and left me standing in the middle of that dance-floor?' I sobbed.

'I know. God, I'm sorry. I can see the stupidity of it now. I'm sorry I hurt you. It was the last thing I wanted to do. I thought I was doing you a favour, saving you from pain. I wanted you to be happy,' he said.

'Do I look happy?' I asked sarcastically.

'I've seen you better.'

'Oh, Colm, you're such hard work.'

'I love you to bits, you know.' He smiled a warm,

loving smile at me. 'I love everything about you, the way you chew your lip, the way your hips sway when you move across the office, the way you make a mountain out of a molehill but you're really enjoying yourself, and the way you try to hide the love in your eyes when it's plain to see you care,' he exhaled. 'I even love the way you slurp that Energyade stuff and the way you hide your sweets in the torn pocket of your uniform jacket . . .'

I blushed.

'What's wrong with you? Are you deaf and blind as well as everything else? Do you not understand that I've always loved you?' he implored.

'You hurt me, badly,' I mumbled.

He put his hand over my mouth so I couldn't speak. 'Listen, my pet. You're not the only one who got hurt. You're not the only one who trusted and got messed up, dumped, deserted. I know all about people fucking off. My Mam fucked off on my Dad ten years ago for a man twenty years younger than her. She left me to deal with the aftermath. Look at my Dad. Look at the state of him. How do you think a kid handles a thing like that, eh?'

I was speechless.

'Every day I've had to sit there and watch him die slowly of a broken heart. He's given up. He might as well be dead. She killed him. I wasn't going to let the same thing happen to me.' His voice was cracking.

'But . . .' I tried to speak, but his hand was still over my mouth and I gave up.

'I've tried to tell you all this before. I run away from anything I get attached to. I didn't want to end up like my old man, so I played it safe. I kept my distance, never got involved. Until you came along and messed it all up for me.'

He didn't need to keep his hand over my mouth any more. I had nothing to say. The penny dropped. I felt stupid and ashamed.

'I just did what I thought was the best thing to do, but I never expected life would throw me here beside you. I never allowed for that, do you understand? Nod once for yes, twice for no,' he joked.

I nodded once.

'Eventually I gave up too. I gave up everything I loved because if I didn't it was going to come after me and bite my ass anyway. I just made sure I was one step ahead.'

I noticed he was shaking. He took his hand away from my mouth.

'The football? Why did you give it up?' I asked in a whisper.

'There wasn't time for it. I was trying to keep my Dad alive. I guess everything I loved died in that fight.'

'That I understand,' I offered.

'What?'

'I used to play the piano, remember?' I sniffled.

'Why did you give it up?' he asked.

'Same reasons, I guess.'

'You can start again. You're so talented. I never heard anything as beautiful as you playing that piano in McCullough Piggott's,' he said, resting his hand on my cheek. 'There's no good reason why you should have given it up. Such talent is a gift. It's a waste not to use it,' he finished.

'I know that now, but I think it's too late,' I admitted.

'I'll make a deal with you,' he whispered, a wicked grin on his gorgeous face. 'I'll play ball if you get the piano tuned.'

'Why should I do anything you say?' I asked, like a child.

'Because you love me,' he said.

'I do?'

'Sure.'

'Do you love me?'

'Skinny?' He threw up his hands.

'Is that a yes or a no?' I pouted.

'It's a yes. Do I have to spell it out?' He laughed.

'That might not be a bad idea.' I grinned.

'Are you ready to love me now? Are you as ready as I am?'

I looked down at my chest. 'I'm ready. No more the shrinking violet, I promise,' I whispered.

'Great. When can we start?'

I took his hand and held it. It felt right. Like when you get into your own bed. 'Come here, Colm,' I commanded.

He looked like a teenager, all gawky and awkward. There was only one thing left for me to do and that was to show him I really did love him too, to show him I was ready to take the chance, ready to risk being loved. What had I to hide now? What was the point in hiding anything? He was standing there before me with his heart in his hand. I wasn't going to abandon him now. I was going to show him in the only way I knew how. I pulled at the bandages on my chest. I didn't care about the pain. I unrolled each one.

'What are you doing?' he asked.

I ignored him, just as he had ignored me.

'Finn, should you be doing that?'

I paid no attention and he knew it was pointless to argue with me 'Come here,' I urged him.

Reluctantly he lay on the bed beside me.

'Help me.' I beckoned.

His hands joined forces with mine and together we

unravelled the long white bandages. As we drew nearer to my skin, we slowed, deftly unrolling the last strips of gauze. I savoured each second: I was peeling away the last strips of shame, of pretence, of illusion. The last piece made me wince with pain, but that made sense: it was closest to the bone and they say the first cut is the deepest.

I let Colm pull it off slowly. It seemed only appropriate. I took his hand and kissed it. He bent his head and kissed my chest. I was stunned. He had kissed my chest. I drew my arms round his back and held him close for the first time. I felt him flinch and withdraw, but I wouldn't let him. I knew instinctively I was probably the first woman to have 'really' been allowed that privilege. I let him become familiar with my touch. 'Stay,' I whispered, holding him near me. I smiled and closed my eyes.

He remained silent. I understood perfectly. He didn't need to respond. I didn't need to say any more. We were like Siamese twins, welded together through *karma*. It was a paradox, really, because it was our connection that would lead us to discover our separate selves, and at long last bring us home, to where we had always belonged.

# Chapter 29

The road to Glenthulagh was more like a dirt track. I had set out in the morning to catch the early bus from the depot. I queued for my ticket but only a handful of people was making the trip. I took a backpack with me and stuffed it with all my favourite things, marshmallows, Walnut Whips, fruit pastilles and, of course, Energyade for the journey. I had also come bearing gifts for Mam. Silly things, like scented pot-pourri bags and hand-painted stones. I had also made her an enormous card of the type I used to give her when I was a toddler, the type that used to make her eyes light up with love.

The bus trundled along, swerving to avoid the muddy potholes, some the size of a small backyard. I let the steady gurgling of the engine lull me into a peaceful trance. I had taken a book, but couldn't read a single page. My concentration was shot. I wondered how I was going to be received. I had not called Mam to say I was coming, but I knew she would be there – she never ventured further than the local supermarket. I prepared my speech and read the text over and over in my mind. I had many questions, needed many explanations. I had planned to confront her head on.

We jigged along the dirt tracks and dusty lanes. The bus ran parallel to the rolling landscapes, all bursting with explosions of autumn colour. The sheep and cattle grazing on the hillsides looked like miniatures from a toy farm. I laid my head against the window and drank it in, the rich country scent of apple orchards, peat briquettes and pine needles. Haystacks reflected the morning sun like yellow pyramids and I could hear the hum of combine harvesters rattling through the fields.

Overgrown branches brushed the roof of the bus, then scratched against the window rousing me. I had fallen asleep. It had been a long time since I had done that with such ease. Then I realized that the bus had halted. I was back in Glenthulagh. I was home.

I stepped off and took a long look round. Nothing had changed. Kelleher's was still there, the only big supermarket that sold fishing tackle, cereal, coal, ham, shoestrings and tyres from the one shelf. O'Riordan's pub, tucked away in the corner where you had to bend down to enter its tiny Snow-White-and-the-Seven-Dwarfs wooden door, its Welcome sign flapping in the wind. Murphy's petrol station looked deserted, until a car rolled in looking for fuel, but the old GAA centre where my Dad had taught the boys Gaelic and hurling was all boarded up and barbed-wired. Kiely's, the little newsagents was still doing trade.

I trudged towards Mam's, a small ivy-covered, three-bedroomed bungalow that nestled in a half-circle of beech trees. Had it always been so quiet, I wondered? I let my hand run through the privet hedging as I walked up the garden path, breathing in the green of Mother Nature, allowing it to enfold me. I knocked at the door loudly. There was no answer, but I knew she was in there. I poked my nose through the letterbox and saw her slippers peeking out from the kitchen door. I knocked again, louder this time.

'Go away!' a tiny voice replied. 'I'm not buying anything today,'

'Mam? It's me, Fainche,' I called, through the letterbox.

The little slippers twitched a bit, then poked out from behind the kitchen door. They slithered towards me and abruptly stopped again.

'Mam? It's me, Fainche! Will you open up, Mam?' I urged her.

I heard the clanking of the locks. First the top bolt being slid back, then the Chubb lock in the middle being turned four times, the bolt at the bottom and, finally, the safety latch. The door came ajar, just a couple of inches.

'Fainche?' the little voice whispered.

'Yes, Mam, it's me. Don't be afraid, open up the door.'

'Fainche?' she repeated. I pushed against the door gently and she moved backwards. I was inside the hallway.

'Mam.' I stared at her. She was thin and gaunt, her eyes sinking backwards, her jawline protruding, making her look like she had aged twenty years. Lines had taken up permanent residence on her face, and her eyes crinkled as she smiled.

'Oh, Fainche dear, it is you!' she said, beaming.

'Mam, are you OK?' I asked, placing my hands on her shoulders. She looked up at me with watery eyes. She seemed so vulnerable, so frail, her skeletal frame hunched over, as if she was shrinking before my eyes. When did she get to be so small?

'Is it really, really you, Fainche?' she checked again.

'Of course it's me!' I exclaimed. 'Don't you recognize me?' I asked, puzzled. She looked me up and down as if I were an alien. I felt guilty – and stupid into the bargain. Perhaps it was too much to expect her to recognize me. She was old now, I hadn't called in God knew how long, and I had changed, drastically.

'I haven't my glasses on me,' she mumbled, twiddling her thumbs and shifting from one foot to the other.

'Come inside, Mam, and I'll make us a cup of tea. Would you like that? A cup of tea, Mam?' I took her arm and slowly led her to the kitchen. She looked old and sick. She wore her old fruit-patterned pinny but it was stained and frayed at the edges. Her beautiful mane of rich plum-coloured curls had turned grey. She had pinned the sides back carelessly with two old brown clips. The house was a mess, the paint peeling off the walls, the kitchen lino scuffed and torn, the furniture threadbare and colourless. The smell of old cooking wafted through the rooms.

'When was the last time you saw the boys?' I questioned her, worried.

'Let me see now . . .' She paused. 'Christmas. Yes, I saw Padraig at Christmas,' she said finally, but I knew she was unsure and was probably making it up.

'What about Fearghal?' I went on.

'Easter,' she said immediately. I suspected she was lying.

'Has Mrs Farrell next door been in to see you?'

'Of course, every day she comes in. God bless her.' Mam nodded. I noticed her whole body trembled constantly; even her head shook like a puppet's. I had thought it was fear, but now as I studied her movements about the kitchen I realized it was permanent.

I put the kettle on and told her to sit down, which she did. I poured two cups of tea and placed them on the table. She took the cup to her lips and it shook violently. I felt a wretch. Sickening remorse rose up in my belly. I remembered how I had prepared for this moment: how I would challenge her about why she had allowed my stepfather to rule the house with an iron rod, how she had allowed him to treat me as if I was invisible, how she had denied her only daughter in favour of his sons, but somehow that all seemed unimportant now.

'Mam, I'm worried about you being here all alone,' I said.

'Oh, there's no need to worry, sweetheart. I'm fine, just fine.' She waved a hand at me.

'I'm sorry I didn't visit earlier, but with the job . . .' I trailed off, knowing that was no excuse.

'I loved the flowers,' Mam interrupted, as if she herself did not want to enter into that particular conversation.

'I ordered them for you specially. I know you love lilies.'

I felt overwhelmed with guilt. I had wanted to say so many things. I had wanted to ask her why she had given up and given in? I wanted to ask her why she had put up with such a terrible life, but I already knew why. Hadn't I done the same thing in my own? Hadn't I put up with the Mickahs, the Shanes? Who was I to preach? It wasn't long ago that I would have settled for anyone . . .

Mam had done the only thing she thought she could. She had put a roof over my head, made sure I got an education. I could see the same haunted look of loneliness and regret in her eyes, the look of loss, of recognition that she had been cheated by life. What right had I to bring all this old stuff up now? It was the last thing she needed.

'Did I tell you Mrs Brady passed on?' she said, the cup of tea rattling in her hand.

'No!' I exclaimed, trying to look interested.

'Oh, indeed. Only sixty-eight. In her prime. God be good to her,' she finished, and clicked her false teeth back into place. Her hand jerked back and forth as if it had a mind of its own.

I scolded myself severely. I should have telephoned the boys to check they were making regular visits. I bet they haven't even called to see her, I thought. A fat lot of good it had done Mam to give in to their every whim while my stepdad had been alive. Where were they now? I asked myself. *And where were you, Fainche? Her only daughter. Shame on you . . .*

She had suffered enough. She had paid the ultimate price for what she had done, all in the name of sacrifice. All for me. She could have taken a boat to England and had an abortion, she could have handed me up to the sisters for adoption and never looked back, but she hadn't. She had stayed with me. She had tried to give me a life.

Mam stood up and went to the kitchen window. The endless fields rolled on, an expanse of yellow corn, grass and lush vegetation. How selfless she had been, I thought now. Her life had been a nightmare, dancing to my stepdad's tune, tiptoeing around him for all those years just to keep me in a home. No wonder she didn't stand up to him about me. She must have been terrified he would throw us out. He must have known that, and played on it time and time again.

'You know, your Dad always said that the sun rose up over Kelleher's but went down over O'Riordan's. Do you remember, Fainche?' she asked suddenly.

'How could I forget?' I replied. 'Didn't I have to hear him say it every morning before I went to school?'

'Well,' she turned to me, 'did you know that he was dead wrong, Fainche? Dead fucking wrong!' She folded her arms defiantly.

I choked on my tea. I had never heard my mother curse, never mind publicly denounce my stepdad.

'Come, see for yourself,' she demanded.

I walked to the window and she pointed to the sun glaring down over Kelleher's.

'God! You're right, Mam.' I laughed.

'Of course he couldn't be told, Fainche. He couldn't be told anything, especially that he was wrong! He was always bloody right, no matter what,' she said angrily.

'I know, Mam,' I said. I put my arm round her shoulders. 'It wasn't your fault, Mam.'

She began to shake even more violently as I held her tiny little body against my shoulder. Great big sobs of remorse, regret and sorrow rose from within her and gushed forth. I wiped the stray strands of hair off her face and caressed her gnarled fingers. 'Look at me, Mam,' I implored her.

She looked up at me.

'What do you see?' I asked.

'I see. . .I see. . .a beautiful young woman.' She dried her eyes.

'That's right, Mam!' I hugged her close to me. 'But I'm still your little girl. I'm here for you now and I'll never leave you. Do you want to know why?'

She nodded.

'Because you never left me, Mam,' I finished.

She smiled. I could see the relief my words brought her, cleansing her, setting her free.

'You know I have a good job, a flat, and I have met the most amazing man who I'm probably going to marry, and I know he's going to love you, Mam . . .' I pulled back to hold her little scrunched-up face. 'I'm very happy. Do you hear me? I'm very happy!' Tears were brimming in my own eyes now.

'You're not going to follow in my footsteps?' she warned.

'No, Mam, I have a choice. Things are much different

for women now. You made the right decision at that time.'

'I never stopped loving you,' she whispered.

I reached into my backpack and took out a perfectly entwined daisy chain. I placed it over her head and arranged it till it sat comfortably round her neck. 'I never stopped loving you either . . .' I hugged her. 'From now on, it's you and me, always together, and nothing will keep us apart again.'

I had solved the mysteries of love and life. I had discovered there was no mystery. In fact, it was all too simple for me to comprehend. It went straight over my head. It was so fucking easy a baby could have figured it out. I didn't have to be *something*. All I had to do was be *me*. I wasn't alone in feeling bad about myself. We were all flawed in some way or another. We were all fumbling – the blind, the crippled and even the beautiful. We were all on the same road, climbing up the same mountain, heading towards the same summit.

Every time I undressed I understood that I was the maker of my own state of consciousness. I could be happy or I could be miserable. I chose to be somewhere in the middle. Content to love and be loved in return. I was available to all who wished to get to know me. Just this simple decision, to join the living again, brought new friends, new hope and new beginnings.

I had been back in work for some weeks when I made my third and final trip to Arnott's department store. I didn't do any cartwheels through the door: I walked. I wasn't interested in the lingerie section. I was looking for aftershave. I asked the woman for 'Pi'. I didn't have to make any hand signals. She knew the name and pulled out a shiny new box. When I saw the price I hesitated, but then I thought of all the moments without Colm.

There hadn't been many lately – I hadn't been able to lose him since that day in the hospital.

There was the rare occasion when he had to go home, like to change his clothes after a game of football, and during those free hours I would tinkle on the piano. I hadn't decided whether to get lessons or not, but I had had it tuned. I needed something for such emergencies. For the moment, this was the perfect substitute. *My own private bottle of Colm.* He would never receive it as a gift, of course. It was for my pillow, my nightclothes or the evenings when he left. For quick visits to the loo at the Credit Union when I couldn't go up to him and sniff him. I had to have it.

I dished out the cash and put the box into my bag. I was about to leave the shop, but God hadn't finished with me yet. I found myself smack-bang in the middle of the lingerie department. I couldn't help wondering why a crappy thing called a bra had dominated my life for so long. I picked things up, rubbed them between my fingers, then put them back. They didn't feel the same any more. They felt like – like – pieces of cloth.

I thought of all the pain, the misunderstanding; the searching for what was under my nose. I still felt ashamed for having been so gullible. I stood staring at a mannequin clad in black silk. I perused the department and couldn't find a single woman in it who had the figure to match it but it didn't stop them queuing up to buy it. Nothing had changed. The illusion was still worming its way into younger victims' hearts. Mine had been torn out because of it, but I was grateful: at least I could see it now. I walked around with it in my hand, proudly displaying it like a badge of honour.